THE RIGHTEOUS WITCH

Nicholas Lincoln

First edition May 2025

Cover design by GetCovers
Edited by Gareth W. Rosewood

ISBN: 979-8-218-66771-9

PART ONE

1

Hidden deep in the snow-dusted Pyrenees was a small, verdant valley, carved into the surrounding rock over eons by a snaking creek. The meltwater creek wound its way down from the pine-covered montane, flowing through forested foothills, before reaching small fields separated by dirt paths that led to the pastoral village of Estrelle.

Estrelle's most noticeable feature was the steeple of its church, which broke the monotony of gray stone buildings and towered over the village center like a watchful guardian. A square schoolhouse with several windows in its stone facade sat beside the church. A woman's voice echoed off the stone walls loud enough to be heard outside.

Inside the schoolhouse, Isabella, a thin elderly woman in a plain gray dress and matching bonnet, lectured a classroom of variously aged children: "The serpent told Eve that eating the fruit from the tree would open her eyes and make her like God. When she heard this, she saw how succulent the fruit looked, and she desired the wisdom it would give her, so she took it and ate it. This was how the serpent tempted her."

The students stared blankly as they listened to their teacher, except for one. In the front corner of the class sat a twelve-year-old girl with long, bronze hair. She had been staring into the wall behind her teacher with her head tilted to rest on her hand. As Isabella spoke about the serpent, she narrowed her eyes. She suddenly sat up and raised her hand.

"Yes, Cora?" Isabella permitted her question.

Cora lowered her hand. She inquired in a slightly incredulous tone, "Why wouldn't God want Eve to be like him? He didn't want to share his wisdom?"

Isabella smiled and lowered her head to think, but before she could reply, Cora followed up with another question, "And why did God blame the serpent for tempting her? God put the tree in the garden and made the fruit look super tasty."

Her questions had aroused her classmates, and her last comment had sparked a snicker from the back of the classroom. Leora, the nine-year-old blond-haired girl sitting to Cora's left, was particularly interested in what Cora had to say. She stared at Cora with curiosity.

Isabella replied, "God let Adam and Eve obtain wisdom from the tree. But He told them not to eat the fruit to give them a choice: to obey or disobey."

"But if they didn't have wisdom, how would they know it was bad to disobey?" Cora continued.

"God told them not to. They did not need wisdom from the tree to know how to obey God's word."

"No, yes, they knew they were told not to, but they didn't know *why* it was bad to disobey. They only learned why once they gained the wisdom from eating the fruit, right?" Cora asked.

Leora expectantly looked at Isabella. A few other students now seemed intrigued as well, and they also looked at her for an answer.

"That is correct. They did not know why it was bad to disobey God until after they ate the fruit. God gave his creation the ability to choose a destiny, like a test to see what they would do, and they chose to disobey. Thus, humankind was inclined to sin from the beginning, and that is why we can only be saved by faith. We are born into sin."

Cora pondered her teacher's explanation as she continued the lesson. "Now the serpent, as we all know, was Satan, and Satan wanted to corrupt God's creation as an act of defiance. So when he..."

Cora interrupted her, "So then, why is it

wrong to disobey God?"

The room fell silent, except for a chirping bird outside. Every student in the class turned their head to gawk at Cora. Most wore looks of disbelief. A couple appeared surprised, half smiling as if they thought she was joking. But Leora again looked at her with curiosity.

Isabella frowned. "Cora, God created us to know and love Him. He wants us to choose Him. We chose Him by obeying Him, and we do it out of love and respect, in the same way you should obey your mother and your elders. God is the path to salvation. If we do not follow Him, we are damned. The souls of disobedient sinners will be condemned to burn in hell for eternity."

"Duh," a fourteen-year-old boy named Francisco remarked from the back of the class. His comment sparked laughter from the boy sitting next to him and Clara, the twelve-year-old girl sitting behind Cora.

"It's common sense, Cora," Clara said.

Leora furrowed her brow at Clara.

Isabella said, "Be kind, Clara. Every question is welcome in this class. Now let us get back to the reading."

As Isabella began reading from the Bible, Leora leaned over and whispered to Cora, "Good questions, C."

Francisco teased, "Good questions for an idiot, maybe."

Leora turned around and spoke loudly, "She's

not an idiot, you're the idiot! My sister is smarter than all of you!"

"Leora!" Isabella reprimanded her. "That was uncalled for. Apologize to Francisco right now!"

"But he said..." Leora began.

"Right now!" Isabella repeated.

Leora's face turned red. She turned around to Francisco but could not look him in the eye when she spoke. "I'm sorry."

Francisco smugly grinned and spoke with pompous benevolence, "I forgive thee."

Isabella glared at him and addressed the class. "There will be no name calling in this classroom. Remember Matthew five, verse twenty-two: But I say to you that everyone who is angry with his brother will be liable to judgment; whoever insults his brother will be liable to the council; and whoever says, 'You fool!' will be liable to the hell of fire."

Cora quietly sighed. She rested her face back on her hand and resumed staring into the front wall.

Isabella finished the story of Adam's and Eve's fall from Eden, which concluded the lesson for the morning. "Well, children, it is time for lunch. I know some of you will help your fathers with the grape harvest in the afternoon, so while you work, take time to reflect on what you have learned today. Remember, tomorrow we will practice growth enchantments in the forest, so get a good night of sleep. You will need your energy."

* * *

As the students filed out of the schoolhouse, Cora followed Leora. "You didn't have to say those things," Cora whispered, trying to avoid eye contact with Clara and the other girls. "In fact, I wish you wouldn't. It's embarrassing."

"But it's true!" Leora insisted, turning around. Cora nudged Leora's shoulder, forcing her forward and turning her away from their classmates.

"It will only make things worse," Cora warned, coming around to walk beside Leora.

"No, it won't. You have me to protect you."

"I don't need your protection," Cora said, maintaining her focus on the path ahead.

Leora studied her sister's face and said no more.

They continued along the road parallel to the creek until they reached the wooden bridge, the only crossing in the valley. On the other side was a vineyard where an old man was working with a donkey. The man waved at the girls as they passed. They waved back. Further from the village, the vineyards and crop fields faded into grassy meadows.

Leora skipped ahead to look at some flowers along the side of the path. She lingered as Cora caught up and passed. Cora turned around and beckoned for her to catch up. Then Leora skipped ahead again, passing Cora and turning around to wait for her.

"Hey C, I bet you can't beat me to that tree up

there." Leora pointed to a tree that grew alongside the path.

Cora dismissed her sister's challenge. "I bet I couldn't either. You're already halfway there."

Leora ran back to meet Cora and tried again. "How about now?"

Cora kept walking.

Leora tried one more time. "On the count of three. One. Two. Three!" She took off running, but stopped before reaching the tree, when she realized Cora was not chasing. "What's wrong, C?"

"Nothing. I'm just thinking. If you want, you can run there and back. I'll time you."

"You're always thinking!" Leora proclaimed. "What are you thinking about?"

"Oh, just...about what Mother Isabella said in class today." When she saw the perplexity on Leora's face, she added a diversion to her reply. "And the enchantments tomorrow."

Leora smiled excitedly. "Oh! Do you think you will be the first one to grow something? Maybe you can grow a brain for Francisco!"

Cora laughed, "That would be extraordinary. But I don't know if I'll be first, silly. That depends on you!"

"What do you mean?"

"You're always the first to master a new enchantment."

Leora laughed. "Yeah. Maybe I'm just lucky." She thought for a moment, "But maybe you'll get lucky tomorrow!"

"Maybe," Cora dubiously replied.

The girls had reached the outskirts of the village where the path narrowed and trailed into the wilderness. The village was no longer visible behind them, not even the church steeple. Traveling beyond this point would take at least two weeks on horseback to reach the nearest settlement to Estrelle. At the narrowing of the path, there was a smaller path that branched into the meadow and toward the forest. The girls took it. The smaller path ended at the forest's edge, where there was a humble roundhouse with a thatched roof.

A dark-haired woman in her mid-thirties stood near the back and side of the roundhouse, hanging wet clothes on a line between two trees.

"Mama!" Leora shouted and ran up the path to the house.

Thalia turned her head while fixing a dress on the line. "My girls! How was school today?"

Leora launched into a description of her day. "It was wonderful! First we practiced Latin, and then some arithmetic, and then Mother Isabella told us the story of Adam and Eve! And tomorrow we are going to practice growth enchantments in the forest!"

"Good, that sounds like fun!" Thalia said. "Cora, how about you? Did you have a good day?"

Cora lagged behind her sister on the path and had not yet reached the house. She replied, "Yeah, it was fine," and walked straight toward the door of the house.

"Are you sure?" Thalia asked.

"Yes. I'm going to read for a while." She went inside.

Her mother looked back at Leora, as if to ask for more information, and Leora instinctively provided it. "Francisco made fun of her again."

"I see. Honey, why don't you squeeze the water out of the rest of these and toss them over the line? I will talk with Cora for a bit." She gestured to a basket full of wet clothes.

"Ok." Leora agreed. As Thalia walked to the house, Leora asked, "Hey mama, later can we practice fire spells again? It was so much fun trying them out last night."

"Leora, remember what I told you about that? You didn't talk about it at school, did you? Sister Isabella could tell Aunt En and the rest of the coven, and they would be upset with me."

"No mama, of course not. I haven't even talked to Cora about it."

"Good. Now give me just a few minutes to speak with Cora. Then I will start preparing dinner, and later we can practice fire spells together. Ok?"

Leora triumphantly raised her arms in the air, "Yay! Ok mama." She spun around quickly and went over to the basket of clothes. Her mother walked into the house.

Cora was sitting next to an open window and

looking out at the meadow, lost in thought, when her mother entered the house. Thalia walked over to her bed, knelt down, and began looking for something under it.

The round house was just enough of a dwelling to call a shelter. It was a single room with a fire pit in the center and beds and other furniture along the walls. The windows were head-sized holes in the walls that were filled with bundles of straw when the shutters were closed. The beds were pine log framed with straw-filled mattresses. It was one of the simplest houses in the valley, and a house that matched the family's status among the villagers.

Thalia dragged a cedar chest out from under her bed. She opened it and rummaged through her belongings, retrieving a rolled-up piece of parchment. She held the scroll in her hand, staring at it for a moment before taking it over to Cora. "I have been meaning to read this to you for quite some time, but I think now you are old enough to understand."

Cora had been expecting to be interrogated about her day at school, but her mother's tactics caught her off guard. She curiously glanced at the scroll. She moved her feet so her mother could sit down beside her on the bed. Thalia held the parchment up to the light coming in from the window. Cora noticed the choppy handwriting, which caused her to suspect that a man penned the words on the paper. She noticed the format was that of a letter.

Thalia brought the letter down to her lap. "The day your father..." She paused and lowered her head, clenching her eyes and pursing her lips while swallowing. After a moment, she had collected herself. "He left this letter for me. I had always planned to read it to you when you were old enough. When Leora is ready, I will read it to her, too."

Cora was now completely engrossed in what her mother had to say. Thalia rarely spoke of their father. In fact, nobody ever spoke about him. The only details Cora knew about him were that he was from a German village named Coburg and had died shortly after Leora was born. She also got the sense that the villagers respected him, and that he was important to the coven.

Thalia read the letter:

My dear Thalia, light of my life,

As I sit here with the quill trembling in my hand, I am enveloped in the silence of finality. The words I must write are an anchor in my heart, dragging it into a despondent abyss. Each stroke of ink feels like a tender farewell that carries me further away from you, and I am struggling to complete them. But when you read them, I hope they might ease the burden of this moment.

Life has cast us upon a tumultuous sea, and I now must sail into the unknown. This final journey must be mine alone. Please know that my decision is born of obligation to a promise I once made; a trade that I once could not fathom, but is now soberingly clear. But that promise stole a blink of happiness with you from the treasures of eternity, and I regret nothing of it.

Our children, dear Thalia, are the blossoms of our shared dreams. Cora has my insatiable curiosity, but she also has your patience, and I hope that will temper her restless heart. Leora has the light of our laughter in her heart, and such kindness that could only come from the purest of beings. I implore you, my beloved, to nurture their spirits. Teach them to embrace the beauty of life in every fleeting moment. Introduce them to the magic of the world around them, so they may dance in the rain and find joy in the simplest of things. Instill in them a deep love for others, for empathy will be their guiding star, just as you have been mine.

As a parting gift to you, I leave you with a pendant; a powerful star to be your guardian in my stead. Wear it close to your heart, and may it remind you that when darkness reigns, the light to tame it must come from within. The pendant is a symbol of the purest love that binds us across space and time, and it will keep you safe.

Though my destination is uncertain, my thoughts will forever linger on you and our precious children. Carry my love with you, as I will carry yours, and know that you are never truly alone. I believe in your strength, Thalia, and I trust that you will guide our children to become the very best

versions of themselves.
With all the love my heart can hold,
Your Faustus

When Thalia had finished reading, the two of them sat in silence for several seconds. Thalia wiped tears from her eyes.

Cora gathered from the letter that her father knew his death was imminent, and that it would be his own fault. She wondered if he did it himself. To avoid further upsetting her mother, she asked delicately, "Did father...take his own life?"

Thalia shook her head no, took a breath, and then spoke. "Your father was a scientist. Like you, he was always curious about the world. He thought there must be something more to life, some higher meaning or purpose, but he did not accept the meaning provided by Christianity: that we were made to serve God. He spent years searching for answers. It was during this time when he learned how to connect with nature and channel magic. But he also found something else. I never learned what he found, but I can only imagine it was something terrible, because it cost him his life."

"So you don't know how he died?"

"No. Your father was adamant that I should never know, for our protection." Thalia stopped to let Cora process the barrage of information.

Cora stared into the fire pit with a look of confusion, her mouth slightly open as she thought. "You said he learned magic...was he a member of the coven?"

Thalia smiled. "He was not a member: he was the founder. He made an agreement with Father Julian and the village to teach magic to a small group of us. Magic scared people, though, and only señora Mendoza, your teacher Isabella, and your Aunt En and I were willing to learn." She paused, reminiscing in her mind, and added, "He opened our eyes to the true beauty of this world."

"But if he learned so much, and if he was so powerful, why are we..." Cora looked around the inside of the meager roundhouse.

"Why are we so poor?" Thalia finished her question. She knew her daughter well.

"Yes!" Cora affirmed. "Everybody else is better off. Even Aunt En lives in a large house."

Thalia sighed and put her hand on Cora's shoulder. "Your Aunt En is my older sister, so she inherited everything from our parents. But that is why I wanted to read you your father's letter, so you could hear his own words. He valued his quest for knowledge more than all else, but in the end, he gave it up for us. Cora, your father was a great man. He was not famous, or rich in possessions, but he was rich in love, and his recognition of that was his salvation. Our promise to each other was to share that love with you and Leora. I have tried my best. And this..." she grasped the star pendant around her neck and held it out to show Cora, "this is more valuable than anything else he could have left us. It's not just a pendant, it's a symbol. It reminds me every day of our promise. You are special, and you have the potential to do amazing things with your magic, or very terrible things. It is important that you learn how to love, so that you do not go down a dark path. The Bible does a good job teaching us how to love. That's why I send you to school, despite your doubts about God, and I know you have them. After all, you are so much like your father."

Cora turned her head away. She knew the lecture was coming, eventually. "If he loved us so much, then why didn't he leave us with anything more than a stupid pendant? Or at least make sure you wouldn't have to barter for food for us?"

"Cora, I..."

"All I know is if I were that powerful, I would take care of the people I love and make sure they never have to live in shame."

Thalia was about to reply, but Leora, who came bursting through the door, interrupted her. "I'm all done!" she exclaimed. Leora noticed Cora's body language and their mother's look of concern. "Is everything ok, mama? Are you still talking about school?"

"Yes, Leora, we're fine," Thalia replied, forcing a smile. "Cora has a strong mind, and we don't always agree on things, but we are finé. Come sit with us for a minute."

Cora thumped her forehead against her palm and brought her head up into a forced smile. Leora cautiously approached them and squeezed herself into the space between Cora and Thalia on the bed. Thalia had stashed the letter away before Leora could see it, and placed her hand on Leora's back.

"We were just talking about school, and how important the lessons are," Thalia told Leora, but her eyes were on Cora.

Leora asked, "Did she tell you about Francisco? He was mean to her again today."

Cora butted in, "He's just a fool. His words are meaningless to me."

Thalia commended her, "That's good, Cora. We should not burden ourselves with the opinions of others. Leora, you would benefit from your sister's example. Aunt En has told me how quarrelsome you can be."

"Only when they tell lies about you and C!" Leora insisted with indignation.

"Even so, you must recognize them as such and let them go. You are strong, both of you. If you let anger cloud your mind, you could accidentally do something that you would come to regret."

"Yeah, I know." Leora sighed.

Thalia continued, "Then promise me you will be mindful and treat your classmates with care, even when they do not do the same. You must be strong and be an example. They will come to respect you in time. Promise me."

"I promise," Leora replied.

"Cora?"

"Yes mother, I promise."

"Alright, then get cleaned up and help me prepare our supper. Later we will practice fire spells, as I promised." Thalia stood, and the girls followed suit. Leora jumped up with glee, and Cora reluctantly dragged herself to her feet.

2

Isabella let the heavy iron gate swing closed behind her as she entered the courtyard. Her shoes clacked on the cobblestone as she approached the manor house of the Ortiz Estate. The soft glow of a fire lit the window of the room to the right of the large oak entry doors. She peered through the glass as she stepped closer, hoping to see Enheduanna to confirm that she had not yet gone to bed. She did not see anyone, but rapped the brass door knocker, anyway. After a minute, she raised her hand to knock again, when she heard a metal bar being removed from the inside, and the door being unlocked.

"Good evening, señora Domingo," the butler welcomed her.

"Good evening, Enrique," Isabella replied.

"Please, come in from this frosty night." Enrique stepped aside and held the door for Isabella. "What can I do for you, señora?"

"I came to speak with Enheduanna. I pray I have not come too late in the evening."

"No, señora Ortiz has not yet gone to bed. If you would please have a seat in the foyer, I will let her know you are here."

"Thank you, Enrique," Isabella said. Enrique bowed his head and left the room. Isabella slowly strolled through the foyer, looking at the paintings that hung on the walls in between the candelabras. The first was a portrait of Enheduanna with her late husband, señor Ortiz, and their son Geoffrey. Isabella stopped in front of the second, a painting of the Madonna and Child. Even in the dim light, she could admire the deep blue color of the Madonna's robe.

"It's a Botticelli," Enheduanna announced as she entered the foyer. "My father was a patron of his."

"Hmph. Beautiful," Isabella remarked, suspecting that Enheduanna expected her to recognize the artist's name. She did not.

Enheduanna continued, "Did you know he painted the walls of the Sistine Chapel in the Vatican?"

Isabella's eyebrows rose, and she shook her head.

"Yes, everyone talks about Michaelangelo and

the ceiling, and they forget Boticelli's frescoes." She walked up to Isabella's side and looked at the painting with her. "But father simply adored his style."

"I can see why. It's marvelous," Isabella praised.

"So what urgent matter did you need to speak to me about that you had to come here at this late hour?"

Isabella's face flushed. "Yes, I'm so sorry, sister. I would have waited until tomorrow, but it's a matter that you specifically requested I bring to your attention, should it ever occur, and I..."

Enheduanna smiled and touched Isabella's shoulder. "Oh, not to worry! Dear sister, you are welcome here anytime. Especially if you have information that I have previously requested. Please, let us go to the library."

Enheduanna guided Isabella around the corner and into the library, where the fire that Isabella had seen from outside was still burning in a resplendent fireplace. Carved into the wooden mantle were depictions of cherubim guiding crusaders into the holy land. Shelves of books lined the surrounding walls that extended up to the second floor. A large chandelier hung from the ceiling in the middle of the room, but it was not lit.

"Please, sit," Enheduanna offered a seat on one of the upholstered couches around the fireplace. When Isabella sat, Enheduanna sat across from her. "Now what was it you wanted to tell me, sister?"

Isabella sat on the edge of her seat, unable to get comfortable. "It's...it's about your niece, Cora. I would never presume to involve myself in the matters of another family, least of all one of my students, but you did ask that I let you know if either of your nieces ever behaved unusually."

The corners of Enheduanna's mouth tightened into the very slightest smile as she sat, leaning back, with her arm outstretched and resting on the back of the couch. "Go on," she encouraged.

"Well, today in class, she was quite curious about the story of Adam and Eve. First she insinuated God tempted the couple by making the fruit look succulent, and then she asked a very peculiar question: she asked why it was wrong to disobey God."

Enheduanna leaned forward, her eyes widening. "She asked what?"

Isabella repeated herself. Enheduanna's face twitched, then she breathed in slowly and leaned back again. "I knew it," she mumbled.

"I beg your pardon?"

"Nothing. Thank you, sister, for bringing this to my attention. Walk safely on your way home." She picked up a bell that sat on a table beside the couch and rang it, summoning Enrique. "Please see Isabella out," she requested.

Isabella remained seated for a moment, perplexed by Enheduanna's reaction and surprised at being suddenly kicked out. But Enheduanna remained silent, staring into the stacks of books in contemplation. Isabella stood and departed. Enrique locked the door behind her and asked Enheduanna if she needed anything else. She declined.

Enheduanna waited until Enrique was out of earshot before she asked, "Did you hear that?"

"I did," a woman's voice came from a chair in a dark corner of the room that Isabella had not seen. The woman stood and came into the firelight. She was a tall, thin, old woman with deep marionette lines and gray hair that was tightly pulled back into a bun. She put her hand on the back of the couch to steady herself. "I knew it would only be a matter of time before that harlot handed those poor girls over to Satan."

Enheduanna snorted and said, "Oh Mary, you're so dramatic. I'm sure Cora is not in league with Satan," she paused, "but she may be starting down that path."

"And if she is, something will need to be done about it," Mary warned.

"If it comes to that, then yes, but I will make that determination myself."

"We cannot allow her to continue practicing witchcraft if she follows that path."

"Indeed," Enheduanna agreed, "It would threaten everything I...*we*...are trying to build."

"And if Thalia is doing nothing about it, or worse, encouraging it, then she is equally guilty," Mary asserted.

"Yes. But I cannot do anything without more evidence. My sister has too many allies in the coven. We need to show them who she really is."

"How will you do that?" Mary asked.

"My sister is very protective of her daughters. I will provoke her and let her damage her own image." Enheduanna stood and took Mary's hand to help her out of the library, picking up Mary's cane from the corner on the way. "Don't worry, we will purge our coven of Thalia if necessary. But we do not yet know for certain whether her daughters are truly lost to us. They would be tremendous assets for our cause."

Mary agreed as she departed. "I trust your judgment. May the peace of Our Lord Jesus Christ be with you, sister."

"And also with you," Enheduanna replied.

***

The next morning, Thalia accompanied her daughters to school, carrying a basket full of herbs and mushrooms that she had collected in the forest. An eagle circled overhead, following the creek up the valley. Leora ran, giggling as she tried to keep up with it. Thalia smiled as she watched her daughter. Then shifted her gaze to the eagle. She followed it with her eyes until it was out of sight.

Isabella stood outside the schoolhouse in her usual gray attire, welcoming the students as they entered. This morning, however, Enheduanna joined her. Enheduanna wore the white robes of the coven leader, tied with a golden pin in the shape of an oak tree with an umbrella canopy.

Thalia addressed her sister and Isabella as they approached the schoolhouse. "Good morning, sisters!"

"Sister Thalia!" Enheduanna acknowledged. "I see you have brought some herbs to trade."

Cora and Leora observed the interaction. They both noticed a subtle change in their aunt's voice whenever she spoke to their mother in front of the other coven elders. She lowered her voice, elongated her vowels, and enunciated her consonants more acutely. They had discussed the change in Enheduanna's mannerisms before, and while Cora interpreted it as a deliberate slight to their mother, Leora considered it an unconscious effort to mask her insecurities and appear more confident to the elders.

"Yes, the forest was generous this week," Thalia replied.

"The forest is always generous for those with keen eyes," Cora added, smiling at her mother.

"Mmhmm," Enheduanna responded and flashed Cora a smile with her mouth.

"Cora, why don't you and Leora go inside and prepare for your enchantment lesson today? I need to catch up with your teacher and Aunt En before I take the forest's gifts to the market."

"Yes, mother," Cora replied as she took Leora's hand.

The women waited until the children were

inside before continuing their conversation. Thalia spoke softly, "Sisters, you must have seen the eagle in the sky this morning. Do you think it belonged to the inquisitors?"

Isabella stepped closer to hear better. Enheduanna replied, "Yes, I saw. It is possible they are venturing close to the valley."

"They have never come close to our valley before. Why would they do it now?" Isabella asked rhetorically.

Enheduanna continued, "It could just have been a hungry predator. But in case it was more than that, we should gather the elders tonight. We can convene after the Vigils bell at the prayer circle. We may offer a prayer for the Lord to protect us."

"A prayer is fine, but perhaps we can cast a cloaking enchantment," Thalia suggested.

Enheduanna spoke loudly out of embarrassment and incredulity, "Certainly you are not diminishing the power of prayer, sister, or suggesting that the Lord would forsake His faithful servants?"

Thalia took a deep breath to hide her dismay. She opened her mouth to speak, but before she could, Isabella asked, "A cloaking spell? We have never tried that before. How would we do it?"

Enheduanna jumped in to demonstrate her knowledge of witchcraft, since Isabella had ignored her previous accusation, "It is no different from enchantments to conceal small items. It would just be on a larger scale, so it would require all of our combined strength. You have nothing to fear. I will guide everyone through it." She glared at Thalia for a second, before telling Isabella, "Go, sister. The students are eager to practice their witchcraft."

Isabella bowed her head with her hands together as if to pray. As she went inside, Thalia began walking to the market. Enheduanna followed with her.

"Thalia, I must confess I have heard concerning news about Cora. She has always had a curious mind, always asking for proof of the divine, but Isabella told me that yesterday she challenged the authority of the Almighty, in the same way Lucifer did, before God cast him down into the pit."

Thalia sighed, "Eh" in protest to Enheduanna's choice of words, but Enheduanna continued, speaking louder to get her point across before Thalia could respond. "We all just want the best for her, and I think it would be prudent for her to come live with me for a while."

Thalia turned away, visibly perturbed. Enheduanna qualified her suggestion, "At least until she has learned to respect the will of God."

Thalia finally weighed in, "She is at that age where we all begin to question things. Truthfully, I support her efforts to find her own path."

Enheduanna protested, "But if that path leads to darkness…"

"It will not! En, you remember how Faust was when I first met him? I see so much of him in Cora.

He walked a fine line, but in the end he found peace through our love. Whether he believed in God or not, he decided what gave meaning to his life and how he wanted to live it. Cora deserves that same chance. We all do."

"A fine line, for sure. That man's craft took him to the brink of desolation! He easily could have dragged us all with him."

Thalia did not know whether the memory of Faustus had distracted her sister, or if Enheduanna had deliberately ignored her point. Either way, she knew her sister was unconvinced.

Enheduanna continued, "All I'm asking is if she strays from the righteous path, who will shepherd her back? And if she uses her abilities for evil, who would stop her?"

"I will. As her mother, that is my responsibility, and my promise to her father."

"Then she will be your burden. If she strays, the coven will have no choice but to hold you equally accountable for her actions."

"So be it," Thalia accepted.

The sisters stared at one another, each waiting for the other to concede. Enheduanna backed down in frustration. "Fine! But if that happens, even I, as your sister, will be unable to help you. You know the punishment for witches who break the vows of the coven. It would be the end of both of you."

Thalia smiled and put her hand on Enheduanna's shoulder. "I would not expect any less."

"Hmph," Enheduanna uttered. "Well, I need to get back to the church to help Father Julian prepare for Sunday's service. Good day, sister."

"Good day," Thalia replied. As she continued to the village square, she tried to remember the moment she and Enheduanna began drifting apart. Enheduanna had always envied her, since Thalia was more beautiful. Her envy only increased as they learned how to connect with nature and channel magic. Thalia was better at opening her mind and thus became more powerful. But she decided it was when Faust began showing an interest in her. *Our love changed everything*, she thought.

3

The birds chirped in the lush canopy above Cora as she knelt on the damp forest floor with her eyes closed. A cool, late summer wind blew the scent of the coming autumn through the trees. Cora inhaled deeply and the sounds of the forest faded into silence. She put her hands on the ground and leaned forward until her forehead touched it, too.

Isabella observed and advised. "Open your mind."

Cora heard her teacher's words like a distant echo.

"Feel the earth beneath you. Find the roots of the plants twisting and burrowing through the dark soil like veins, reaching deep for hidden moisture. Follow those roots with your mind until you find a wellspring of energy. When you find it, welcome it into you."

With her eyes closed, the physical world yielded to ethereal darkness. Cora's other senses elevated to compensate for her loss of vision. She felt the earth slightly shifting beneath her fingertips, as if it were breathing. It connected to her surroundings, both living and nonliving entities, and encircled her with limitless energy. The energy flowed up from the ground through her and warmed her, as if she were basking in the morning sunlight. She perceived innumerable roots and seeds scattered in the soil. As soon as she noticed them, they became tiny packets of multi-colored lights that populated the darkness. The lights clustered to form recognizable structures, like trees, blankets of moss, and animals. She traversed the space in her mind. As she moved, the packets of energy whizzed by her like drops of rain. Cora focused on the energies that she recognized as seeds. She tried to latch onto one as they passed her by, but it was like trying to catch a single raindrop without getting touched by any others. She tried repeatedly, to no avail.

While Cora was concentrating, Isabella turned her attention to a younger girl with long, mocha colored hair. "Listen carefully, Maria. Magic is not something we conjure, it is something we channel. Don't try to force it into existence, just listen for it. It is all around us. When you learn to quiet your mind, you open yourself up to feeling things that you otherwise could not."

Maria inhaled deeply and exhaled slowly. "Good," Isabella said, "When you start to feel the natural energy around you, do not try to control it straight away. Just be present with it. The better able you are to listen to nature, the more powerful your magic will be."

As she concentrated with closed eyes, Maria furrowed her eyebrows.

"No," Isabella said. "You are trying too hard. You have to relax."

Cora heard her teacher's voice in the distance. She realized her attempts to seize the surrounding energy were as unproductive as flailing in the water and hoping to swim, so she stopped trying to do anything and just observed her environment. Gradually, the speedy packets of energy slowed until they were motionless. They surrounded her like stars in the night sky, but many were close enough to touch. She chose one of the shining seed orbs and reached out to it through the ether. When her own energy connected with it, she felt it acknowledge her, and she welcomed it into her, like Isabella had instructed. In a single instant, her being became one with the energy of the seed, and she understood it completely, as if they shared the same body and mind. The seed she had chosen was a dandelion. Cora drifted back toward consciousness, like waking from a lucid dream. She maintained a connection with the dandelion as she returned and brought the energy of the seed with her. When she opened her eyes, a small sprout came out of the soil in front of her: her dandelion.

Cora inhaled and exhaled slowly, smiling with delight. The way she felt about the appearance of the dandelion was like answering a knock at the door of her home to find a good friend waiting outside. Her energy fueled its growth, as if it were her child.

Slowly, Cora's mind returned and re-acclimated to the physical world. Her sense of self resurfaced; her hopes, fears, and every intrusive thought re-populated her mind. Her happiness for welcoming the dandelion into the world gave way to the realization that she had successfully cast a growth spell, which excited her and filled her with pride. The moment pride consumed her, her communication with nature was severed. Her energy had redirected away from the sprout, and it stopped growing.

"No!" Cora shouted, to no avail. "Noooo!" Sadness overtook her as she realized why she had failed to grow the sprout any further. She slumped over and looked at the ground, feeling dejected.

Isabella came over and inspected the sprout. "Not bad, Cora. It is a good start. Dust yourself off and try again."

Several meters behind Isabella, Francisco was pounding the ground in frustration. "Grow, you stupid plant! Do what I tell you!" he shouted at the dirt. Isabella left Cora to calm him down and try to help him.

Clara stepped through the underbrush to see what Cora had accomplished. "Oh! Not bad!" she remarked upon seeing the sprout. "I got one to grow too. It's taller though." She pointed to a sapling that grew a meter out of the ground on the other side of the brush.

Cora forced a smile. "Good job!"

"Thanks, bestie!" Clara looked to make sure Isabella was out of earshot, leaned in, and spoke quietly, "You know, I could try to help you if you want. So at least you could grow something big enough to pass today's challenge."

"No thanks," Cora declined, "I just need to keep practicing. If I had help, it would only make it harder to do other spells on my own in the future."

"Yeah, you're probably right. You need all the practice you can get. Maybe you should pray more or, you know, ask God to help you, like your cousin does." Clara pointed between the trees to Cora's right. Cora followed Clara's finger to see her cousin Geoffrey, a few meters away. He was in the same child's pose that Cora had been in, repeatedly reciting the Apostle's Creed loud enough for them to hear.

Cora rolled her eyes. "Maybe."

Clara shrugged. "Ok, well, I'm going to see how everyone else is doing."

Ricardo, a ten-year-old black-haired boy, was a short distance away from Cora in the opposite direction. Ricardo had given up trying to grow anything and was running around, playing in the trees. He ran through a thick patch of brush, down an embankment, and into a small clearing.

"Watch out!" Leora shouted at Ricardo. He had wandered close to the patch of dirt that Leora had planned to use for her growth spell.

Ricardo spun around, and when he realized he was not in danger, he retorted, "Watch yourself!"

Leora stuck her tongue out at him. He did the same and then ran away to find an unoccupied space in the forest, leaving Leora sitting alone at the base of a large, hundred-year oak tree. The dirt patch she had chosen for her growth enchantment was lit up by a ray of sunlight that came through a small gap in the canopy. A ring of fern covered embankment surrounded the clearing. It was a picturesque spot, and the same one Leora always chose when they practiced witchcraft in the forest. It felt private to her, even though Isabella and the other students were scattered amongst the nearby trees.

She closed her eyes and sat silently, with her legs crossed, slightly swaying side to side, as she unconsciously synchronized with the movement of the oak leaves in the gentle wind. With her eyes closed, she could hear all the sounds of the forest coming together in a symphony: the melodies of the birds, backed by the whistle of the wind, the percussion of crickets and a few falling acorns, and the rustling of a squirrel. She slowly placed her hands on the earth, gently sliding her fingertips over the soil, like a mother caressing the cheek of her newborn. Gradually, she heard low droning chords. They were nearly imperceptible at first, but she silenced her mind and concentrated until she could understand them. They reverberated energy in distinct ways, as though communicating. Leora welcomed the energy. She could feel vibrations within her, some from the outside and some originating from within herself. Her own chords, higher in frequency, playfully mingled with the lower ones. Although her eyes were closed, she perceived colors as wisps of smoke that moved in time with the progression of the chords. Her higher energies were bright colors of blue, white, and indigo, while the lower energies from the earth were deep browns and yellows. The musical energy and dancing colors filled her with incredible peace. As she lingered in communion with the earth, her senses wandered into a world beyond the physical, where she felt everything, and nothing, at the same time. The living and non-living things around her blended into one complete existence.

Among the sounds, Leora heard a unique tone. She recognized it coming from the frequency range of other plants, but it was unlike any she had ever heard. She zeroed in on it. As she did, she felt it notice her, and they harmonized. Somewhere in the fabric of space in the world beyond, Leora sensed the energies of Isabella and the other students from her class gathering at the opposite end of her glade. She slowly drifted back to her body, bringing the plant with her. Then she opened her eyes.

"Whoa!" several of the children exclaimed at once. Isabella gasped. Leora's body radiated a soft blue glow that fluctuated like the aurora borealis. Her eyes emanated the purest white light. The other students watched her in awe, as she lifted her right hand from the ground, rotated it so her palm was facing the sky, and raised it up. Suddenly, the dirt patch in the middle of the glade cracked like glass, and up through the middle shot a single translucent sprout. The sprout grew toward the sky, sprouting offshoots of leaves as its stem thickened. When it reached approximately a meter in height, it blossomed into a flower so beautiful that its appearance overwhelmed all who looked upon it. A kaleidoscope of diamond-like petals emerged, spinning and morphing with the complexity of a fractal.

Leora had given her energy to the plant to help it grow, and when she felt it had matured, she finally let it go. The light that Leora's body emitted dimmed, and her eyes returned to their natural blue. She smiled at the flower she had brought to the forest, admiring its beauty. For several seconds, it swayed in the wind, dazzling Isabella and the other students. Its flowers gradually spun off toward the sky, fading and evaporating with glints of light. When the flowers had all floated away, the rest of the plant aged within seconds. The leaves curled up, fell off, and decayed almost instantly, and the stem curled over and sank back into the earth. Finally, the cracks in the ground smoothed over, and the patch of dirt regained an unassuming appearance, as if nothing had ever emerged from it. Leora was still smiling, but tears streamed down her face.

Her classmates and teacher were at a loss for words to describe or question what they had just witnessed. There were no plants like it that grew anywhere in the world.

Leora sensed their confusion and explained, "It was my friend. I found it out there, and we lived years together. It knew how much I loved this place. To know me better, it wanted to experience my world, but it could not last long, so I had to let it go." She sniffled and looked at the sky.

"Leora..." Isabella struggled to find her words. "Leora, that was incredible!" She looked at Leora, still trying to process everything. She exhaled and smiled widely. "God has blessed you! I believe we have just witnessed a miracle!" She suddenly rushed over to Leora and took her hands. "Child, you are truly special." She helped Leora to her feet and turned to the other students. "Come! Let us go back to the schoolhouse. We have all learned much from today's practice. We must spread the good news about this miracle from God!"

The students cheered and rushed over to Leora, bombarding her with questions. Cora, however, held back. She smiled as she watched her sister's joy at being the center of attention. She walked to the dirt patch, knelt down, closed her eyes, and touched it. Residual energies lingered in the soil. She recognized one of them as her sister's. Its familiarity comforted her. The other was gentle and calm, like an old soul. She could sense the friendship between the energies, and what her sister said began to make sense to her. Cora gleaned an impression of time. Wherever Leora had gone, she truly had spent years' worth of time bonding with the being she brought back to grow here in the forest. Cora thought, *But to bring it here only for a few moments of life...* A dagger of sadness struck her heart as she fully realized the meaning of her sister's words. She opened her eyes, sat on the ground, and wept.

"Cora!" Isabella called out. "This is not a sad moment - this is a gift from God!" Cora was deaf to her teacher's words. Isabella tried a different way to reach her. "I know you tried hard with your enchantments, but we all fail sometimes. I can devote one-on-one time with you to help you, if you'd like, and the next time we come back here, you can grow something wonderful. Would that help?"

Cora finally heard her teacher and laughed incredulously. "What?"

Isabella repeated, "I said I could schedule one-on-one time with you and..."

"No, I'm fine. I'll be fine. I just need to practice some more." Cora said what she knew her teacher wanted to hear to placate her.

"That's right. That's the best way to look at it. Now come, let us go back to school."

Cora stood and joined the others. What she had discovered about Leora from reading the residual energies filled her with awe and pride for her little sister. Plants were not the only creatures that grew that day.

4

It took Thalia a while to settle her daughters from the excitement of witchcraft practice, but the girls had finally gone to sleep. Thalia exited the roundhouse and cast a protection spell over it, before departing for the coven's prayer circle.

She made it to the village center roughly forty minutes earlier than their planned meeting time, but that was what she had intended. She passed the entrance to the Ortiz Estate and proceeded to the graveyard behind the church. The graveyard stretched out in quiet rows with older headstones worn by time near the entrance, while the newest markers stood at the farthest end. Thalia approached one in the second to last row that read: *Here lies Faustus Neumann, beloved husband and father*. She stood in front of it in silence for a minute.

"I know your body was never laid here, but I don't know where else I would go. I miss you terribly, my love. Everyone told me time would heal the pain...but all time has done has turned the stabbing pain into a duller ache. You took half of my heart with you, and I am reminded of its absence every day. You are now my shadow. Every time I pass our oak tree in the forest, every time I make your favorite stew, every time I lay down to sleep and feel cold where I once felt your warmth, every time I look at them..." Thalia choked up.

"You should see them now, Faust. Leora is ten! And she's still just as playful as ever. You knew, didn't you? Even in the little time you had with her, somehow you knew how easily she would find delight in life's gifts. And Cora...she's just like you, Faust. Just as headstrong and curious. She's so smart." Thalia smiled, thinking of the parts of her husband that lived in their children.

"That's actually why I'm here tonight, my love. I am trying my best, but I feel like I am letting Cora down, and therefore breaking our promise. The other day, I read her the letter you left me. I thought it would help me reach her. She interpreted it...differently, to put it lightly. She places too much value on knowledge and power. I see her struggle with her faith. I know you never agreed with Christian doctrine, but it's the best way I know how to teach her the importance of love and compassion. If you can hear me out there, somewhere, I beseech you for guidance. I have asked the Lord for help too, but I must admit I have my own doubts as well. Perhaps she can sense that in me. She is very perceptive. Very sensitive. She cares a great deal about how the villagers see us, and especially about what the other children think of her." She paused and looked up at the moon.

"I know how hard it is to be a teenager trying to find one's self and one's place in a world that rarely makes sense. I only hope that she finds a path that brings her joy."

Thalia went over and knelt beside the headstone. She placed a single red rose on the ground in front of it, resting her forehead against the cold stone and closing her eyes.

She stood to leave and noticed a patch of dirt where the grass had worn away, in the next row back. Ortiz was the name on the stone beside it. "You hide it well, En," Thalia remarked to herself.

As she departed, she passed the grave of her parents. She felt its presence, as if the headstone were watching her, although she did not look, refusing to acknowledge it.

The Ortiz Estate was a stone's throw away from the church. The manor house was the only structure in the valley that could compete with the church steeple in height. Its light gray stone facade matched the color of the rock wall that surrounded it, except for the iron gate at the entrance from the village's main road, where Thalia's and Enheduanna's maiden name had been stricken from the engraving on the post.

The entrance led into a grand courtyard, which contained the only garden in the village that was for decoration instead of food. The house was two stories tall, and wrapped around itself in the shape of the letter C. The courtyard extended into the middle of the C, where a statue of John the Baptist stood atop a pedestal that rose from the middle of a fountain. The house had fireplaces at each end, on both the top and bottom floors. The top floor was filled with bed chambers, including the master at the front of the house, and rooms for house servants and guests around the side and back.

Thalia knocked on the oak door. Enrique opened it and welcomed her. He led her to the library. When she entered the room, the smell of burning cedar greeted her. She saw the other coven elders seated around the fire, and from the sparsity of the hors d'oeuvres tray, she surmised they had been there for some time. Her arrival caused an immediate cessation of all discussion. The first and only one to respond to her presence was Elise.

"Thalia!" Elise stood up from her seat to approach Thalia and greeted her with two kisses. Elise's light brown hair draped over a black velvet dress with golden embroidery, that sat low on her shoulders and revealed the top of her ample bosom. Her free-spirited personality and provocative attire would often catch the wandering eyes of the village men, and earned her the ire of the other elders. At twenty-two, Elise Bellarose was the youngest of the elders. Despite her youth, she was a widow. Her husband had died under mysterious circumstances, which left her with a substantial inheritance and often made her the topic of village gossip. Thalia had suspected that it was this inheritance, and not her skill with witchcraft, that caused Enheduanna to nominate her to become an elder.

"How are you? How are the girls? Here, come sit with me," Elise offered.

Before Thalia could respond, Mary cut in, "We do not have time for idle chat. It is late and we have work to do."

Enheduanna stood up and turned toward Thalia. She wore a navy blue bodice with white decorative trim that flowed into her navy skirt and its white hemline. The golden oak was pinned to her breast, as usual. Her braided hair was like a crown. She supported what Mary had said, "Yes, you are late, sister. We have all been waiting for you."

Thalia was certain she was not late. She felt a creeping suspicion that the elders were hiding something from her, but she apologized, regardless. "I'm sorry. The girls did not want to go to sleep tonight, and you know how long the walk is for me."

Elise looked down, feeling embarrassed for her friend. The other elders stared at Thalia, unrelenting. She repeated, "I'm sorry."

"All is well. Come join us, sister Thalia," Isabella said in a light tone of voice. She smiled and held out her hand in a welcoming gesture.

Josephine, who was sitting beside Mary, scowled at Isabella's kindness toward Thalia. Like Elise, Josephine Matisse's family had emigrated from France, however, her family joined Mary's and Enheduanna's families as the wealthy elites who made it possible for the children of the village to get an education. She had weak skills with magic, but her conservative nature and tendency to pander to Enheduanna and Mary elevated her status among the group. She was also dressed well for the occasion.

Constantina Sierra-Mendoza, the fourth of the original elders, remained silent, as usual, sitting beside Josephine on the couch opposite the one Elise had come from. Constantina was a small woman in her late-thirties, with jet black hair and pale skin. Her brown garment was covered with cat hairs of various colors. She and her husband had a cottage that was filled with all varieties of cats that came and went as they pleased.

Thalia joined Elise on the couch where Enheduanna had been sitting. Enheduanna explained the situation. "As we all know, the Spanish monarchy holds the misguided view that witches are heretics and inquisitors have been scouring the country for women like us. We have been fortunate to have remained undiscovered so far. This morning, however, there was an eagle sighted near the village. Now, this does not mean inquisitors have found us. The bird could have simply come down from the mountains in search of food. Nevertheless, we will take no chances. We have gathered here to combine our power to cast an enchantment over the entire village. We will cloak it from view. Anyone who comes to the mountain pass, where the road forks down into our valley, will see nothing - no buildings, no fields of crops, no people, and not even the roads that pass through here. This will help keep us safe from those who would seek out and kill witches like us. If you would all now follow me into the courtyard, we will cast the spell under the moonlight."

The women followed Enheduanna. She lit a lantern and led them from the library to the breezeway in the middle of the house, and then out into the courtyard, where the fountain statue stood. They walked beyond the fountain to a landscaped circle of apricot trees in the garden. When they got to the middle of the circle of trees, they formed a circle themselves by joining their hands, thus forming a concentric circle of humans amid a circle of fruit-bearing trees, beneath the light of a waxing crescent moon. Their positioning and timing would enhance their connection with nature, which would make it easier for them to cast their spell.

The coven elders closed their eyes. Enheduanna led them in prayer. She spoke, and the elders repeated. When the prayer had finished, they stood silently with their eyes still closed and their hands still interlocked. To an outside observer, it would have seemed like nothing was happening. The women remained in their silent vigil for roughly one minute, and then opened their eyes and dropped their hands, all at the same time.

Isabella, who had stood between Thalia and Enheduanna, wore a look of sorrow that went unnoticed. When they harmonized their energies to cast the spell, she completely connected with both sisters. She saw into their hearts, and what she saw filled her with sadness.

Enheduanna said, "It is done. This enchantment will last until the moon is full, which will buy us enough time to let anyone who may be seeking our village pass by without noticing. Thank you, sisters. That will be all for tonight."

The women bid farewell to one another and departed from the courtyard through the iron gate.

Isabella lingered. She desperately wanted to help the sisters understand each other better, but she was unsure of what to say, and reluctant to meddle with the affairs of another family. "Sister Enheduanna?"

"Yes?" Enheduanna turned toward her.

Isabella stood stupefied for a moment, trying to think of what to say. "Next time we cast a spell together, you should hold Thalia's hand. It only seems right for the coven leader to harmonize with her own blood." She was pleased with herself for thinking of that recommendation. It would let the sisters connect on their own, without her having to do anything.

Enheduanna smiled lamely. "Ha. Yes, I suppose you're right. Maybe we will next time."

Isabella smiled. "Good."

"Ok, well, good night sister."

"Good night," Isabella replied.

Enheduanna turned back toward the house and scowled. "That would be a cold day in hell," she muttered to herself as she trudged to the door.

5

The early morning sun graced the valley and lightened the inside of the roundhouse. After a late night of spell casting, Thalia had struggled to wake up at the early hour she needed to. It was Sunday, and they needed to get ready for church.

Cora folded her pillow over her head to dull the sound of her mother banging around the house.

"Wake up, sleepyheads!" Thalia called out.

"But mama, it's so early!" Leora protested, "The sun isn't even up yet!"

"Yes it is, dear. And that means we have to get ready for church."

"Can't we skip today?"

Cora rolled over and answered, "You can't skip the Sabbath. It's literally impossible. It's a day for resting and doing nothing. So even if you don't do anything, you're still observing it."

Leora giggled. "If that's true, then why do we need to go to church on the Sabbath?"

Cora smiled. "Good question."

Thalia turned away so they would not see her smirk. "Rest doesn't mean doing nothing, it means breaking from our usual daily labors for spiritual renewal. Now come on, let's go, girls."

"So we rest by spending the morning worshiping God. Very refreshing indeed," Cora quipped.

"Does church not make you feel spiritually re-energized?" Thalia asked.

"I suppose it does re-energize me," Cora answered. "When it ends and we can go home," she muttered under her breath.

"What was that?"

"Nothing." Cora groaned and swung her feet out of bed. "Ok, time to get up." She began brushing her hair.

"Put this on, Leora, quickly!" Thalia tossed a dress onto Leora's belly as she lay in bed. "Or we will be late again and Father Julian will reprimand us sinners."

"Yes, if there is one thing God detests, it is tardiness," Cora said. She looked at her mother and sister, and they all burst out laughing.

"Seriously though, at the very least, it will be embarrassing," Thalia said. "So come on! Finish brushing your hair, Cora, and put that dress on, Leora!"

The three of them scrambled to get dressed. Thalia rushed the girls out the door. As she closed the door, she realized she had forgotten her star pendant, and went back inside to get it.

"Come on, mother!" Cora shouted.

"Yeah, you're making us late again!" Leora added. She and Cora laughed.

"Just give me three seconds!" Thalia shouted from inside. She then rushed back outside and shut the door. She straightened the pendant on her chest and joined the girls on the dirt path.

Leora stared at the pendant as it sparkled in the sunlight. Her mother tossed her long, dark hair back behind her shoulders, its layers unfurling like the feathers of a raven, contrasting her porcelain skin. The shining white star between her breasts was the perfect accessory for her church dress. The dress was as dark green as the surrounding pines, and it made her emerald green eyes look even greener. *Beautiful*, Leora thought.

They arrived at church just as Father Julian was closing the grand wooden doors at the entrance, and after exchanging a few hurried pleasantries on the way in, took their usual seats in a pew beside Enheduanna and their cousin Geoffrey. Beside Geoffrey sat Mary, the coven elder, with her husband and their adult son and his wife.

Father Julian began his sermon. "Welcome, children of the Lord, on this wonderful Sunday. A few days ago, I visited with the Herrero family and blessed our sister Rosa, who is still bedridden from her tragic horse riding accident. I found myself wondering why God, in his infinite wisdom, would allow such a sweet woman to be so afflicted. It is in moments like these that we are tested, so today I would like to speak about doubt, and describe how the Scriptures say we should deal with it."

Father Julian gave the slightest glance to Enheduanna, but it did not go unnoticed by Thalia. She recalled her sister's comment from the other day about helping Father Julian prepare for today's sermon, and she surmised Enheduanna must have told him about Cora's questions in class. She glared at Enheduanna, who pretended not to notice. Then she remembered the awkwardness of the coven elders when she met them the night before. *How much have you been gossiping about my daughter?* She wondered to herself.

Father Julian continued, "I will begin by reading from Proverbs three, verses five through eight: Trust in the Lord with all your heart, and do not lean on your own understanding. In all your ways acknowledge him, and he will make straight your paths. Be not wise in your own eyes; fear the Lord, and turn away from evil. It will be healing to your flesh and refreshment to your bones." He paused to let the congregation reflect before expounding on the verses. "As sinners, our own understanding of the world is flawed and filled with biases from our emotions and impulses. This passage tells us that when we are uncertain, we should trust in God, whose logic is infallible. We put our faith in Him to guide us, as is written in Isaiah fifty-eight, eleven: And the Lord will guide you continually. So even when we are lost, or confused, all we need to do is put our faith in God to show us the way. He always reveals the truth to us, even if it sometimes takes us days, months, or even years to recognize it. We trust in God because He is trustworthy, and because He is righteous and holy. This is also why we follow God's plan. By obeying Him, we follow the purity in His law."

He continued to preach about the virtues of a life of servitude to God, occasionally glancing at Cora, Thalia, and Enheduanna. Then he addressed the witches sitting in the pews, "I know many of us wonder why God, in His infinite wisdom, gifted some of His children in our humble village the knowledge to wield magic. Most of Christendom treats witches as the concubines of Satan. But here, we have recognized that it was God's will to bestow these gifts. Our village is a private sanctuary to those among us who wield them. When the Bible tells us to trust in God's plan, it tells us to trust that the witches among us are here because He wants them to be. Whatever the reason, it is a righteous one, and we will be a paragon for the world. When the time is right, we will teach the world how witches can live peacefully and piously."

"Hallelujah!" Enheduanna shouted. She had been nodding vigorously as he spoke.

Mary smiled with her eyes at Enheduanna. *She did it! She convinced the old man*, Mary thought.

Father Julian looked directly at Cora as he preached, "It is confusing, and perhaps even frightening, to learn that magic exists, or that there are forces in this world we do not understand; forces that are not written about in the good book. But fear not, for nothing is beyond the understanding of God. The existence of magic, and its absence from the Bible, does not mean God does not exist, or that He does not love us, or that He does not have a plan for every one of us, and therefore it should not change our faith."

Cora noticed his focus on her, and her face turned red with embarrassment. She looked down at her feet. Thalia noticed Cora's reaction and put her hand on Cora's, comforting her. Thalia's face was red too, but with anger. Regardless of her belief in Father Julian's words, she was not happy that Enheduanna had taken it upon herself to set up a thinly disguised lecture for her daughter.

Father Julian repeated himself a couple more times in different ways before wrapping up his sermon. At the end of the service, Thalia restrained her anger and decided to confront her sister privately. "En, would you please wait here with me? I must speak with you."

Enheduanna smiled politely, "Of course, sister, anything you need. Mary, would you mind walking Geoffrey home? Thalia wants to have a word with me."

Mary accepted, and Geoffrey followed her out of the pew.

Thalia turned to her daughter, "Girls, would you please wait for me outside? I need to speak with your Aunt En for a minute."

"Yes, mother," they both replied. They joined the other villagers who were filing out of the church. Father Julian waited by the doors in the vestibule to bid farewell to each person as they left.

Thalia took Enheduanna to the side of the church. She whispered so the villagers who had not yet left would not hear, but her anger made it a harsh whisper, breaking slightly as she emphasized some words, "The other day, I told you I would raise my children my own way, and you agreed not to interfere. You agreed, and then you went straight to Father Julian to manipulate his sermon."

Although she had tried to be quiet, her voice caught the attention of a woman who was making her way toward the church doors. She looked back at them, but tried to be discreet about her eavesdropping. Enheduanna listened with her head tilted and smiling with her mouth. She noticed the woman looking back at them, so she replied a little louder than Thalia had spoken, to make sure the woman heard her, "Thalia, I don't understand. I don't know what you are talking about. I would never presume to interfere with the way a woman raises her own children, even if they are my nieces."

Thalia's face flushed red, and she glared at her sister. "You..." she lowered her head, trying to corral her fury before responding. "You know exactly what I'm talking about. All I will say is that this is the last time I will be cordial about this. I trust you will leave my children's parenting to me."

Enheduanna forced her smile wider. "Of course, dear sister. Honestly, there is no need to be upset. If I did anything to offend you, I apologize."

The woman who had been eavesdropping was now exiting and far enough away not to hear them. Thalia was still furious, but she had gotten her point across, so she turned to leave. Enheduanna grabbed her arm and forcefully pulled her close. She whispered into Thalia's ear, "You would do well to remember what I promised you the other day too, sister."

Thalia whipped her head around to look into Enheduanna's eyes. "Let go of my arm!" she commanded, abandoning her attempts to contain her anger.

Enheduanna squinted her eyes and challenged her. "Or what?"

Thalia's lips curled back in contempt. The church dimmed as if thick clouds had blocked the sunlight from outside. The candles around the altar, and in the wall sconces along the sides of the nave dimmed too; their flames weakening as though being absorbed by the surrounding air. The orange glow of their light became burning rings around the centers of Thalia's emerald eyes.

Enheduanna looked around nervously. If she provoked her sister now, nobody would witness it. She also realized this meant facing Thalia's wrath alone. She quickly released Thalia's arm, as if pulling her hand away from a hot stove.

Thalia's eyes returned to their brilliant green, the candles regained their vivacity, and sunlight returned to the church. Enheduanna chuckled meekly, but then regained her moral authority. "Such a temper. And you wonder why I worry about Cora."

Thalia scowled, but said nothing more. She simply left the church, briefly shaking Father Julian's hand as she departed.

Enheduanna followed. As she shook Father Julian's hand, she commended him, "Excellent sermon today, father."

"Thank you, sister."

Thalia walked briskly down the church steps and collected her children. "Let's go, girls." They noticed her irritation and followed her without a word.

Cora mis-attributed her mother's irritation, thinking it was because her questions in class caused Father Julian to preach about doubt and obedience to God. *She's embarrassed by me*, Cora thought.

As the sun set Sunday evening, the morning church service had already become a memory. Cora and Leora were playing in the tall grass at the edge of the forest by their house. They chased each other around, laughing.

Leora tripped and fell, cutting her knee on a rock. "Ow!"

"Are you ok?" Cora asked.

"Yes, I'm fine. It's just a scratch. I can heal it. Come help me."

Cora sat next to Leora in the grass and took one of Leora's hands in hers. Leora placed her other hand on her knee, and Cora put her other hand on the ground. They closed their eyes.

Immediately, the two of them had their senses multiplied. They felt themselves merge with the environment, as if it were an extension of their own bodies. They felt the warmth of one another, like two flames flickering in harmony.

Cora was surprised how quickly she entered this state with Leora. If she had tried on her own, she would have had to concentrate on quieting her mind, but with Leora, it was instantaneous. *Is this how it always is for her*? She wondered.

The vibrations of the earth and the surrounding creatures blended into a symphony. Everything from the largest tree down to the smallest bacterium, and even the rocks and other nonliving material, joined in the gentle music. Glowing star-like lights accompanied the acoustic energies, whimsically drifting like snowflakes.

The girls looked at their surroundings with their minds' eyes, admiring the beauty of this hidden world that lay beyond their normal existence. They looked at each other and giggled. They could see into each other the same way they could see into the creatures and things around them. In that moment, the sisters understood each other completely, as if they shared one body, and that body was also part of the earth. Everything connected as one whole.

God, Leora thought, *this must be how God sees everything.*

Cora did not know how to explain her experience in the world beyond, but she doubted it was God. After everything she had learned about God's perfection and the fallibility of humans, she did not think it would be possible for them to directly connect with God, or experience what it would be like to see the world through God's eyes.

Leora sensed her sister's skepticism and telepathically explained herself, *God is no different from us. He is us. He is everything. To be connected like this is to be one with God.*

I don't know, Cora thought, *that is a flexible interpretation of the Scripture. I don't think Father Julian or Aunt En would agree with that.*

They don't need to. You don't need to. We can each experience God in our own way, Leora responded.

Cora laughed, causing a wave of glittering euphoria that expanded from her being into the universe. The surrounding energies seemed to laugh with her. *You're just making up your own rules now. Father Julian even said it himself when he read from Proverbs today: do not lean on your own understanding.* Her memory recalled Father Julian's voice and caused it to materialize in both of their minds.

Leora capitulated. *Well, I don't know how else to make sense of what we experience, in this state or otherwise, in life.*

Leora's thoughts resonated with Cora, and she realized their father must have struggled with these same questions.

While the girls were telepathically communicating with one another, energy had flowed from the earth into Leora's hand and throughout her body. Her knee was healed. Upon realizing this, the girls began to let go of their connection with nature to return to their normal states of consciousness.

Leora suddenly stopped drifting back, yanking Cora's consciousness back with her. Cora would have wondered why, but since they were still connected, she instantly understood why Leora had lingered. Just behind the tree line in the forest, there was an unusual energy. What made it unusual was that it was actually not energy at all. It was more like an absence of energy, like a small void of darkness. It was only perceptible because of the energy that moved around it, in the same way water would flow around a boulder in the creek. The girls marveled at the void, wondering what it was. It filled them with a slight malaise that was shared by the other living entities around it. They sensed that whatever it was did not belong.

Let's go, Cora thought, hoping it would disappear when they severed their connection with nature.

They quickly awakened from their dreamlike, meditative state, and saw that the sun had gone down. The grass was becoming damp from the night air, and a fog was descending from the mountains. Leora turned to look into the trees where they had detected the void. The hairs on the back of her neck stood up. She saw nothing, but she felt something watching them from the darkness. She turned to Cora, "Do you see anything?"

Cora's uneasiness had disappeared. She felt and saw nothing in the trees. "No. Maybe it's just an empty spot in the forest." She stood and helped Leora to her feet. Leora kept her eyes trained on the trees, and Cora tried to reassure her, "I'm sure it's nothing, but we can investigate it tomorrow morning before school, if you want. Let's get inside. Mother probably has dinner ready by now."

6

Monday morning, Isabella stood outside the schoolhouse ringing a bell to welcome the students into the classroom. She stopped ringing it when Cora and Leora walked up to the door.

"Cora, may I speak with you privately for a moment?" Isabella asked.

Cora nodded and waited outside for the rest of the students to enter the building. Her body tensed up as she anticipated another lecture.

Isabella closed the door. She smiled kindly at Cora and touched her shoulder. "I wanted to apologize if I seemed dismissive of your questions last week. It's perfectly normal for people your age to start questioning the world. You have every right to, and...I hope that you have not been...

discouraged or ashamed by certain people who may not understand why you would ask such questions." Isabella tried to choose her words carefully.

Isabella's empathy surprised Cora. She did not know how to respond, so she stayed quiet.

Isabella continued, "It occurred to me that Father Julian might be able to answer your questions better than I would. I have asked if he could speak with you privately this afternoon, and he agreed. If you would leave class a bit early, he will be available in his office at the back of the church. Would you like that?"

"Sure, I guess," Cora said. She was skeptical that Father Julian would do any more than chastise her for her skepticism, but she lacked the confidence to decline Isabella's invitation.

"Very well. Very well." Isabella was pleased with herself and hoped that Father Julian would help Cora. She opened the door, and they entered the schoolhouse, leaving the door open.

As Cora took her seat, the other students watched her, wondering what Isabella had said to her. Isabella addressed the class, "Before we begin today, I would like to remind everyone that all questions are welcome in the classroom, and any ridicule will not be tolerated. Is that understood?"

"Yes, Mother Isabella," the students responded.

Isabella picked up her lecture from the previous week by progressing through the book of Genesis, teaching the class about the story of Cain and Abel. In the afternoon, they studied mathematics.

The students were in the middle of practicing addition on their own, when Geoffrey broke the silence. "This is so boring! Why can't we practice more enchantments? Why do we always have to wait until Saturday?"

Isabella rebuked him, "Now Geoffrey, you know it's impolite to break your classmates' concentration. And you also know we must honor the agreement between the coven and Father Julian."

"But magic is actually useful. When are we ever going to need to know how to add numbers?"

Isabella explained, "Our village is fortunate. We only have magic because of the discoveries of Faustus Neumann, who migrated to our village and taught us how to connect with nature and channel its energy. Father Julian saw his arrival as God's will, and his discoveries as gifts from God, so he made an agreement with the coven that we can practice magic, and teach magic, as long as it is always secondary to the Scripture, and as long as our students learn deference to God above all. So I teach you all the same subjects you would learn anywhere else, and we limit our craft to Saturdays. Witches are persecuted in most of the world, so we must be careful with our magic, and only use it within the valley, or when absolutely necessary. Mathematics, however, is useful anywhere in the world, and for a variety of different reasons."

"But my mother says I need to practice more. She says I am too slow to quiet my mind and connect with nature," Geoffrey lamented.

Francisco snorted and snickered with his friend, Miguel, from the back of the class. "My mother said..." he mocked.

Isabella scolded Francisco, "Enough! Geoffrey's mother has a point. Many of you struggle to connect with nature, especially you, Francisco."

Francisco slouched back in his chair. Miguel laughed at him, and he hit Miguel's arm. Isabella did not see.

Isabella continued, "With practice, it will become easier for you to enter the state of mind necessary to use magic. But you can always practice on your own after school. In time, it will get easier. Eventually, your connection will become automatic. You will be able to connect with nature instantly whenever you please. When that happens, you may channel magic at will, just like us coven elders."

Cora asked, "How long will it take to get that good?"

"Well, it depends. Some people are naturals. Your mother, for instance, was always adept at it, and she learned within a few years. Your Aunt Enheduanna, our coven leader, was also a quick learner. It took her a couple of years longer than your mother, but she is now a very powerful witch. It took me longer still, about ten years, and Constantina and Elise were about the same. So most of you should get to that point by the time you are sixteen years old. Some of you may get there sooner, and some later."

"Why doesn't Father Julian know magic? Why don't my parents know it? Why is it only the coven that knows?" asked a fourteen-year-old girl with neatly tied back black hair, who sat in the middle of the class, next to Ricardo.

Isabella answered, "Many people dislike the idea of magic or witchcraft. As you know, Anabella, as you all know, the inquisition seeks to kill witches. They see the craft as blasphemy. Even though Father Julian and your parents have more progressive perspectives, most of them are still not comfortable learning it, or participating. For others, it is very difficult for them to quiet their thoughts enough to connect with nature. Those types of people never develop abilities, but in theory, anyone could. We, as a village, decided that we should teach you all, because some of you likely would have learned anyway, and it would be too dangerous to develop magical abilities without religious guidance. Just think of the harm a wayward witch could do. But witches who spread the good word and follow God's plan...imagine what a wonderful world we could build!"

"It would be a world in which witches are the instruments of God." Enheduanna's voice boomed through the classroom as she entered the building. Isabella bowed her head, backed into the wall in the front of the class, and allowed Enheduanna to take command of her classroom. Enheduanna continued, "God has chosen us to be His emissaries. There are witches scattered throughout the world practicing in hiding, because they are hunted by those who do not understand us. But our village is a sanctuary. We can practice here, unafraid. So it is of utmost importance that you never demonstrate your abilities outside of this valley, and that when you use your gifts, you do so in the service of the Almighty. If Satan tempts you to use them for selfish or evil means, your soul will burn for eternity in the pit of fire."

She paced back and forth in front of the students, with her hands behind her back. "Our coven will ensure that you grow to be God fearing witches. One day, you will join the coven. We will grow stronger as we increase our numbers, and when the time it right, we will spread the good word throughout the land." She waved her hands in broad, sweeping gestures to illustrate her words.

She looked out a window at the village center. "People are fickle. They fear the unknown and bow to anyone who provides certainty. When they see our power, they will turn away from their priests and pastors. The monarchy will heel to us and abandon their inquisition. Everyone will look to us for guidance, because they will think we have the answers and can provide security. So it will be up to us to keep the faith and maintain peace through order. Do you understand?"

Nobody answered, so Enheduanna repeated her question louder, in a more intimidating manner,

"Do you understand?"

"Yes, Mother Enheduanna," the class answered in unison, except for Cora and Leora who called her "Aunt En," and Geoffrey, who simply replied "Yes, mother".

Isabella looked at Enheduanna meekly as the coven leader worked herself into a fervor. She was skeptical of Enheduanna's revolutionary ideas and uncomfortable with indoctrinating the children, but she dared not voice any opposition. She was also conflicted, as she could see the merits of a world where witches could live peacefully among common people, and she wanted that world.

Some of the children were enraptured by Enheduanna's speech, while others watched her with stifled amusement, unconvinced that they wanted to join her cause, or that such a crusade would actually change the world. But they all assumed learning witchcraft meant ultimately joining the coven.

Enheduanna left the class with a final warning. "I will say this again. It is vital that you put your faith in God's plan..." She stopped walking for a moment in front of Cora's desk. "And that you obey God, and your elders, as we teach you His will." She stepped away from Cora's desk. "Thank you, sister Isabella, for allowing me to interrupt your class. I was on my way to see Father Julian, and I heard you speaking as I passed. Exemplary as your lecture was, I thought I would add my voice."

Isabella replied, "Of course, sister, the voice

of our coven leader is always welcome here." She bowed again.

"Good day," Enheduanna said to Isabella. She turned to the class. "Good day, children." Then she left, closing the door behind her.

Isabella drew the class back to scholastics, "Now please, let us return to mathematics."

Shortly before the end of the school day, Isabella excused Cora, who walked the short distance from the schoolhouse to the church next door. She found Father Julian in his small living quarters at the back, which were separated from the church by a wall and had a private entrance.

"Ah, Cora, welcome!" Father Julian said as Cora entered. He offered her a seat at a small table and sat across from her. "Would you like a glass of water?"

"No, thank you," she replied.

He tried to make small talk. "How is your mother doing?"

"She's fine."

Father Julian smiled. He suspected Cora was uncomfortable and possibly annoyed with being there. "I suppose I'll be direct. I have heard from Isabella and your aunt that you may be questioning your faith. They each had their own interpretation of the intent of your questions. Your aunt's interpretation was...negative. However, I choose to believe the best in people, and I think your questions originated from innocent curiosity rather than deviance. It is perfectly normal to have doubts about one's faith. I have had my own to wrestle with. I'm not going to lecture you or judge you. I just want to hear what you are thinking. If I can answer your questions, then I will. If not, I will do my best, and leave the rest to the Lord. Is that alright with you?"

Cora relaxed a little. "Yes."

"Very well. Why don't we start with your question from last week? Isabella told me you asked why it is wrong to disobey God. Tell me about that."

Cora shifted in her seat, remembering Father Julian's promise not to judge her. She explained herself, and as she did, she gradually unloaded the thoughts she had kept in her head. "Mother Isabella didn't explain why it is wrong to disobey God. She just said that disobedience has consequences - burning in hell, whereas obedience presumably has a reward in the afterlife. If it's not inherently good or bad, then obeying God is just a matter of choosing consequences. So I don't understand why people say sinners are evil. Maybe sinners accept they are going to hell, and have decided to sin, anyway. What's wrong with that? Mother Isabella said God gave us the choice, and he wants us to choose. So what if a person does not choose God?"

Father Julian listened with surprise as he realized there was more to the girl who sat across from him than he imagined. He put his hand on his chin, leaned back in his chair, and considered her questions. "But God is good. So not choosing God is choosing evil."

Cora responded immediately, "But *why* is God good? What does it mean to be good?"

"Goodness is life, love, compassion, selflessness...it's all the things that give you a warm feeling inside when you do them. Evil is the opposite - it's hatred, selfishness and anything that makes you hurt inside."

"But evil can feel good, too. Revenge can be satisfying, for example. And good can feel bad, like when you love someone who doesn't love you back," Cora asserted.

"Yes, but that is the devil tainting your perspective, tempting you to abandon good and pursue evil."

"So if I love someone, which is good, but they do not love me back, how is that the devil tempting me?"

Father Julian raised his eyebrows and looked up to the right. "How would it make *you* feel if you loved someone and they did not love you back? What would *you* want to do?"

"I would be sad and angry. Maybe jealous. I'd want to cry or scream, or pound my pillow."

"Exactly. You would turn to destructive behavior. That is what the devil wants. You pound your pillow and feel a little better, so you are tempted to do more dark things."

Cora scrunched her lips together. "That

doesn't seem fair. There are so many things in life that hurt. It's like we're set up to fail."

"The path to righteousness is not meant to be easy. But God knows this. That is why He gave us His only son, Jesus Christ, so that even when we try our best and fail, we can accept Jesus' sacrifice, and still make it to heaven."

Cora nodded. "Ok, but again, there's a reward. Shouldn't good and evil be the ends? Forget the afterlife. Shouldn't God want us to choose Him because it is intrinsically good, not because we're afraid of going to hell and want to go to heaven instead?"

Father Julian smiled. The conversation fascinated him and gave him a newfound respect for Cora. "You are a sharp one, aren't you? Your father's daughter, for certain. If only you were born male, you would have made an excellent scholar."

Cora also found herself enjoying the conversation, but she indignantly rejected his last statement. "I can be a scholar if I want to be. And you're dodging my question, old man," she teased.

Father Julian guffawed. "This old man needs time to think. And I'm sure you could do whatever you set your mind to, dear Cora. You and your sister. The world is changing. But one thing that is constant is causality. Every action has a reaction. That was how God made the world, and that is why I believe He offers reward and punishment. Heaven is not a reward, it is a consequence. But so much of the world is uneducated and incapable of thinking like you, Cora. When we, the representatives of the church, preach, we must do it in a way that the common people understand, and rewards and consequences are the easiest ways to convince them." He paused. "Does that make sense?"

Cora nodded. "I think so."

"Let me ask this. When you do as your mother asks, why do you do it?"

"Because she would punish me if I didn't."

Father Julian smiled. "Yes, I'm sure she would. But even if she didn't, you would still listen to her, would you not? Most of the time, anyway?"

"I suppose."

"Why?"

She imagined what it would be like to be her mother. "Because...because she probably has good reason for asking me to do something."

"Yes, that is one reason. Because she has higher knowledge that you might not have as a child. But why else?"

"Because I respect her."

"Yes, you respect her. And why do you respect her?"

"She cares for me and Leora. She works hard for us."

"She loves you. And you love her. So you do as she asks because of your love. The same is true of God."

Cora thought, *But what if I don't love God? How can anyone love someone they've never known?*

She could not bring herself to ask Father Julian the question.

Father Julian interpreted Cora's silence as acceptance. He went on, "Isabella does her best, but a mind like yours ought to be given every opportunity to learn. I have several books here, mostly about the Scripture..." He reflected on their conversation, "But there are a few translated Greek texts that you might find more interesting. Let me see." He scanned the spines of the books on his shelf. "Ah, here," he picked one out. "This is called The Republic, by the Greek philosopher Plato. Start with this one. When you read it, do not care so much about the outcome of the discussions, but pay more attention to the style of thinking."

Cora took the book.

Father Julian gestured at the other books. "You are welcome to borrow these any time you please."

"Thank you," Cora said.

"You're welcome! You had better go home now, before it gets too late."

Despite her lingering doubts about God, Cora left feeling hopeful and validated. She had never spoken with an adult like that before.

That night after dinner, Cora and Leora sat by the fire with their mother and told her about their day.

"She said, *or else your souls will burn for eternity in the pit of fire!*" Cora spoke in a harsh voice, straightened her back, and pulled her hair back tightly to mock her aunt. Leora and Thalia laughed.

Thalia defended her sister. "She was just trying to emphasize the importance of using magic for the right reasons. She can come across as a little draconian, but she means well."

"She said one day everybody in the world will look to us to guide them," Leora said. "Is that true?"

Thalia shrugged. "Your Aunt En has bold dreams. However, when you are old enough to venture out into the world, people will probably gravitate toward you, not because you can use magic, but because you will know how to connect with them. When people feel understood, they notice and appreciate it. They might like you and not be able to explain why. Especially men."

"Ooooh! Like how Francisco likes Cora!" Leora teased.

"Shut up!" Cora said, slapping her sister's arm. Leora laughed

Thalia smiled and remarked, "If he teases you a lot, he probably does like you, Cora."

Cora cringed. "Ew! He's repulsive! He's such a big oaf. And he has goofy hair. And an enormous nose. And he's an idiot!"

Leora pushed her finger on the tip of her nose to flatten and widen it, and spoke in a low voice to impersonate Francisco, "Why do you ask so many questions, Cora? Why don't you ask me on a date in the forest?"

"Stop it!" Cora said while trying to hold back her laughter. She tried to slap Leora again, but Leora pulled away, rolled over, and laughed.

"Alright girls, that's enough," Thalia said.

Leora sat up and settled her laughter. "So Cora, if you don't like Francisco, who do you like?"

Cora crossed her arms in front of her and stared into the fire. She remained silent.

"Come on! Who do you like?" Leora persisted.

Thalia glanced at Cora. She would never admit it, but she was just as curious as Leora.

"Nobody," Cora responded. "None of the boys in this village appeal to me."

Leora considered ragging Cora for her response, but when she saw the seriousness in her sister's eyes, she realized it was the truth. Thalia noticed too. None of them spoke for a few moments. Then Leora asked, "Well, if there is nobody here you like, what do you imagine your prince to be like?"

Cora half-smiled and thought about her sister's question. "I suppose he would be quiet and thoughtful. Maybe dark hair and eyes. He would be tall, slender, and confident. We would have a grand manor house like Aunt En's. It would sit on a hill overlooking some city, like Toulouse. And we would have plenty of servants. I would teach him magic, and he would teach me how to farm. In the winter, he would bring us wood to keep the fire warm, and in the spring, he would bring me roses. We would have several children, four boys and three girls...

and we would have everything we ever needed. Our magic would keep us safe and provide us with abundance."

"Wow!" Leora remarked in amazement.

Thalia's heart filled with sorrow and doubt for her daughter's desires. She masked her feelings with a hopeful smile and summoned words of encouragement. "I hope you get all of those things, sweet Cora." She shifted the conversation to Leora. "Well, Leora, how about you? Is there someone who you like?"

"I kind of like Ricardo."

Cora snapped out of her reverie. "Ricardo!? But he's so immature! And he's terrible at magic!"

Leora blushed. "But he's cute! And he makes me laugh."

"You were just complaining about him the other day because he interrupted your growth enchantment."

"Yeah, I know," Leora said meekly.

Thalia chuckled. "That's perfectly fine, Leora. Boys often make girls upset, but as long as their hearts are pure, that is what matters."

Thalia's words encouraged Leora. "He doesn't always make me upset. Only sometimes. Other times, he's sweet. Like this one time, we were practicing thunder spells, and I accidentally summoned a lightning bolt too close to me, and it knocked me down. He saw, and he came to help me up and make sure I was ok."

"Aw, that is sweet," Thalia remarked.

Cora laughed. "Yes, very sweet. Did you ask him to kiss you to make you feel better?"

Now it was Leora's turn to retaliate. "Shut up!"

"Alright, alright," Thalia said. "It's getting late. Why don't we follow nature's lead and join the rain with some water spells tonight? Maybe you can use them to clean the soup pot for me."

"That's what I'm talking about," Cora said, "using magic for practical purposes!"

Thalia laughed. The girls closed their eyes and began to concentrate.

7

Rap, rap, rap. The girls jolted awake. A crack of thunder shook the house.

Rap, rap, rap, rap. They looked around in confusion.

"Stay in bed," Thalia commanded. "Someone's at the door."

Rap, rap, rap. The knocking was loud and hurried, conveying a sense of urgency. Thalia threw fur around her shoulders and opened the door. Immediately, the sound of heavy rain and rumbling thunder filled the house. A large man stood at the entrance, enshrouded in darkness as the rain poured down on him. In his arms, he carried a body.

"Señora Neumann!" the man's voice called out. "I beg your forgiveness for intruding upon you so late. I would not have come if I thought I had another choice."

"Señor Herrero? What is it?" Thalia was reluctant to invite him inside, even to get out of the rain.

"It's my wife, Rosa. Tonight I awoke to hear her gasping for air with a horrible gurgling sound. When I went to her, I found a wolf had broken through our door and...it tore into her neck! I scared it off, but my Rosa, she's...I didn't know where else to go," the man said, his voice breaking. "Please..." He held his wife's body out before him.

Thalia looked at Rosa's body. Rosa's eyes were open, but she was otherwise limp. Her neck had a blood-soaked cloth wrapped around it. Thalia gritted her teeth as she stood in the doorway, debating what she should do. *Even if I heal her, it may be too late*, she thought. Finally, she stepped aside and spoke quickly. "Bring her inside. I'll see what I can do. Girls, clear a space on the floor and get some blankets for señora Herrero."

Carlos Herrero carried his wife into the roundhouse and set her on the floor that the girls had quickly cleared. Thalia used a stick to steal fire from the fire pit and light a few candles. She heard Leora gasp behind her. She turned around to see Rosa lit up by the firelight.

"Oh, my God!" Thalia gasped, putting her hand on her heart. The cloth around Rosa's neck had fallen away to reveal that her neck had been torn to shreds. There were only a few threads of tissue connecting her head to her body. *How is she still alive?* Thalia thought.

Cora gagged and covered her mouth. Leora stood, frozen in horror, with her mouth agape.

"Please!" Carlos pleaded. "Can you help her?"

Thalia blinked rapidly, took a breath, and collected herself. "Cora, take Leora outside. Wait there until I tell you to come back."

"But it's raining!" Cora protested.

"Go around the side. Stay under the thatching," Thalia demanded. "Do it now!"

As Cora took Leora's shoulders and led her outside, Thalia rushed over to the Herreros.

"I will do what I can, but so much blood has been lost. I don't know how she is still alive. Why did you take her all the way out here? I am no surgeon, and the Serranos' would have been closer and faster."

Carlos cried, "No. No, you misunderstand. A surgeon cannot help her now." He grabbed Thalia's hands and looked her in the eyes with great sorrow. "She is in tremendous pain. Her accident on the horse paralyzed her from the neck down and made her mute. She has been dying slowly, and now she is in so much pain. I came here to beg you..." he struggled to speak. "I came here to beg you to end her suffering."

Thalia pulled her hands away from Carlos's and took a step back.

He persisted, "Please, I know God would not approve. But I cannot stand to see her like this."

"You are asking me to kill your wife?" Thalia asked as more of a statement than a question. There was anger in her voice, and as she spoke, it grew stronger. "You carried your suffering wife to the sinner; the outcast at the edge of the village, because you thought she would be the only one who would do it. The village gossip says I am the whore who slept with Faustus Neumann to become a powerful witch, right? So you thought, what's one more sin for that harlot? That's why you're here, right? You brought this horror to my doorstep and forced my daughters to bear witness! Why should I do anything for you!?"

Carlos turned away from her and buried his face in his hands in shame. "I'm sorry!" he sobbed. "I'm so sorry."

Thalia could not determine if he was talking to her or his wife. She looked at Rosa lying on the floor. Rosa's eyes looked up at her, pleading. Her neck no longer gushed any blood, and her body was still, as if she were no longer making any attempt to breathe. If it were not for her eyes, Thalia could have mistaken her for being dead already. *How is she still alive*? Thalia thought again. There was something unnatural and unsettling about her condition, beyond the gore.

On the outside of the house, Leora sat with her back against the wall. Her eyes were closed and her hands covered her ears. She had heard her mother shout, and it scared her. Cora, meanwhile, stood beside Leora, looking in a window. She had pushed away the straw just enough to open a crack to see inside. She had heard everything that was said.

Carlos sobbed. Thalia put her hand on his shoulder and pulled his hands away from his face. She turned him toward her and saw the despair on his face. She took pity on him. It made her angry that she pitied him.

"God damn you, Carlos," she swore in exasperation. She looked at Rosa again and relented. "I will do this for her, not for you. But I will only do it under one condition: you must never speak of this to anyone. Swear that to me. Swear on your wife's eternal soul." Thalia's fear was that a careless word from Carlos's mouth would kick the hornet's nest of the coven, or worse, stir up more gossip that would ultimately hurt her daughters more than her.

His sobbing subsided. "I swear," he promised. "I'm so sorry. God bless you, Thalia. I swear, I will tell no one."

Thalia looked up at the ceiling with grave concern. "May God have mercy on us." She turned back to Rosa. Standing over her, she told Carlos, "I sense there is something evil about what happened to your wife, but it does not excuse what I am about to do; what you have asked me to do."

Carlos said nothing and resumed crying. Thalia knelt beside Rosa.

Rosa stared intensely at Thalia. A dark, empty sorrow filled her eyes. She knew what Thalia was about to do, and she accepted it. She wanted it. A tear ran down the side of her face.

Thalia looked into Rosa's eyes while taking one of Rosa's hands in hers and putting her other hand on Rosa's cheek. "I'm sorry. Your suffering will be over soon and you will be with God. You will be in paradise, and it will seem like the blink of an eye before your husband joins you there." She spoke both to comfort Rosa and to hold her attention. Behind her, a log had risen from the pile of firewood and floated toward her, as if carried by a ghost. Thalia positioned it in the air above Rosa's head, with the cut ends of the log vertical so that one of them was facing Rosa. Rosa must have noticed it, but she kept her eyes locked on Thalia's. Thalia pulled her hand away from Rosa's face and leaned away from her. Rosa smiled at her with her eyes.

The log hit the floor of the house with a heavy thunk, accompanied by a crack of lightning. Pieces of Rosa's head splattered on the floor and sprayed into Thalia's face. She clenched her eyes together and frowned as a wave of emotional agony washed over her. She screamed. When the feeling had passed, she opened her watery eyes and quickly thrust her hand out towards the fire. As she gestured, it was like she had grabbed a ball of fire from the air. She spun her wrist around and flicked the ball of fire onto Rosa's body, immolating the entire thing immediately. The fire consumed her body and quickly reduced it to ash. The putrid smell of burned flesh filled the house.

From outside, Cora's wide eyes watched with equal parts of horror and awe.

Thalia stood and retrieved a broom. She swept Rosa's ashes into the fireplace and tossed the log she had used into the fire too, using magic to move it without touching it.

Carlos had sat on the floor crying the entire time. He did not move until Thalia went to him and commanded him to stand up. She grabbed his shoulders to look at him face to face. Though his body towered over hers, he seemed small.

Thalia closed her eyes and cursed him. "Carlos Herrero, you will remember this night until your dying day. You will carry the guilt of what you have done. May it burden your days and haunt your nights. May it cause you to reflect on your character and strive to be better. And may you keep your promise to tell no one of what happened." Her voice sounded as if several people were speaking through her, with various pitches and timbres. At once, Carlos stopped crying. Thalia's curse permeated his mind and solidified itself like words etched in stone to endure through time. He walked out of the house in a trance and went home.

Thalia wiped her face in her nightgown and changed her clothes, throwing the blood-soaked ones into the fire.

Cora pulled the straw back into place and sat next to Leora, who was crying.

"Why did she do it?" Leora asked.

Cora was surprised that Leora had known what happened, despite not watching or listening. "How did you..."

"I felt her fade." Leora answered before Cora could ask. "And I felt mother do it."

Cora hugged Leora to comfort her, and they cried together. The rain fell harder, pattering on the ground where it fell from the thatching, and splashing on their feet.

"Girls," Thalia called from inside.

The girls went back inside and sat on Leora's bed. Despite Thalia's efforts to clean up, a foul smell lingered in the air. Thalia saw the state her daughters were in and it broke her. "I'm so sorry girls," she cried. "You should never have had to see that." She sat between them and put her arms around them.

"It was the right thing to do," Cora said.

"No! Nothing about this was right. But I chose to do it, anyway."

They laid down together in an embrace, crying softly until they fell asleep to the sound of the rain.

8

Rosa stood in front of Cora, blood flowing down her tunic like rain. She reached her arm out and tried to ask for help, but could only gurgle as blood spurted from the chasm in her neck. Fear paralyzed Cora, and she could not move as Rosa's gaunt, emaciated body stumbled toward her, reaching out to her. Cora felt warm, sticky fluid in her hands. She held them up to find them covered in blood. She lowered them enough to look back at Rosa, but found Leora standing where Rosa had been, her neck torn apart like Rosa's. Blood soaked her white nightgown.

"C!" Leora sputtered.

Cora jolted awake with a gasp. Her sweat-soaked body trembled as her mind took a second to realize she was dreaming. She looked over at her sister's bed and saw her sleeping peacefully in the firelight. She whimpered and laid back down, pulling a blanket over her face.

The next morning, Carlos told the rest of the village that a pack of wolves descended on Rosa while she worked in the stable, and dragged her into the forest. The village marshaled a search party for her. After a few days without success, they capitulated. Father Julian organized a funeral that the entire village attended. They buried an empty casket in the graveyard behind the church.

The entire village mourned, but the Neumanns were particularly somber and listless. Leora tried to ask her mother what God would do to her for what happened, but Thalia refused to talk about it.

Cora was more concerned with Carlos Herrero than God. After school one day, she crafted an excuse to stay late and walk back alone, without Leora. Before going home, she took a detour to the Herreros' farm. She hid behind a tree, just off the dirt path leading to their house, and spent several minutes spying on Carlos as he tended to his horses in the pasture. She watched him with hatred and hoped he was suffering from what he made her mother do. She had seen the guilt weigh on her mother, and she hoped he felt it just as much. It made her angry to see him walking around outside. He was not acting joyful, or doing anything to suggest that he was unburdened with grief, but the fact that he was not sequestered inside mourning filled Cora with rage. She watched him, studying him, as though she would see something that would help her come to terms with what happened, or at least feel as though he were justly depressed. As she watched, she unconsciously clenched her fists.

"Animals are special." Father Julian startled Cora, and she jumped.

"Apologies, Cora, I did not mean to frighten you. I was just coming by to check on señor Herrero." He walked off the path to the Herreros' house and joined her by the tree. Cora remained silent, not knowing what to say, as her mind locked with surprise and anger. Although there was no way Father Julian could have known her inner thoughts, she felt as though he had caught her.

"Do you know why animals are so endearing to us?" He did not wait for her to reply. "It's because when we gain their trust, they show us unconditional love. They don't care what we look like or what we've done. They play with us when we are happy. They comfort us when we are sad. They calm us when we are angry, and invigorate us when we are excited. Even if we treat them poorly, they do not abandon us. What is most remarkable is that they do all of this without uttering a single word. Their love is pure, like God's love. It brings me joy to see señor Herrero comforted by his horses. Wouldn't you agree?"

No! Cora thought, but she nodded.

"Of course." Father Julian smiled and put his hand on Cora's shoulder as they watched Carlos together. "It is rude to spy on our neighbors, even if we just want to make sure they are doing alright. So I will go speak to him. Would you like to join me?"

"No," Cora declined.

"It's alright, God will smile upon you for harboring concern for your neighbor in your heart. But next time, it would be more polite, and I'm sure señor Herrero would appreciate it, if you spoke with him."

Cora took the hint from Father Julian that she should leave, so she did. She walked home alone as the sun was setting, reflecting on her anger in consideration of what Father Julian had said. *If he only knew how I really felt, what I was really thinking*, she thought to herself, *he would not have been so nice.* A wave of shame washed over her. She meandered to the side of the road, dropped to her knees, and sobbed. She buried her head in the grass and screamed, balling up her fists and tearing the grass out of the ground. All the shock, horror, sadness, and anger that she had held inside all week erupted from her at once. Her mind raced, bouncing from the pain in Rosa's eyes to the pain in her mother's, then to the helplessness and despair in Carlos', the sight of the log, the mess on the floor of their house, the smell of incinerated human flesh, and the nightmare she had had every night since. Cora sat in the moonlit grass and cried until she could no longer.

Cora and Leora remained glum throughout the next week, although most of the villagers had moved on from mourning. This was especially true of the other students in school, since none of them had known Rosa well.

The following Monday, Leora overheard Clara talking with Anabella and Maya about getting together to try on various clothes that her mother made. Clara's mother, Josephine Matisse, the coven elder, designed clothing and employed a handful of skilled seamstresses. Josephine thought it would brighten the girls' moods to have a dress up night after school. Clara invited Cora, but not Leora. Later that evening, Leora brought it up with her mother and sister. Cora did not want to go, but Thalia thought it was a wonderful idea and pressed her to join them. So Tuesday evening after dinner, Cora begrudgingly departed for Clara's house.

After Cora left, Leora picked up Plato's Republic from Cora's belongings. As Thalia cleaned up after dinner, Leora lay on her bed, reading parts of the book.

"None of this makes any sense," Leora complained. "Why did they talk so differently back then? Every sentence is like a riddle."

Thalia shrugged. "I don't know, dear. You will have to ask Cora when she comes back."

Leora gave up and closed the book. She had her legs propped on a pillow, with one crossed over the other, twirling her foot in a circle as she stared at the ceiling, thinking. She glanced at her mother and decided to try bringing the subject of that night up again. "Ma?"

"Yes, dear?"

"Why did you do it?"

Thalia frowned as she scrubbed a plate in a bucket of water. Although Leora's question was ambiguous, Thalia knew what she meant. Several seconds passed before she replied. "She was dying. Slowly. She was suffering, and I thought it would be merciful to end it."

"But the Bible says it is wrong to kill."

"And yet, people kill every day in the name of God, and that makes it ok."

"Does it?" Leora asked.

"No. And yes. It depends who you ask. The commandment that God gave to Moses was *thou shall not kill.* There were no exceptions. But Saint Augustine said there are times when killing is justified. When the crusaders killed the Muslims, the church defended it by saying it was a just cause."

"So, is ending someone's suffering a just cause?" Leora asked.

"I don't know. Only God knows, and only God will judge me for what I did."

Leora thought for a moment. "But if you didn't know..."

Thalia stopped what she was doing and

interrupted her, "Leora, often in life, it is hard to know what is right and wrong. One saint will say one thing, and another will contradict it. Ultimately, all we can do is try our best and decide for ourselves. One day, you might find yourself in a situation where your own morality conflicts with the church, the coven, the monarchy, or any other authority. If that day comes, you will need to decide whether you want to remain true to yourself, and if you do, whether you are willing to accept the consequences." She wrung out the rag she had been using into the bucket.

Leora said, "Father Julian says God is merciful. So I think he would agree that what you did was right."

Thalia shrugged. "Perhaps. I have prayed and will continue to pray for forgiveness. I leave the rest to Him."

Leora wanted more certainty that her mother did right by God, so she optimistically interpreted her mother's words. *God will forgive her. She did the right thing.* She could not tolerate any thought to the contrary; that her mother could go to hell for it.

Thalia had stopped short of betraying her most immediate fears to her daughter. Regardless of what God might think, she had used witchcraft to kill, which was strictly forbidden by the coven. If they found out, it would not matter why she had done it: her punishment would either be excommunication or execution. To ensure they would speak no more of the subject, she distracted Leora. "Leora, why don't we practice some spells together? Would you like that?"

Leora grinned. "Yes! Of course! Can you teach me how to put a hex on someone?"

"I can...but you must use hexes and curses with caution. They are the darkest spells and can tempt you to use witchcraft for evil."

"All the more reason to learn how to master them properly!"

"You have a good point. Alright, let's start with something simple: preventing someone from moving."

***

"Cora! Welcome! Come on in!" Clara greeted her friend.

Cora smiled sheepishly as she walked inside. It had been years since she had last been to the Matisse's house. It was not the Ortiz Estate by a long shot, but it was still a respectable house with glass windows and two floors.

"Come on, let's go upstairs to my room," Clara said.

Anabella and Maya were already there. They welcomed Cora warmly.

"Cora, you have got to see this bonnet," Anabella said, producing an amethyst colored, rounded bonnet. "Clara said her mother had two of these made, and its twin was given to Queen

Consort Catherine de' Medici of France!"

"That's right!" Clara smugly confirmed. "It's a royal bonnet."

Anabella handed it to Cora. "Try it on!"

Cora put it on her head, and Anabella helped straighten it.

"Here," Clara said, handing Cora a small, rectangular metal mirror.

Cora looked down with fascination at the mirror she held in her hand.

"What's wrong?" Maya asked.

"Nothing, it's just..." Cora began.

"Oh, my! Have you never seen a mirror before!?" Clara asked. "I forgot how little your family has. But I would have thought you would at least have seen one at your aunt's house." She smiled, taking delight in remarking how much poorer Cora was than the rest of them.

"No, I've seen a mirror. It's just that it has been a while," Cora replied. She had seen mirrors at the Ortiz Estate and would often look at her reflection in still bodies of water, but it had been nearly a year since the last time Cora had seen her reflection in a mirror, and she was nervous to look. She slowly raised it and peered at her reflection. When she saw her face, she smiled, bringing her hand up to touch her cheek. She recognized some of her mother's features in herself. They were stronger now than the last time she had seen her reflection.

"Well? What do you think?" Clara asked.

"I...I love it! It's a beautiful bonnet," Cora replied.

"See! I told you!" Anabella said. "I knew it would look good on you."

"Yeah, yeah, now let me try it on!" Maya insisted. She removed the band from the top of her head that she always wore to keep her hair in place.

Cora handed the bonnet and mirror to her. They continued trying on different garments and put together entire outfits. Even with the occasional jab or backhanded compliment from Clara, Cora enjoyed herself. For a short while, she forgot about her troubles.

"Ooh, if only Miguel could see you in that. He would lose his mind," Clara teased Maya, as she tried on a thin white petticoat. The outlines of her legs were visible through the material in the candlelight.

Maya grinned. "You think?"

Anabella smiled and looked at Cora and then at Maya. Cora had not known that Maya liked Miguel, but it become apparent to her through this interaction.

"Of course!" Clara said.

Maya pushed her breasts up. "Maybe if these were as big as Anabella's."

Anabella blushed. "You'll get there. You're only twelve. I have two whole years on you."

Clara looked at Cora, realizing that she had been quiet. "So Cora, why don't you tell us who you like?"

Cora blushed. "Oh, I don't..."

"Come on, we all know Maya likes Miguel and I like Francisco, and Anabella likes that older boy who works on the Alvarez farm. So who do you like?" Clara urged.

"Yeah, come on, tell us!" Maya piled on.

Cora debated to herself how she should respond. She did not think they would believe she was not interested in any of the boys in the village, but she did not know what else to say. "I don't really like any of the boys in our village."

Her friends looked at her, speechless. Clara broke the silence. "That's a lie. Come on, you can tell us. We won't tell anyone. Right?" She looked at Maya and Anabella.

"Maybe she really doesn't like anyone," Anabella suggested.

"No, there is someone she likes. She's just too embarrassed to tell us," Clara said. "Oh, maybe it's her cousin, Geoffrey!"

Maya laughed.

Clara mocked Cora in a high voice. "Oh Geoffrey, you're such a fancy boy!" She and Maya laughed.

Maya squinted at Cora. "No. I know who she likes."

The girls looked at Maya.

"Esteban!" she said emphatically. The girls laughed, except for Cora.

"Gross, can you imagine?" Clara said. "None of the women even look at him. I've heard it's because he prefers the company of his goats." Clara and Maya howled, laughing until Clara lost her breath and coughed.

Anabella laughed until she noticed Cora's embarrassment. "Actually, I think she's telling the truth. She's too smart for any of the men in our village, anyway."

The smile fell from Clara's face. "No, there has got to be somebody. Just tell us! What are you afraid of? Who is it, Cora?"

Cora remained silent, looking down at the floor.

Maya cleared her throat and said, "You know, as much as Francisco likes to make fun of her, I have seen him glancing at her from time to time."

Anger flashed across Clara's face. Maya continued, "Is that who it is, Cora? You like Francisco, but you don't want to upset Clara?"

Cora's face went red. "No! He repulses me! I could never like him!"

Clara's anger boiled over. "You could never have someone like him! You know what? I bet the reason you don't like anyone is that you know you're so poor that no boy would ever want you. And everybody knows how your mother only slept with your father so she could learn witchcraft. Like mother, like daughter, right? No respectful boy would want someone like that."

Tears welled up in Cora's eyes. She pushed

Maya aside and ran from the room, bolting down the stairs and out of the house.

"Cora, wait!" Anabella called after her, but it was no use.

Cora cried as she ran down the main road of the village. She kept running until she reached the point where both sides of the road were fields. Then she stopped and collapsed to her knees. Her chest heaved as she tried to catch her breath while crying.

"It's not fair!" she shouted to no one. She looked up at the night sky. "I hate you! Do you hear me? I *hate* you!" Her words echoed in the darkness of the night. A cold wind blew out of the forest and brushed the surrounding fields.

She sat on the road until she had calmed down. Then she wiped her eyes dry and walked home.

***

Wednesday morning, the students were raucous as they waited for Isabella to enter the building. She was outside talking with Enheduanna about another eagle that had been spotted on the southeastern side of the valley, where the mountain pass led to the nearest road that connected to the Mediterranean and down to Barcelona. It was one of two paths into the valley, the other being on the western side near the Neumanns' house, but it was the path more commonly used by anyone coming from larger towns and cities.

Cora and Leora sat in their usual seats at the front of the class, silently waiting for the class to begin. Leora rested her chin on her hand, and Cora was face down on her desk.

Clara tapped Cora on the shoulder. Cora picked her head up and turned around.

"You know I was just joking last night, right? You didn't think I was serious, did you?" Clara asked.

"No," Cora replied softly.

Clara smiled. "Good. You know how I like to jest? We're still friends, though."

"Sure," Cora said. She turned around and put her head back down.

Cora's and Leora's behavior caught the attention of Miguel, who was tossing a potato back and forth with Francisco. "Hey Neumanns! What's wrong with you?" he asked.

The girls did not respond, so he tried again. "Don't tell me you're still sad about señora Herrero. You didn't even know her! You're just faking it to make Mother Isabella take it easy on you."

Leora looked at him and scoffed, rolling her eyes. Cora continued to ignore him.

Francisco joined in. "Eh, don't waste your time talking to them. They're probably going through their special time of the month." He and Miguel laughed.

"No, they're probably sad that nobody likes

them," Miguel suggested. The girls continued to ignore them. Clara and Maya snickered, which encouraged the boys.

"Hey, check this out," Francisco said. He chucked the potato at Cora, pelting her in the back of her head. It bounced off and rolled to the side of the classroom.

Cora sat up and turned around, but this also caught Leora's attention, who said, "Knock it off, you big dumb idiot! If you do that again, you will wish you hadn't."

"Hahaha, oh no, I'm so scared!" Miguel mocked her.

Leora's insult struck a nerve with Francisco. His smile drooped and twisted into a sneer. He got out of his chair and stepped toward her, trying to intimidate her with his size. He made his voice lower than usual. "No, I know what their problem is. They're sad that their daddy died and left them with a whore for a mother. She can't be that good at it though, because they're still so poor."

Clara covered her mouth, but she was clearly smiling with her mouth open, surprised by Francisco's boldness.

Leora's face darkened with anger and contempt in a way that Cora had never seen in her sister, and it frightened her. The atmosphere in the classroom seemed to darken, too. The other students had stopped whatever they were doing to watch the interaction between Leora and Francisco.

Leora's sapphire eyes illuminated with a soft, icy-blue ring of light. She stood up to meet Francisco, so that they were inches apart. He towered over her, and she glared up at him with unbridled rage.

"Aw, did I make you upset? What are you gonna do about it, twerp?" Francisco taunted, poking his finger in Leora's chest.

"Leora, wait!" Cora said, but it was too late. Cora expected Leora to push him, or kick his shin, which would inevitably cause him to hit back harder and hurt her. But she did not expect Leora to simply put her hand on Francisco's chest. Almost immediately, a blast of fire came from Leora's palm, burning off the front of Francisco's tunic and branding the shape of her hand onto his chest. The force of the fire spell lifted the much larger boy off his feet and tossed him back a few meters into the wall of the classroom. His body slammed into the wall with a thud that shook the building. He collapsed to the floor, unconscious. The spell radiated heat through the classroom, as if an oven had been opened. The accompanying shock wave sent desks, chairs, and students tumbling to the sides of the room. A few of the students screamed. Cora fell from her chair and looked up at Leora in shock.

Isabella and Enheduanna rushed into the room to see what had happened. They found Leora standing with her arm still outstretched, and a clear channel through the collapsed desks and chairs that ended at Francisco's body lying face down on the floor.

"LEORA!" Enheduanna shouted, as she realized what Leora had done. She rushed over and slapped Leora's arm down, then roughly grabbed her shoulders and spun her around. "What work of Satan have you done?" she spat into Leora's face as she demanded an explanation, shaking Leora hard enough to cause her head to bobble.

Cora could see her aunt's fingertips turn white as she gripped Leora hard. Seeing her aunt treat her sister that way pushed Cora over the edge. She stood up and stepped toward the two of them. "Stop it! Let her go, bitch!"

Enheduanna's eyes grew wide, bugging out of her head. She shoved Leora aside, causing her to double over a desk. She stepped forward and backhanded Cora's face, causing a hard smack to echo through the room. "Don't you ever speak that way to your elder!" she shouted so violently it was nearly a scream.

Cora stepped back and opened her mouth in pain. She put her hands on her cheek. The classroom was silent, except for a groan from Francisco, as he regained consciousness, slowly positioning one of his hands beneath him to push himself up. Isabella stood, stupefied, in the corner by the door, unsure of what to do.

Enheduanna closed the distance to Cora again, put her pointer finger in Cora's face, and continued to rebuke her, "I have had it with your insolence and blatant disregard for God's law! I will make sure you are punished for your wickedness!"

She turned to Leora, who was stunned and unresponsive, and reproached her too, "And you! You have always been respectful, but I see now that your sister's and your mother's influences are tainting your soul!"

Father Julian appeared in the doorway. "Sister Enheduanna, what is going on here?" he asked.

Enheduanna stepped toward him and gestured at Leora with one hand and the disarray of the classroom with the other. "This child has been swayed by Satan and used her magic to carry out the devil's work. Look at what she has done to the classroom! Look at what she did to her poor classmate! She burned him with hellfire!"

Father Julian observed the scene in front of him. He walked past Enheduanna, calmly knelt beside Leora, and gently put his hand on her shoulder. "Are you ok?"

His touch caused Leora to jump. She snapped out of her shock, looked into Father Julian's eyes, and began to cry.

He embraced her. "There, there."

"Father, she viciously attacked one of her classmates!" Enheduanna said. "You should..."

"Did you see it happen?" Father Julian interrupted her.

"Well, no, but..."

"This village is in pain. We are all still healing

from what happened to our sister in Christ, Rosa Herrero. It is only natural to make mistakes in such times. But the Lord is merciful, and so too should we be."

"Father, I..." Enheduanna tried once more, but Father Julian stopped her, more forcefully this time.

"Sister Enheduanna, you will lead by example and check that the students are not hurt. Sister Isabella, you too, please check on Francisco."

Isabella obeyed, and Enheduanna went over to check on her son, Geoffrey.

"Mama, she...she...she used magic without... she didn't need to connect with n-nature!" Geoffrey trembled. Enheduanna looked back at Leora with surprise. Nobody had ever achieved such mastery of witchcraft at such a young age. Enheduanna turned her attention back to Geoffrey and inspected him to see if he was hurt.

Father Julian stood and took Leora's hand. He held out his hand for Cora. "Come girls, I will walk you home." He turned to Enheduanna and Isabella. "I am taking Leora and Cora home to their mother. Sisters, please take care of the students and the classroom." He then escorted the girls out of the classroom.

When they arrived at home, the girls went inside and sat on their beds.

Father Julian told Thalia what happened. "Sister Enheduanna said it was fire magic. I know this is a hard time for everyone, but would you please talk with them about it? We cannot abide such use of witchcraft."

"Yes, father, thank you for understanding and walking them home. I sincerely apologize. I will pray with them for forgiveness," Thalia replied.

Father Julian accepted her apology. Before leaving, he quoted the Scripture, "For His anger is but for a moment, His favor is for life; weeping may endure for a night, but joy comes in the morning. Psalm thirty, verse five."

Thalia went inside and closed the door to their house. She sauntered to the girls' beds and sat down on the floor. "Girls, I am so sorry."

Leora got out of bed and hugged her mother. She started crying again.

Cora laid in bed looking at the ceiling, with tears streaming down her face into her ears and soaking her pillow. Cora did not care about what happened to Francisco. She was sad that he pushed Leora enough to cause her to use magic to hurt him. *That's just not who she is*, Cora thought.

"It's ok, sweetheart." Thalia said to comfort Leora. "This is all my fault. I should have turned señor Herrero away. I should have..." she trailed off and buried her face in Leora's hair.

Cora had never seen her mother break. Thalia always had to be strong for them. In that moment, it was clearer than ever before to her that the three of them were, and always would be, all they had. *We will carry the burden of that night together. Not even Father Julian can help us. Not even God,*

Cora thought. *There is no casting your burden on the Lord. Despite all our prayers, we are left to deal with life ourselves.* She squeezed her eyes closed and clenched her fists to squeeze away the pain. When she opened them again, her resolve was firm. She got out of her bed and joined her mother and sister on the floor, embracing them. It was her turn to be strong for them.

9

Cora awoke the next morning to a warm, bright ray of sunlight that snuck into the roundhouse through the open door, and formed a vertical line through the house that ran directly up her face as she laid in bed. She moved her feet to the side of the bed with great effort, as she tried to will herself awake after a late night of talking with her mother and sister. To help them settle, Thalia had sung them to sleep in the early hours of the morning, which were only a few short hours ago.

Thalia came into the house with a basket of berries that she had collected for breakfast. She removed the straw to open a window on the opposite side of the house, above her bed.

"Rise and shine!" she proclaimed.

Leora groaned. "I don't want to go to school today."

Thalia set the basket down on their dining table. "I know it's hard, sweetheart, but the best way to be resilient is to pretend until it is so. If you go to school today, it will feel like a normal day. That's what we all need right now. Plenty of normal days."

Cora got up and stumbled over to the basket of berries. "Come on, Leora, if I have to go, then you have to come with me."

Leora groaned again. "But if I go, Francisco and Miguel might want revenge on me. And Aunt En will punish me somehow."

"No." Thalia said definitively. "She will do no such thing. I will not stand for it. For years, that woman has done nothing to cultivate the relationships between our families. She has no right to suddenly start acting like an aunt now."

Leora looked at her with skepticism and confusion.

Thalia went to her and knelt by her bed. She sighed. "Ok, I'll tell you what. I will let you wear my star pendant."

Thalia's offer perked Leora up. "Really!?"

Cora looked at her mother to see if she was serious. A trickle of envy ran through her.

"Yes. It will keep you safe." Thalia took it off her neck and put it around Leora's.

"But not from Aunt En," Cora asserted, allowing her envy to poison her empathy for her sister. "It's blood magic. It only works with those who are not blood relatives, right?"

Thalia corrected her, "Not exactly. The pendant was enchanted with blood magic, but it represents the purity of the love your father and I shared. So the pendant protects its wearer from anyone whose love for the wearer is not pure. Ordinarily, that would be one's closest family members, but just between us, I don't think Aunt En would make the cut." Thalia smirked at Cora. Cora snorted and grinned.

"So as long as I wear this, nobody can hurt me?" Leora asked.

"That's right," Thalia confirmed.

"What about emotional hurt?" Leora asked.

Thalia frowned. "I'm sorry, honey, but there is no magic that can prevent that."

Leora looked down at the pendant. "Well...I guess it will do. Thanks so much, mother! I've always thought it made you look even prettier when you wear it."

Thalia exploded with laughter. "Thank you, Leora."

Cora rolled her eyes and popped a blueberry into her mouth. Thalia helped Leora get up, and they got ready for school and left.

As the girls walked to the village, Cora glanced at the pendant on Leora's chest. It sparkled as the sunlight struck the diamond's facades at various angles, flashing rainbows through the interior, reminding Cora of the colors she would see when she connected with nature to channel magic. *It's like father compacted an entire universe to fit inside of it*, Cora thought.

Leora bounced along, smiling, as they walked. She imagined the pendant made her look as beautiful as her mother.

They arrived at school a few minutes early and saw Anabella and her brother, Ricardo, arriving at the same time.

"Hey Cora!" Anabella said. Cora smiled and waved, but quickly made her way inside. Anabella's face fell. She felt sorry for Cora. She turned to Leora. "Hey Leora, how are you doing?"

"I'm fine," Leora replied. She made eye contact with Ricardo and quickly looked away.

Anabella glanced at her younger brother, who was awkwardly shuffling his feet. "I'm glad you're ok after yesterday. It was brave of you to do what you did."

"Thanks," Leora said.

Anabella noticed the star pendant. "That's such a beautiful pendant you have. Ricky, isn't it pretty?" She was fully aware of Leora's interest in her brother. She knew that he had a crush on her too, but he was being shy. She discreetly nudged him with her elbow as she complimented Leora.

Ricardo made eye contact with Leora, and they both blushed. "Yeah," he said. "Pretty. I like how it shines in the sunlight."

Leora beamed, "Thanks, Ricardo."

Isabella stepped out of the building with the school bell just as Father Julian approached from behind Anabella and Ricardo.

"Ah, Father Julian! You are just in time!" Isabella said. She looked at Leora. "Leora, Father Julian and I will escort you inside today. We want to discourage retaliation and make sure everybody feels safe here at school. Ok?"

Leora nodded. They all went inside.

Cora rushed to her seat without making eye contact with anyone.

Clara already sat in her usual seat behind Cora. She took notice that Cora came in alone, without Leora. As soon as Cora sat down, she asked, "Did you get home alright last night, Cora?"

"Yes, why?"

"Oh, I was just concerned for you. Leora was in such an unhinged mood. I worried she might burn you, too."

"She didn't."

"Thanks be to God! I wouldn't know what to do without my best friend." Clara smiled, searching for any emotional response from Cora. Cora remained stoic, so Clara continued, "If Leora were my sister, I don't know how I could sleep at night after what she did to poor Francisco. Of course, I don't imagine it's easy to sleep anyway on the floor with the bugs and mice. Your family sure is hardier than mine!" Clara smirked, glancing over at Maya.

Maya piled on, "Yeah, that must be hard. Even

our animals have hay to sleep on. The only creatures that sleep on the floor are wild dogs!" She began giggling as she spoke the word "dogs," and Clara snorted.

Cora sighed, "We don't sleep on the floor. We have straw beds like most people in the village."

Clara smiled and looked at Maya. "Oh! Well, that's great Cora! I always just assumed that was why your hair was always stringy - because you had to sleep on the dirty floor."

Maya burst out laughing. Cora glanced at the part of her hair that rested on her right shoulder. *Is my hair really stringy*? Her face became red with embarrassment.

Clara noticed Cora's shame and put her arm around her. "Hey! Don't worry! That's why you have friends like us! Here, let me help." Clara retrieved a brush from her bag. She took some of Cora's hair and pulled it down behind Cora's head. She began to brush it roughly.

"Jeez, Cora, your hair is as stiff as the mane of a horse!" Clara remarked. Maya giggled. "But don't worry, I'll fix it for you."

While Clara brushed her, Cora looked down at the floor with equal parts embarrassment and anger. Clara suddenly stopped as Anabella, Ricardo, Isabella, Leora, and Father Julian entered the classroom.

"Take a seat, everyone," Isabella ordered.

Everyone sat down, but Isabella kept Leora in front of the class. Father Julian stood behind Leora and put his hands on her shoulders. Isabella motioned for Cora to come stand with them in the front.

Leora noticed Francisco was in the classroom, which surprised her. She was also surprised to see a bruise on his cheekbone around the side of his face. *That wasn't me*, she thought.

Father Julian addressed the class, "Children, I know yesterday was frightening for all of you, and I know there were disagreements that resulted in an unfortunate accident. I want you all to look at Leora and Cora here. They are not outsiders. They are not your enemies. They are your sisters. I will not put blame on any of you for what happened yesterday, but I want you to know that your sisters care deeply for you all, and I hope you would treat them with the kindness you would show any family member. Remember what God said to Moses in Leviticus: You should not hate your brother in your heart, and you shall love your neighbor as yourself. I ask you to remember God's will, follow Christ's example, and forgive. In return, the Neumann girls have promised not to use witchcraft to harm anyone, ever again." He helped Leora and Cora to their seats. "Peace be with you, children," he said on his way out.

"And also with you," the children replied in unison.

Neither Cora nor Leora recalled promising never to use witchcraft to harm anyone, but they went along with it.

* * *

Isabella began the day with geography, showing a map of the known world and pointing to New Spain and its capital, Mexico City. In the back of the class, Miguel was whispering to Francisco, trying to rile him up to take revenge, but Francisco was not having it. So Miguel took it upon himself. He closed his eyes, blocked out the sound of Isabella's voice, and sought the inner peace that would allow him to connect with nature to channel magic. In his mind's eye, he saw his classmates and Isabella as auras; outlines of various colors that illuminated the surrounding darkness. He searched through the energies in the classroom until he found Leora's. Leora's bluish-white aura unfurled into the shape of a lily. He focused on it. He had decided on a kind of growth enchantment to embarrass her, so he tried to conjure horns to grow from the top of Leora's head. Something was wrong, though. No matter how hard he tried, he could not get his enchantment to work. So he gave up on Leora and turned to her right. He now saw Cora's dark fuchsia and violet aura folding up like a rose. Miguel focused on it and tried growing horns from Cora's head instead. This time, he made it work.

Cora's head began to itch. As she scratched her hair, she felt nodules form under her skin. They began to protrude and grow until sharp points emerged from her skin. She shrieked and stood up, holding her head. The goat-like horns grew quickly and curled around on themselves.

Isabella stopped teaching, stricken with horror at first, but then grew stern. She glared at the students. "Who did this? This is not funny."

Despite her scorn, the class erupted in laughter.

"Look at Cora! She's the spawn of Satan!" Miguel jeered.

Leora turned around and glowered at him. The moment he saw Leora's face, the blood in his veins went cold, and his laughter died.

Isabella noticed Leora's posture and hastened to prevent another incident. "Leora! Girls, please everybody, just stay calm. I will handle this." She walked around Leora's desk as she spoke to stand in between her and Miguel. "Miguel!" Isabella shouted. "Was this your doing?"

Miguel shook his head.

"Miguel, lying will only make your sin worse. Remember the eighth circle of hell from Dante's Inferno? Is that where you want to end up?"

Miguel shook his head and swallowed. "I did it," he said sheepishly.

"You ought to be ashamed of yourself! Gather your things and leave this instant! Report to Mother Enheduanna and tell her what you did. You had better be honest, or I will know, and then your punishment will be tenfold worse!"

Miguel hurried out of the classroom. The other students had stopped laughing. Cora had covered her face in embarrassment and crouched under her desk to hide the hideous horns on her head. Isabella went around the side of her desk and created a barrier with the slack in her dress, so that the class could not see Cora.

"It's ok child, I will fix this," Isabella said. She touched one horn and closed her eyes. The horns shrank until they disappeared entirely, and Cora could no longer feel them. "There, all better." Isabella helped Cora up and back into her chair, running her hand through Cora's hair to straighten it. Then she turned to face the rest of the class. "There will be no more use of magic in this classroom, or else I will cancel Saturday's practice. Understood?"

Several students nodded yes, and Isabella resumed her teaching.

After school ended, Cora and Leora walked out together.

"I'm sorry, C," Leora said.

Cora did not reply.   They walked silently down the main road through the village, passing the Ortiz Estate. At the iron gate, it was possible to see into the courtyard. Leora passed without looking, but Cora looked through the gate. She saw her aunt in the courtyard outside, along with Miguel and Geoffrey, the latter of whom had just returned home. She stopped to get a better look. Miguel was sitting on a swing that hung from a tree in the courtyard. Enheduanna was pushing him.

"Did Miguel tell you what he did at school today?" Geoffrey asked as he approached them.

"Yes, he did. Quite inventive!" Enheduanna

said. "Was it really a growth enchantment, Miguel, or was it a spell to show one's true colors?" She laughed at her own joke.

Miguel roared. Geoffrey chuckled, too. It appeared to Cora as though her aunt had not punished Miguel at all. Rather, she had applauded him for what he did and rewarded him with a day off from school.

Cora scowled and rushed to catch up with Leora before anyone could see her spying from the gate.

When the girls arrived home, only Leora went inside.

"Are you coming, C?" Leora asked.

"No, I'm going to stay out here for a while."

"Ok, hold on." Leora went inside briefly to drop off her satchel and then came out to meet Cora in the tall grass.

"Are you ok?" Leora asked.

"No."

Leora sat down next to her sister, and they remained sitting there together in silence for an hour.

The last light from the sun poked out from behind the stratus clouds in the distance, painting the sky in shades of violet, red, and orange. It had already dipped behind the mountain peaks. Finally, Cora spoke, "Did you enjoy the protection of the pendant today?"

Leora looked at Cora, attempting to read her,

but Cora was stoic. "Yes."

"At least one of us did," Cora said.

"You can have it tomorrow, if you want. Here." Leora took it off and handed it to Cora.

Cora held it in her hand and looked at it intently. She held it up to the sky and looked through it, admiring its luster. She lowered her hand and closed her fingers around it, feeling the cold rock against her skin. It felt good to her to hold the last remaining piece of her father. "It's mine now," she teased.

Leora did not find her declaration amusing. "No, it's not. It belongs to mother."

"Nope, it's mine now." Cora stood up and pressed it against her chest.

"No, it's not!" Leora stood up and tried to grab it away from her. Cora held it up high, out of Leora's reach, but Leora reached up and jumped. Cora held it as high as she could, rising onto her tiptoes and leaning back. Leora landed on Cora's foot and tripped, falling to the ground.

"Ow! Watch it!" Cora said.

Leora landed hard on her side, knocking the wind out of her. She began to cry, but not because of the pain.

"Cora!" Thalia shouted from the entrance of the house. "What is the matter with you!? Help your sister up right now!"

Embarrassed and dejected, Cora tossed the pendant down next to Leora. "Fine, you keep the stupid thing." Her eyes filled with tears, then she ran into the forest.

"Cora!" Thalia called after her, but she kept running.

Cora ran deep into the forest, climbing higher into the mountains until conifers outnumbered the deciduous trees. She ran until exhaustion replaced her anger and frustration, and she had to stop to catch her breath.

She leaned over and braced herself on a large boulder that jutted up from the earth. As she looked around, she noticed a break in the canopy where the moonlight fell onto another large boulder. She continued looking and noticed there were several of them, oddly arranged in a circle. They were ancient and had unusually smooth surfaces, with runes carved into the sides. Cora deduced the boulders must have been worked by man-made tools. She walked between them and studied them with fascination. As she did, she felt an odd sensation; a presence. A wind blew through the trees, carrying with it a faintly audible whisper, calling out her name.

She looked around, trying to find the source of the sound. She heard it again, but louder and more clearly this time. It was a man's voice.

"Who's there?" she called out.

"I have wanted to meet you for so long," the voice said.

Cora nervously looked around. The voice seemed to come from behind the boulders, moving between them with great speed, as if it came from all around her.

"Who are you?" she asked.

"I'm here to help you."

"Help me with what?"

"You desire knowledge, and power," the voice stated confidently, as a statement of fact rather than a question. "I can help you acquire them."

"How?" Cora did not know how the voice knew her inner desires. She was intrigued, but also cautiously skeptical.

"I was here long before this valley was green, when ice covered it, and before then, when it stood as high as the surrounding mountains. I will be here when the ice returns to cover it again, when it erodes away completely into the ocean, and even longer still. I have seen much, and there is no knowledge of man that I have not been privy to. I can teach you this knowledge, and more." The voice collapsed to a single source behind the dense growth of the forest.

Cora stood in the center of the circle of monoliths, surrounded by moonlight, and stared deeply into the darkness of the forest.

"Who are you?" she tried again. "Why don't you come out so I can see you?"

"No. I will appear to you when you are ready to see me." The voice again ignored her question about its identity.

"If you won't tell me who you are, what should I call you? Are you...God?"

"Hahaha," the voice roared, once again echoing through the forest, and it spooked Cora. Sensing her unease, the voice settled quickly back to a single source. "You may call me teacher, but only if you choose to be my student."

"What will you teach me?"

"I will teach you what no other can. I will tell you how to break the shackles of your life, how to make your enemies bow to you, and how to take anything you ever want. And if you're willing, I can bestow more power upon you than that coven of yours has ever dreamed of."

"Are you a witch too?"

"I am beyond man, and beyond witches; I am greater. I will not teach you witchcraft. I will give you the skills to become a powerful being."

Cora thought about the offer. It appealed to her greatly, but she was apprehensive. She recalled the story of Adam and Eve. "What's the catch? Power and knowledge always have a cost."

The voice chuckled. "You are a clever girl, and you will make a fine student. Loneliness is the price I pay for my greatness; for there are no others like me. In return for knowledge, you will give me companionship."

Cora grinned. "So all I have to do is come here and talk with you, and you will teach me? I can do that."

"Good," the voice purred. "You will become my student and my companion. Put your hand on the rock and swear this to me."

Cora did as she was told. "I swear it. Now teach me something useful." She was growing impatient. "Ah!" She pulled her hand back from the boulder to find her finger punctured. Her blood trickled down the boulder, filling a shallow channel carved into the rock that had previously escaped Cora's attention. As her blood flowed through the channel, it pooled around the rune, filling it. A gust of wind blew through the trees and blew Cora's hair around her face, blocking her vision. For a brief moment, she saw a dark figure in front of her, but by the time she brushed her hair aside, it was gone. The wind settled, and it was once again silent in the forest. Her blood had vanished from the stone, and her finger had magically healed. *Did I just imagine that*? Cora wondered.

"Hello?" Cora called out, but received no response. "Hello?" she tried again, but again received no response. So she left, disappointed, and walked home.

She arrived back at the roundhouse late. She opened the door as slowly and quietly as she could, to avoid waking them, but Thalia had not yet gone to sleep.

"Where have you been?" Cora could hear the anger in her mother's voice, even as she whispered the question.

"I just went for a walk."

"Your sister and I were worried sick about you. You have some apologies to make. But get yourself into bed. It is late. We will talk about this tomorrow."

"Yes, mother," Cora replied sullenly as she slunk into her bed.

Cora bounced her knee, waiting for time to pass. It was hard to see the position of the sun from where she sat in the classroom, but it appeared not to have moved since the last time she checked.

Leora interrupted her own studious note-taking to see why her sister kept looking her way. She smiled at Cora.

Cora smiled back as she recalled their conversation from the morning. She apologized to Leora for "accidentally knocking her over while they were playing", or so Leora described the event to their mother. Leora carefully chose her words to lessen any punishment Thalia might dole out to her sister. Cora could not help but feel guilty after that, although she continued to eye the pendant dangling around Leora's neck.

Cora heard Isabella's end-of-day instructions for Saturday's witchcraft practice, in the back of her mind, as she daydreamed. Finally, school was over. She rushed home and anxiously waited for the sun to set. The very moment it ducked behind the mountain tops, she told her mother she was going for a walk to clear her head. Thalia allowed it, although she made Cora promise to keep it short. Cora ran up the base of the mountain, following the path she had taken the previous night, until she again came to the circle of monoliths.

"Hello?" she called out. There was no answer. She tried another couple of times and was met with silence again and again. She sat down with her back against one of the monoliths, put her hand over her face, and laughed.

"I can't believe it. I must have imagined the whole thing. I'm such a fool. I'll only ever be a fool." Her insecurities seized control of her, and her eyes teared up.

She sat at the base of the monolith for a few minutes and then got up to leave. Before leaving, she remembered the agreement she thought she had made the night before, and decided to give it one last try. "Teacher?"

Immediately, the voice echoed through the forest. "I was beginning to think I had chosen the wrong pupil."

Cora's face lit up with joy. "Teacher! I'm here!" She scanned the trees.

"Very good," the voice said, collapsing into a single source, but still hidden from Cora's view.

"Can we start? What can you teach me?"

"Truth. Let's begin with the truth."

"Ok..." Cora accepted, although she was slightly disappointed because she was unsure how the truth would help her, and she wanted a taste of the power the voice had promised.

"Who do you love the most?"

"Uh...seriously?" Cora snorted. Despite receiving no confirmation of the question, she answered, "My sister and my mother."

"Is that all?"

"Yes."

"Why did you not say yourself?"

"Well, I mean, I do love myself..."

"Do you?"

"Yes! Of course I do!" Cora replied as though it were common sense, as though it did not require explicitly stating.

"So, do you advocate for yourself and defend yourself?"

The question stung Cora. *Not always...ok, not often. But that doesn't mean I don't love myself,* she thought. "Sometimes," she answered.

"Then you only love yourself sometimes," the voice concluded.

"No, I love myself all the time, but I only stand up for myself sometimes," Cora clarified. She was met with silence. "Hello?" She called out, but the voice did not reply. Her mind went back to her last statement, trying to resolve the cognitive dissonance. "I suppose I could stand up for myself more often...but why does that matter?"

"It matters because we are speaking about the truth, and you are not being honest with me or yourself."

"Fine. I...I don't love myself as much as I should."

"As much as you *should*? Who determines how much you *should* love yourself?"

"I don't know. God? The Bible says to love thy neighbor as thyself, so I guess that means you are supposed to love yourself the most, because that would mean you would also love your neighbor that much."

"So you let a book tell you how much you should love yourself, and how you should love others," the voice summarized.

Cora chuckled. After hearing it put that way, she revised her answer, "Well, no...I just..."

"You just do not believe in yourself enough to decide what is best for yourself, so you look for answers from a higher authority. Tell me, Cora, how is it working out for you to let an old book determine how you live your life?"

Cora looked at the ground in shame. *He's right*, she thought. She internally debated herself, *but it's the Bible! It's good to do as it says!* As soon as the thought entered her mind, she recognized her own hypocrisy. *This is the same authority that I challenged when I asked Mother Isabella about disobeying God.* "What are you trying to say?" she asked.

"You are only limited by the boundaries you choose for yourself. You are the architect of your own heaven, or your own hell. Only you are responsible."

Cora considered what this meant. "So if my love for myself is limited..."

"So too is the love you have for your sister and mother," the voice finished her thought.

Cora understood the logic and could not think of a counterargument. She went back to what the voice had asked her before about standing up for herself. "So if I stand up for myself, that would mean I love myself more, and therefore could love my mother and sister more?" The voice did not respond. Cora continued, "And I guess that means I'm supposed to love God that much, too."

"If that is what you want. Do you love God?"

"Not really. I mean, I want to, but how can you love someone you've never even met?" She thought about the question some more. Her answer was not completely honest. "No, wait...I...don't love God. I suppose if I am being honest, I hate God. I hate how he lets good things happen to bad people, and bad things happen to good people. He is supposed to love us, but he does not seem to give a shit. We're all on our own."

"How can you hate someone you've never even met?" the voice's question mocked hers.

Cora snorted. "Yeah, I don't know. I've never met him, but I've seen what he has done, and more importantly, what he has *not* done. So I guess I hate his work."

"If your mother or your sister did something that you hated, would you hate them too?"

Cora thought about the question before answering. "No, it's different with them because I know them. Leora might do something I hate, but I don't hate her, because I can talk with her about it, and because I know her and she might have done it by accident. And mother lectures me, but I know she loves me and tries to do what is best for me, even if she makes mistakes."

"When has your mother mistakingly lectured you?"

"Today, for example, because yesterday I accidentally tripped Leora, and mother thought I did it on purpose. And because I ran off when she called for me and stayed out too late."

"That's not why your mother lectured you," the voice declared. "Try again."

Cora's eyebrows raised in confusion. "I don't... no, that was why she did it."

"Wrong!" the voice boomed. "Why did your mother lecture you? Why did she give her star pendant to Leora and not to you? You are the oldest child. Why did she give it to Leora?"

Cora's heart skipped a beat. "How did you know about..."

"I can see what is in your heart, Cora. You can

hide nothing from me. That is how I know when you speak the truth."

Cora could not think of another reason her mother would lecture her. She suspected she was missing something obvious, but she could not imagine what it could be. Suddenly, Cora's own memories replayed in her head as if put there by suggestion, and her recollection was not under her control. She saw her mother put the pendant around Leora's neck to protect her, and the smile on Leora's face as she walked to school. She saw the cruel smiles of her classmates, as they laughed at the horns growing out of her head. She saw earlier memories and noticed things she had missed before, like the sorrow in her mother's face when she described her ideal future, and what she would accomplish. She saw her mother's delight in hearing Leora describe how Ricardo made her laugh, as if it satisfied her mother more than Cora's goals. *How could laughter be enough for mother? Doesn't she want more for us than a life of poverty?* She heard her own voice echo inside her head. Then she heard herself repeat her thoughts from a few minutes ago: *I'll only ever be a fool.* She saw these memories cycle through repetitively. *I'll only ever be a fool. I'll only ever be a fool.* Cora put her hands on her head and stumbled around between the monoliths, panting. She fell to her knees and screamed to drown out the memories.

"I'm not a fool!" she shouted in defiance.

"Then tell me: why did your mother give her

pendant to Leora and not you?" the voice asked again.

"Because..." Cora felt the answer come to her, but she denied it.

"Yes," the voice encouraged her, "say it!"

"Because she loves Leora more than me." As the words left her mouth, her heart dropped into a bottomless pit. She began to cry.

"And why does your mother love your sister more than you?"

Cora thought about the question for several seconds before responding, "Because I remind her of all of my father's traits that she despised, and Leora has all of his traits that she loved. That's why she gave Leora the pendant." Cora recalled her mother's description of the pendant from the night her mother read her father's letter to her: *it's a symbol of our love...the purest love.* Cora thought, *Leora's like the pendent; just a sweet, innocent girl. She was only forced to deviate from her nature to protect me when I did not stand up for myself.*

"Thank you for your candor, Cora."

"Is that really the truth?" Cora asked in desperation.

"It is your truth. Your self-hatred caused Leora to hurt Francisco, which caused her to be punished. That caused your mother to comfort and protect her by giving her your father's pendant. Your envy hurt Leora and caused your mother to lecture you. Do you see all the pain you have caused?"

Cora cried harder. "Yes," she admitted. She had not expected her first lesson to break her down. She slumped over on the ground in defeat. "I am a fool, after all," she lamented.

"You have not been listening to either of us. What has your truth taught you tonight?"

"That my mother loves Leora more than me. And that I hate myself and let others dictate how I live my life."

"Yes, and that is the source of your suffering, is it not?"

"Yes."

"You. You are the source of your own suffering."

"Yes."

"And how did I tell you to change it?"

Cora tried to remember. "You said...that I create my heaven and hell. I...can choose."

"That is your first lesson," the voice declared, fading.

Cora heard the voice fade and called after it, "Wait! How is this supposed to make me powerful?" There was no reply.

Cora remained in the circle of stones alone. She laid on her back and looked up at the starry sky, reflecting on the conversation. After a long while, she wiped the tears from her eyes and stood. She clenched her fists in determination. "I can choose," she said to herself. Then she walked home.

11

Isabella could hardly contain her excitement as the students arrived at the schoolhouse for their Saturday witchcraft practice. She had decided that, since the last two weeks had been difficult for everyone, she would break tension and uplift the students' spirits by surprising them with a game.

When everybody had arrived, she broke the news. "Good morning, class! As I mentioned throughout the week, today's practice will focus on telekinesis. But what I have not yet told you is that today's practice will involve a friendly game. You will play in teams, and as a reward, the winning team will be let out of school a half day early next Friday!"

Their surprise was audible. Isabella smiled. "I

will tell you what the game is and provide the rules once we get to the forest. Are you all ready to go?"

The students eagerly affirmed, curious and excited about what they would do.

Isabella led the students to a clearing in the forest. In the middle of the clearing sat a murky pond surrounded by tall grass, with a few lily pads and watercress floating on its surface. The pond sat in a depression in the ground so that the surrounding grass, although tall, was still low enough to allow anyone standing on the banks to see over it.

Isabella asked the students to stand aside and observe. She then demonstrated telekinesis and used it to move a long, dead tree branch from the ground to the center of the pond. She rotated it so its length stood vertically above the pond, and then thrust it down into the water with force. The bottom of the branch sank into the muck at the bottom of the pond, leaving the top sticking out of the water like a flagpole. For the flag, she levitated a piece of burlap that she had carried into the forest with her over to the dead branch, and hooked it on a twig coming off from the side like a barb.

She then informed the students about the game, "The game will be: capture the flag. I would like you to organize yourselves into three groups of equal size. Then I would like one group here, another one over there, and the third there." Isabella pointed to positions around the pond that would form a roughly equilateral triangle.

The children began debating who should be on which team. Francisco and Miguel grouped up at once. Leora instinctively paired up with her sister.

"Not today, Leora. Let's make it more interesting and join different teams," Cora suggested.

Leora shrugged. "Ok."

Leora went over to ask Ricardo, who was standing off to the side by himself, if he wanted to be on a team with her. He enthusiastically accepted.

Cora interrupted a disagreement between her cousin Geoffrey and Maria. "Excuse me Geoffrey, I'm joining this team," she declared. "It's a girls-only team. It looks like Francisco and Miguel are looking for a teammate, though. Why don't you go join them?"

Geoffrey looked at the older boys with hesitation and then back at his cousin. He was not used to being told what to do by her. "But I was here first!"

Maya, who had been speaking with Clara behind Maria, said, "You heard her, it's an all girl's team. Get out of here!"

"Fine! I'll be better off with them, anyway. Good luck being a team of wimps," Geoffrey said before storming off to the other side of the pond.

Clara and Maya cackled at him. Clara turned her attention to Cora. "Since you got rid of him, why don't you be our team captain?"

"Yeah, show us some of your family's super magic skills," Maya added.

"Sure, ok I'll try," Cora said. She detected a tone in Maya's voice that made her suspect she and Clara were being disingenuous, but she did not care. She was determined to be assertive and prove that she could handle herself without Leora's help.

"You better do more than try," Maya said. "We're counting on you to get us a half-day off, captain."

The other students joined together, resulting in Cora's all girls' team, an all boys' team with Francisco, Miguel, Geoffrey, and Rafael, and Leora's team with Ricardo, Anabella, and a seven-year-old girl named Emilia. They positioned themselves in a triangle and awaited Isabella's next instructions.

Isabella explained the rules of the game, "The objective of this game is to remove the flag from the branch and pull it to your team. The team who gets the flag wins. No students may enter the water. Your team must remain on the bank in the position you started in. Breaking either of these rules will result in disqualification. Understood?"

The students indicated they understood, and Isabella counted down from five to start the game. As she counted, Cora told her teammates to start concentrating immediately so they could use their magic as soon as possible. The other teams noticed Cora's team settling into positions to focus on connecting their minds with nature and copied them. All the students, except for Leora, had closed their eyes and begun to quiet their minds.

"Begin!" Isabella shouted.

Immediately, Leora raised the flag from the branch, and it began floating toward her team. Cora had anticipated that Leora would be the first to act, as all the rest of the students had not yet learned to connect with nature like she had. As she had secretly planned, Cora focused all of her thoughts on Leora instead of the flag. The flag was almost within Leora's reach, and she leaned out over the water to grab it. Suddenly, her foot slipped on the muddy bank and she fell on her bottom and slid into the pond. The flag fell into the water.

Most of the students lost their concentration as they looked to see what had happened. Some of them had opened their eyes to see Leora sloshing around in the cold, muddy water, trying to get out of the pond. Miguel and Francisco burst out laughing. Ricardo abandoned his efforts to concentrate and charged into the water to help Leora.

"That's it, lover boy, help your girlfriend!" Miguel teased.

"A student has entered the water, so her team is disqualified." Isabella announced.

While the other students were distracted, Maya had remained focused, and she had stirred up a wind that was blowing the burlap across the surface of the pond, toward her team.

"Hey! They're cheating, you're supposed to be using telekinesis, not the wind!" Rafael from the all-boys team shouted. Isabella remained silent and simply shrugged, grinning with delight at Maya's ingenuity.

The boys quickly resumed their concentration to avoid losing to a team of girls. Geoffrey began to pray.

"What are you doing, idiot? We need to use witchcraft, not prayer!" Miguel berated Geoffrey.

"This is how I use witchcraft!" Geoffrey insisted. He had often seen his mother use prayer to connect with nature, and he had adopted the same technique.

Despite Maya's success with the wind, Cora had lifted the flag out of the water to carry it toward them faster. It almost reached her outstretched fingertips when it stopped and began to float back toward the boys. All four of them had focused their energy on pulling the flag. When it got back to the middle of the pond, Cora strained herself and stopped it from moving any further toward them. The disqualified students began cheering for her. Ricardo and Leora were still making their way up the bank, but they cheered too when they saw what was happening. Isabella watched with curiosity.

Clara and Maria were too distracted to focus, so they were not helping. Maya was connected with nature, but struggling with telekinesis. That left only Cora to affect the burlap. Her determination had her matching the magical energy of all four students on the opposing team.

"That's it C! You can do it!" Leora vivaciously encouraged her sister, ignoring how cold she was, as the water still dripped from her saturated clothes and hair.

Hearing Leora's words of encouragement stabbed Cora with a dagger of guilt. *If she knew it was me who pulled her into the water, she would not be cheering for me*, she thought. The flag drifted slightly closer to the boys' team.

Cora spoke without breaking her concentration. "Come on! What are you all doing?" she asked her teammates in anguish.

"I'm sorry, I can't focus," Maria complained. She sat with her legs crossed and leaned over the ground, but her anxiety hindered her ability to open her mind to connect with the natural world.

Maya had her fingertips on the sides of her head. She insisted, "I'm trying!"

Clara did not respond. Her eyes were closed in concentration, with sweat beading on her forehead. The flag started drifting toward the girls as Clara's energy added to Cora's.

"No! We're losing it!" Miguel shouted. "Pull harder!" His words were to no avail, and the flag suddenly whipped up into Cora's hand, ending the game.

"Game over!" Isabella announced. "Well done, girls! God has blessed you."

Leora and her team jumped up and down in excitement. Cora helped Maya up and smiled at her. Maya smiled back, saying, "We did it! You did it!"

"Woo-hoo!" Clara exclaimed, "Good job, Cora!" Cora's teammates cheered her for leading them to victory and high-fived her. Leora, Ricardo, and the rest of their team cheered as well, running over to Cora's team and jumping up and down.

"Nice one, Cora!" Anabella said, "You earned it!"

Leora hugged her sister. Cora stood in the middle of her classmates, smiling with joy.

On the opposite side of the pond, Miguel berated Geoffrey and Rafael, who sat and stared at the dirt, crestfallen. Meanwhile, Francisco laid on his back, staring up at the sky, seemingly apathetic.

Isabella joined the students as they celebrated. She would never admit it, but she was proud of Cora, too.

***

As the students practiced witchcraft at the pond, Enheduanna paid a surprise visit to her sister, Thalia, at her roundhouse.

"Hello, En! What a surprise!" Thalia remarked as she opened the door.

"Good afternoon, sister," Enheduanna greeted her, "I wasn't sure if I would find you here, or if you would be off gathering more weeds to barter."

Thalia half-smiled. She recognized her sister had relinquished any pretense of cordiality, so she did the same. "Well, whether it's my weeds or your gossip, we both like to barter, don't we? What information can I provide you with today?"

Enheduanna returned a plastic smile with clenched teeth. "Actually, today I have some information to provide *you*. May I come in?"

"By all means." Thalia stepped aside, sweeping her palm through the room to invite her sister in.

Enheduanna ducked her head under the doorway and walked in. As she stood up after crossing the threshold, she looked with disdain at Thalia's modest home. Thalia pulled a stool out from underneath the dining table and motioned for Enheduanna to sit.

"Can I get you anything to drink?" Thalia asked.

"No, I won't be staying long." Enheduanna sat on the stool.

Thalia took a seat across from her. "So what is it?"

Enheduanna sighed. "I came here today with a heavy heart. Weeks ago, I expressed my deep concern with Cora's deviance. Against my better judgment, I respected your insistence on guiding her, as her parent. But now your other daughter, sweet Leora, has broken the coven's laws and severely injured an innocent boy with her witchcraft. It is clear to me now that your daughters have been influenced by the devil, and you have failed to prevent it. I fear I cannot sit idly by and allow my nieces to follow the path to damnation."

Thalia slammed her palm down on the table.

She spoke in a low tone of voice, "En, I have had it with..."

"Let me finish!" Enheduanna interrupted. "The hellfire that your daughter projected from her blackened soul almost incinerated my son, Geoffrey! And poor Francisco..."

"My God, you are unbelievable."

"Do not take the Lord's name in vain in my presence!" Enheduanna spat.

"Oh please, En. Your holier-than-thou act, and your prayers to help you perform witchcraft...it's sickening. Since when did you become so devout?"

Enheduanna's face turned red. "I have always been, and will always be, a servant of Christ! Even if it earns me the persecution of my own sister!"

Thalia shook her head in disbelief.

Enheduanna continued, "Your daughters' souls are in danger, and I came here, out of my love for you, out of our family ties, to warn you..."

"To warn me!? To *warn* me!?" Thalia stood, turned away from Enheduanna, and put her hand to her forehead.

Enheduanna placed her hand on the table as if to physically put her words down upon it. "To warn you that the coven elders and I may need to step in. It is too much for you to raise those girls on your own, especially way out here in this...house." She spoke the word "house" as if it were a generous label. She glanced around the room and doubled back, as if noticing something. Her eyes fell upon the floor, in the center of the house, next to the fire pit. She squinted her eyes and stared at the floor with curiosity.

Thalia whipped around, her face flushed with anger, "You talk about *your* nieces and *our* family, but when have you ever acted like we are a family? For years, you have looked down on me, on all of us, from your high castle that mother and father left you, always keeping us at a distance, always judging. What does the Bible say about judging, En?"

Enheduanna rolled her head to the side and opened her mouth to respond, but Thalia kept speaking, "You sit there and manipulate the coven, and manipulate the word of God for your own ends - for your own pride, chief of all sins, and you are either too blind or too delusional to see it. You call my daughters evil, and yet you spread lies about me and what I do to put food on our table. I'm tired of it! If this is what you call a family, then I want no part of it!" She paced back and forth. As she spoke, she felt herself becoming angrier. She decided to end the conversation. "I want you to leave. From this moment forward, you are no longer welcome in this house. And if you ever again threaten to '*step in*', or raise *my* children, or *take* my children, you will no longer be my sister, but my enemy. Is that clear?"

Enheduanna sat, stupefied, with her mouth open. After a few seconds of silence, she responded, "I see now how we have come to this. Your girls have strayed from the path because *you* have led them astray. If you want to make me your enemy, then that is fine, but you have made yourself an enemy of God, and that is something I will not tolerate." She stood, and the sisters faced one another.

A long moment passed where neither of them spoke or moved. Then Enheduanna glanced at the floor again, and said, "Something dreadful happened here...recently. What was it? What did you do?"

Thalia's blood went cold. "Get. Out," she demanded, articulating each word.

Enheduanna studied her sister. She wanted to read the history of the spot on the floor where she felt the negative energy, but she suspected if she tried, Thalia's desire to keep it a secret would lead to confrontation. She noticed Thalia was not wearing her star pendant. While she did not know how the pendant worked, she realized that its absence meant her sister was vulnerable. She imagined how she might incapacitate Thalia, and considered her sister's skill with witchcraft, weighing it against her own. She determined she would prevail if she acted first.

Enheduanna quickly held one hand out over the floor to read the energy before Thalia could protest. She raised her other hand in Thalia's direction, curling her fingers around an imaginary ball. "Heavenly Father, I ask for strength," she prayed.

Before Enheduanna's spells could materialize,

Thalia waved her hand through the air as if swiping away a fly, forcing Enheduanna's arms down to her sides, against her will. Enheduanna responded with anger, thrusting her left hand out, with her palm facing Thalia. A concussive blast of invisible energy emanated from Enheduanna's palm and radiated toward Thalia.

Thalia drew her hand in a circle, as if whisking a bowl of cream. As she did, the air around her hand rippled like she had dragged it through a pool of water. Her hand cut through the wave of energy that Enheduanna had sent toward her, and it dissipated. This caught Enheduanna by surprise. "How?"

Thalia then thrust her hand back at Enheduanna, sending her own blast of energy toward her sister. Enheduanna could not counter it. Her body was thrown backwards and through the door of the house, knocking it loose from its hinges. She landed on her back outside.

Thalia emerged from the house. Enheduanna slowly sat up in pain as her sister approached her.

"God may have given us the gift of magic, but you surely have made a pact with Satan to become so powerful," Enheduanna accused. "You are a danger to the entire village!" She rose and curled her fingers to ready another attack. As she did, she saw a thin ring of fiery orange light flash from the middle of Thalia's green irises. She realized Thalia would beat her and decided to retreat instead. Her body relaxed, and she doubled over, panting.

Thalia stood over her sister. Her eyes returned to their normal color. "Have you had enough?"

Enheduanna groaned and sat back on the ground in defeat. "I'm getting old."

"En, this ends here and now. Go live your life. Be a mother. Be the coven leader. Play your sanctimonious games with the villagers. But leave me and my children out of it."

Enheduanna nodded. Thalia offered a hand and helped her stand up. She left without saying another word.

12

Enheduanna limped up the road to the village. Her back ached from being thrown through the door of Thalia's house, and her hip still throbbed from the landing.

Leave me and my children out of it. Thalia's demands lingered in Enheduanna's mind. She thought about what her life would be like if she acquiesced. *How could I lead the coven if my own sister was off practicing unsanctioned witchcraft? If her daughters grew to be as powerful as her, or even more powerful, people would follow them instead of us. They would challenge the coven's authority, and my position as leader. They could threaten our agreement with Father Julian and the goodwill of the villagers to practice witchcraft, and therefore the very stability of the village! No, I cannot let that happen.*

She strained herself to quicken her pace, opting to speak with Father Julian before going home. *And what was that negative energy I felt from the floor? What happened there that would leave such a lingering presence? She's hiding something. She cannot be trusted.*

Knock, knock. She rapped on the door at the rear of the side of the church where Father Julian's quarters were.

Father Julian opened the door and held up a lantern. "Sister, the sun is setting. What are you doing here so late and without a lantern?" he asked.

"Father, I came straight here from my sister's house at the edge of the village. What I have to tell you cannot wait. May I come in?"

"Of course," he said, holding the door open for her. Father Julian's quarters were plain. His bed sat against the wall opposite the door, taking up the entire width of the room. Beside it sat his desk, with a shelf above it to hold a copy of the Bible and a handful of other texts. There was a table on the other side of the room, just next to the door. The only extravagance was the fireplace in the middle, opposite his desk and dining table. It had a magnificent mantle of gray stone slabs that matched the stone floors, creating a seamless blend of earthy tones. The glowing embers cast flickering shadows throughout the room.

"Sister! You're injured!" Father Julian exclaimed as he saw Enheduanna limp into the room. She trudged in a more exaggerated way than her solo walk back to the village.

"I am, father. I'm hurt deeply, physically and spiritually."

"Please, let me help you." Father Julian closed the door. Enheduanna put her arm around his shoulder so she could lean on him, as he helped her to a seat at his dining table. He sat down across from her. "What happened, sister? What is troubling you?"

The warm glow of the fire lit up one side of Enheduanna's face and cast a dark shadow over the other side. "I lament that the reason I have come to you in this state is because of my sister. My injury was dealt by her hand." She proceeded to claim that Thalia had made a deal with the devil for power, and decry Thalia's corruption of her nieces's innocence. She described Thalia's transgressions, embellishing them to suit her needs, and carefully choosing inflammatory descriptive words, as she always did. She concluded with, "Father, I love my sister, but I implore you to decide on a course of action. We must figure out what to do about her before she causes any more harm to our village."

Father Julian's immediate response was to recite from the book of Matthew, "And a person's enemies will be those of his own household." Then he contemplated what Enheduanna had told him. He spoke after several moments of silence. "I have always lamented that Thalia and her girls live so far away from the rest of the village. It is hard for a woman to raise children on her own, especially in isolation. Jesus said that if a shepherd loses one of his sheep, he leaves the others until he finds it, and rejoices when he does. Now is the time for us to find Thalia. Perhaps we could gather the congregation to build them a new house here. As Jesus told his disciples to love their neighbors as themselves, the question we should ask ourselves is what would we want someone to do for us, if either of us were Thalia?"

The calmness of his voice irked Enheduanna. She had hoped that her words would incite him to action. She countered, "Yes, of course, father, but the Bible also tells us that God is avenging and wrathful. Remember in the book of Samuel how the Lord killed David's child for David's facilitation of the enemies of the Lord to blaspheme? By allowing Thalia to blaspheme, we risk the lives of other children." She leaned back and put her hand on her leg. "We risk others being hurt, or worse. We have built a precious home here in this village. In a world of violence against our kind, we are a paragon of unity between the church and witches. One day, we will teach the world a better way: our way. What she and those girls are doing is jeopardizing that!"

Father Julian admonished her, "Careful, sister. Do not let your own ambitions cloud your judgment. As it is written in James, God opposes the proud but gives grace to the humble."

Enheduanna began to protest, but Father Julian interrupted her, "I warn you, sister, as too often I have heard you twist the good word for your own ends. You speak of blaspheme...may I remind you what Jesus said about the adulterer in John eight, verse seven: Let him who is without sin among you be the first to throw a stone at her."

Enheduanna took a moment to collect her thoughts. She then tried a different approach. "Forgive me, father, for I am guilty of the sin of pride. I regret that it has tainted my testimony, but I saw how terrified the students were on the day dear Leora scarred that poor boy, Francisco. I saw the fear in sister Isabella's eyes, and in my son, Geoffrey. Had I not stepped into the classroom, who knows what else that girl would have done? Satan is a deceiver, and he will wear the mask of innocence whenever he can. Do you not fear for her soul?"

Her phrasing forced Father Julian into a defensive position. "Yes, of course I do! If her actions were ill-intended, it would absolutely warrant intervention. But you know how mischievous Francisco can be. I am not convinced that Leora acted solely out of malice."

"Regardless, she could have killed someone!"

"Perhaps..." Father Julian admitted, before Enheduanna interjected.

"There is no question about it! I forgive your lack of knowledge of fire spells, but let me assure you they can be deadly. That is why we must oversee the instruction of such spells. No witch should teach her children without the oversight of the coven, or it would break the delicate balance we have. Imagine a world where witchcraft is allowed to be practiced without deference to God!"

Father Julian capitulated, "Very well. Your concerns are valid, and yes, our agreement was that witchcraft should never be used to harm another human being. I will take Thalia's confession for her actions today, and she will repent. I will ask her to submit her children to private education. Perhaps a bi-weekly Bible study, with emphasis on responsible witchcraft in the service of our Lord. You and I can lead the instruction. And I will ask the congregation this Sunday about building a pleasant house for them nearby."

"I fear that may not be enough, father. I know my sister. Her forked tongue may repent, while she retains malice in her heart. Her hatred of me will stop her from consenting to have me instruct her children. Is there no more we can do about her?"

"What more would you ask of me?"

Take her children and send her into exile! She shouted in her mind. "Certainly there is something we can do to prevent her from causing any more harm. What will you do about her offering herself to Satan for power?"

"Nothing. Nothing at all," he replied. When he saw the disagreement in her body language, he continued, "I have no evidence of such a transgression. I have only heard your dark rumor, and I suggest you reflect on what you have told me, and ask God for forgiveness for how you spoke of your own sister. Now it is late, Enheduanna, and I must ask you to leave."

Dark rumor? She was taken aback. "Of course, father."

"Would you like to borrow my lantern for the walk home?"

"No. I will walk in *darkness*, since apparently it is my kindred," she jabbed.

Father Julian escorted her out of the door. "You know that is not what I meant. Repent, sister, and I will see you at mass tomorrow."

Enheduanna left disappointed, but not defeated. She made her way to Josephine's house, and then to Mary's. She invited them both to meet in her library.

Julio, the Ortiz estate's young gardener, arranged logs in the library fireplace under the supervision of Enrique. Enheduanna had invited Mary and Josephine without notifying Enrique, so the house was unprepared for company.

"That's fine. Light it! Rapido!" Enrique ordered.

"Enrique, can I get you to move a stool in front of this couch for me?" Enheduanna asked.

"Yes, señora, of course."

Enheduanna put her feet up to ease the

discomfort in her hip.

"Is there not a spell that can help with that?" Mary asked.

"Spells related to the manipulation of the body are remarkably difficult to learn. That is assuming you can even discover how to manipulate a certain part of the body. But you are right. I believe Josephine and I can manage something," Enheduanna replied. She looked at Josephine, who sat beside her. Josephine took one of Enheduanna's hands and put her other hand on the side of Enheduanna's hip. Enheduanna began whispering a prayer. After several seconds, Josephine removed her hands. To Mary, it appeared as though nothing had happened.

Enheduanna exhaled, "Much better."

"Tell us how it happened," Mary said. "What did she do to you?"

Josephine and Mary listened intently as Enheduanna recounted her conversation with Thalia and the fight that followed. "She's hiding something in that house of hers. Whatever it is, she was willing to hurt me to keep it hidden."

"She made an offering to Satan," Mary asserted. "I would not be surprised if she has been grooming those girls of hers to be his concubines, too."

Josephine scowled at Mary's words. "She will see the punishment of the Lord. Let's tell Father Julian what has happened."

"I tried," Enheduanna said, "but the devil has

clouded his judgment. Instead of punishment, he offered to build her a house in the village! He thinks bringing them closer to the church will be enough to lure them away from evil."

Mary scoffed, "That bleeding heart fool will put us all in danger."

Josephine nodded. "If either the devil or Thalia has bewitched him, we cannot depend on him. We must act ourselves."

"My thoughts exactly, sister," Enheduanna agreed.

"But how will we get the rest of the elders on our side?" Mary asked. "Elise has always eaten from the palm of her hand, and Isabella is just like Father Julian. Constantina is the only one who could be swayed."

"Indeed. I am confident that Constantina will see things our way. Elise is hopeless. But Isabella..."

Josephine interrupted, "It depends what you have in mind. Isabella loves those girls, like she does all the children. She gets too close to them. We can use that. If we tell her we must banish Thalia for the sake of the girls, she might go along with it."

Enheduanna nodded, thoughtfully. "Banishment seems like the best course of action, and you're right about Isabella."

Mary asked, "But let's suppose we can only count on Constantina. Would the three of you be powerful enough to subdue Thalia? And possibly Elise and Isabella too?"

Enheduanna responded, "We would need the lower ranked members of the coven to help us. Ronaldo and Rigoberto would do as I ask them. That would give us five. And Isabella may disagree with us, but she would never use witchcraft against us, because it would break the agreement we made with Father Julian, and the promise we made to ourselves. She is too dogmatic."

"Let's be clear. We are talking about breaking the covenant and using witchcraft to subdue one of our own. That could strain the trust our coven has garnered with the village," Mary said.

"Thalia broke the covenant when she assaulted Enheduanna. And don't forget, sister, we broke it ourselves when we inducted you! If we must use witchcraft against them, and they see you are not helping us, they could discover you are not a witch, and that would be just as damaging to our reputation," Josephine said.

Mary blushed and turned away.

"That's enough, Josephine. Mary's status in the village is sufficient protection. If it comes to a conflict, there would be no need for her to be present. Nobody would question it, and her secret would remain safe with us," Enheduanna declared.

Nobody spoke for a few seconds. Then Josephine asked, "But how can we banish her without the consent of Father Julian and the rest of the village? And how could we enforce a banishment?"

There were another few seconds of silence.

"Is there a way to strip her of magic?" Mary asked.

"Magic does not work like that. It's not something you can take away once learned," Josephine answered.

"But there must be some way to stop her from using it. What about wiping her memory?" Mary asked.

Enheduanna and Josephine both shook their heads. "If there is a way to alter memory with magic, none of us know how to do it," Enheduanna said.

Mary proposed one more idea. "What about... getting rid of her, permanently?"

The other women looked at her with incredulity.

"Out of the question," Enheduanna said, "That would lower us to the level of the inquisition. We are better than that."

"I pray my ears heard you wrong," Josephine said.

"No, no, please forgive me, sisters. The devil seized my tongue," Mary back-peddled. "I just fail to see how we would enforce banishment."

Enheduanna replied, "I have contacts in Barcelona. I could write to ask for a prisoner transport, and they could take her back to the port and ship her off somewhere." She felt herself speak, but her words sounded like they came from far away. As much as Thalia angered and challenged her, the thought of her little sister being hauled away in a barred carriage struck her heart. She also realized she would have to execute the banishment herself, rather than someone else. Until she made the suggestion, she had imagined it would be someone else's doing. Before she could process her emotions, Josephine picked up and carried her suggestion.

"That would work marvelously! We would not even need permission from the village!" After a moment, she added, "But what of her children? Would you take them?"

Enheduanna was lost in thought and did not hear Josephine's question.

"Sister?" Josephine touched Enheduanna's shoulder, making her jump.

"I'm sorry. What did you ask me?"

"I said what of Thalia's children? Would they come to live here with you?"

"Yes, I think that would be the best solution. I could give them the discipline they need to grow into fine young women, and the guidance to become righteous witches who would support our cause."

Josephine put her hands together and smiled. "So it is decided!"

Mary scowled, "I suppose so. We shall banish the scourge of our village and Enheduanna will give her foul spawn the upbringing they need."

"Are you not in agreement?" Josephine asked.

Mary frowned. "I am still skeptical of the efficacy, but I will support the plan."

"It is a plan that God will smile upon," Josephine encouraged. "Right, sister?"

Enheduanna nodded, "Yes. It is a just plan that will stabilize our coven and bring wayward children back to the Lord. He will certainly smile upon that."

Mary and Josephine said their goodbyes and departed. Enheduanna sat back down on the couch in front of the fire. She stared into the flames and grinned. "May God's will be done."

13

Cora ran through the forest in the moonlight, her face beaming with unabashed joy. She raced between the trees and skipped over a stream, bounding up the hill with the deftness of a deer. She grabbed a young tree and spun around it with her other arm outstretched, her fingertips running along the tops of the dewy ferns around it. The damp night air cooled the sweat on her body. Despite running uphill, she felt as though she had the energy to scale the entire mountain. Her spirit was one with the world around her. The crickets cheered her, and her feet tickled the earth with every step she took. She felt so alive.

"Teacher!" she shouted as she sprinted into the clearing surrounded by the monoliths. "Teacher,

I had the most amazing day!"

Her teacher acknowledged her, "Good evening, Cora. Tell me all about it."

She paced between the stones, regaling her teacher with the story of her class' witchcraft practice, accentuating with grand gestures and youthful expressiveness. Although Cora did not notice it, she conjured an image of the pond in the air above her, as if it were projected onto the droplets of moisture in the air.

"And they cheered for me! They all cheered for me! I felt like they all saw me for the first time, like I was actually part of the class. It was amazing!" Images of her classmates cheering for her appeared above her.

Her teacher congratulated her. "Wonderful! Absolutely wonderful."

Cora added, "Maybe they will respect me more from now on!" If Cora's smile could emit light, its brightness would have competed with the moon.

"Hahaha. They very well might!" her teacher chuckled. "Cora, have you noticed anything different about your magic since this morning?"

"No. Why?"

"Why don't you try conjuring something? Do it now, without closing your eyes and without trying to connect with nature," he challenged her.

"Ok..." Cora said with a tone of skepticism. She tried a growth spell. To her surprise, she felt the energy of everything around her without concentrating. She detected the presence of a moonflower. Its aura swirled around in a tiny vortex nearby, and she welcomed its energy into her. She raised her palm up from the ground. The moonflower sprouted from the dirt and matured before her wide eyes. Unlike the last time she did a growth enchantment, she did not allow her pride to overtake her connection with the plant. She simply admired it and basked in the sensation of being one with it. Then she glanced around the forest, realizing that she could see and feel the hidden energies of the world.

"I...I did it!" Cora exclaimed. "I'm at one with nature! I can use magic like the elders! Aha!"

"You should be proud of yourself."

Cora looked around with fascination at the energy of the forest. As she did, she realized she could not see her teacher. "That's weird. Where are you? Everything is visible to me, but I still can't see you."

"As I told you before, I am greater than any man or witch," he replied, as if it were a sufficient answer to her question.

"Then what are you?" Cora's eyes fixed on a spot in the surrounding trees where there was a peculiar absence of energy.

"You will learn when you are ready," he promised. As he spoke, Cora felt his words come from the void, and it filled her with a blend of curiosity and malaise.

"Tell me, Cora, do you know why your classmates cheered for you today?"

"Well...my team cheered because they were happy to win, and...Leora cheered because she's my sister and we have each other's backs...and her team cheered because they don't like Miguel or Francisco, and their team lost."

"And that is the same reason they will respect you in the future?"

"Yes, I suppose."

"Why would they respect you more for winning a game?"

"Because I proved I can. I showed I can be powerful too, like Leora. Actually, I can be stronger than Leora, if I try."

"You succeeded on your own today, not because of Leora, not because of your team, and not because you were blessed by God, but because you exerted your will and used your power to enforce it."

Cora thought about her teacher's statement and agreed, "Yes."

"And then everybody cheered for you. They cheered your success; the result of your power. They cheered because they admired it."

"Yes, I guess so," Cora agreed again.

"It is so. This is your lesson tonight: the importance of power. The human mind is fearful. You yearn for safety and certainty from the unknown. Knowledge and power grant certainty and security, respectively. But ultimately, knowledge itself is a form of power. Therefore, your kind seeks those who exhibit power, because you think they have the answers to unanswerable questions, or they can provide the resources you need to survive. You are sheep, so willing to follow. Your classmates saw your power today, and they admired it. They respected it. They may seek your company more often after today, hoping it will benefit them, either through social status, protection, the promise of resources, or whatever else your kind needs. Power provides it."

Cora considered his lecture and argued, "But when Leora and I do things together, it's because we love each other, not because we want to be with someone powerful."

Her teacher countered, "But you would not love each other if you did not feel safe around each other. When you love someone, you entrust them with the power to hurt you. They wield that power however they choose, and because they choose not to hurt you, you feel safe with them. Safety is essential for kinship and love to develop. So you see, even love depends on power."

Her teacher's perspective was unusual to her, but she saw its merit and nodded along as he spoke. She raised a counterpoint, "But not everybody wants to follow someone else, though. Some people want to lead, like my Aunt En. She has this grand idea that she is going to teach the world magic."

"The desire to lead people stems from the fear of being left behind; of feeling powerless in a world where certainty and purpose can be elusive. Your aunt desires recognition, praise, and respect from her peers, because acquiring social status prevents her from being alone and remits her insecurities. The rumors she has heard of the inquisition frighten her, and her solution to overcome that fear is to show people how witchcraft and religion can coexist. That is why she seeks power." He paused. "Why do *you* seek power, Cora?"

Cora did not answer, but she saw where his argument was going. She despised the social isolation of her family and the hardships and humiliation of poverty. *I seek power through witchcraft to deal with my fears*, she thought.

Her teacher answered for her, "I know you know. It is the same reason you seek knowledge. You see the unfairness of the world and the hypocrisy of your teachers, elders, and leaders. You want to know why your world is the way it is?"

Cora nodded.

"It is the fault of humanity. You are children, fumbling your way around in the dark. You previously learned that you must find your own path. But power decides which paths become the trails that the rest of your kind follow."

Cora walked around the inside of the circle of stones, running her fingertips along them. "You're saying if I become powerful, then people will follow me, right? That sounds an awful lot like Aunt En."

"Yes, as long as you demonstrate superior power, or even present a convincing facade. When others see you as powerful, you can determine what is right and wrong, and they will follow you. Your aunt is correct."

"But that goes against everything the Bible teaches. God is the truth. God is good. That's what everybody has always taught me."

"And why does that book determine how you should live your life?"

Cora shrugged.

"Power. Your religion was once a collection of stories and ideas. As people spread and adopted them, they became enshrined as customs and laws. Power decides humankind's truth, whether it is by popular consensus, or by authoritarian decree."

Cora understood her teacher's reasoning but was hesitant to accept it.

He continued, "Think about it, Cora. When has God ever punished a sinner?"

"He doesn't. That happens after we die," she replied.

"Ah yes, your churches are the largest buildings in every village, town, and city. Your religious leaders sit in the Vatican on a hoard of wealth collected through offerings. They alone have the opportunity for advanced education. Follow them. Offer your useless worldly possessions to them, for you will be repaid in the next life. Disobey and you will be punished. That sounds like a good deal, does it not? They maraud around the world, killing those who believe differently, persecuting anyone who challenges them, and they convince everyone else to fall in line by ostracizing them. Blasphemers. Pagans. Witches. Every one of your beliefs was made up at some point, promoted to law, and is enforced with power. And yet, every one of you thinks your beliefs are righteous and true, so much so that you will kill to defend them."

Cora sat down in the middle of the circle. She felt that her teacher was ranting and she could not see the underlying lesson he was supposed to be teaching. "You told me to find my own truth. You told me I can choose how to live my life. Now you are telling me to enforce my truth with power?"

"If that is your desire. I simply want you to see that there is no universal truth. Everything is a matter of perspective, and perspectives are enforced through power. When you understand that, you free yourself to do whatever you desire, as long as you recognize the potential consequences of any nonconforming actions or beliefs."

She picked a blade of grass and twirled it between her fingers, feeling the ridges and watching the top of it spiral around in a blurred visage of a dozen blades. "I think I understand. Part of becoming powerful is removing my own limitations, right? And that includes limitations imposed on me by others?"

There was no reply. Her teacher had departed. She sighed and thought about his lecture a minute longer. "Ok."

14

The entire village gathered at the church for Sunday mass. Thalia led her daughters up to their usual seats and took her seat in the pew next to Enheduanna.

"Good morning, sister," Enheduanna said cheerfully, as though the previous day's conflict between them was a distant memory.

"Good morning," Thalia replied. "How did your conversation with Father Julian go yesterday after our fight?"

Enheduanna's blood went cold, and she looked at Thalia in shock.

Thalia laughed. "Relax, En. I can't read your mind. I just know you. Every time we would fight growing up, you would go running off to mother and father afterwards to tell them what a bad girl I had been."

"Oh, haha, yes," Enheduanna laughed pitifully, "I suppose I did."

Thalia smiled and turned around to greet the family who sat down behind them. When she turned back around, she pressed Enheduanna. "So how *did* it go?"

Enheduanna stuttered, but before she could respond, Father Julian began reciting an antiphon to signal the beginning of the service. Thalia and Enheduanna abandoned their conversation to be respectful.

The service proceeded normally until Father Julian delivered his sermon. The clip-clop of horse treads and the shouting of several men outside the church interrupted his speech. Father Julian stopped speaking, and the villagers turned their heads toward the doors to hear better.

"What's going on, mother?" a girl asked before her mother shushed her.

Father Julian came down from the pulpit. "Excuse me, brothers and sisters, let me just see what is happening outside."

Before he could go any further, the heavy oak doors of the church swung open, flooding the aisle down the middle of the building with a blinding ray of sunlight. The tall shadow of a man stepped into the door frame. Other men quickly flanked him and began swarming into the church and around the sides to prevent anyone from leaving. Their shiny steel armor clanked as they marched in. The tall one strode boldly up the center aisle.

"What is the meaning of this intrusion into the house of the Lord?" Father Julian asked.

The tall soldier unfurled a scroll of parchment. He cleared his throat and read it loudly, announcing so that all could hear, "Villagers of Estrelle, your village is now under the supervision of Archbishop Carlos Sanz Castille, and you are to accept our tercio as his holy emissaries and enforcers. We are here under direct orders of his royal highness, Emperor Charles V of the Holy Roman Empire and King of Spain, to seek out and destroy witches, practitioners of witchcraft or magic, consorts of the great deceiver Satan Lucifer, pagans, heretics, or any who would deny our Lord and Savior, Jesus Christ. Any such people are hereby ordered to surrender themselves unto us, and any who know of such people are hereby ordered to come forth and provide information as to their whereabouts. Refusal to comply, or the withholding of knowledge, is a crime equivalent to heresy, and anyone found guilty will be held accountable under penalty of death."

The villagers looked at the soldiers surrounding them with great concern. The tall soldier scrutinized the congregation in return. "I urge any among you who meet the aforementioned description to come forth. Come forth now," he beckoned.

Father Julian stepped toward the tall soldier,

trembling with apprehension and trying hard to conceal it. "Sir, we are but humble farmers. There are certainly no witches here. Nor pagans, or heretics. We are God-fearing children of the Lord. As you can see, our entire village is here to honor the Sabbath, which is more than I can say for your tercio."

The tall soldier drew his sword, pointed the tip at Father Julian's neck, and admonished him, "Priest, your duty is to assist us. You will speak no further until I deem it necessary."

A woman shrieked at the sight of the sword, and it caused a stir among the other villagers. The soldiers around them put their hands on their swords, readying themselves to draw.

"Settle down!" The tall soldier commanded. He spun in a circle with his sword drawn, looking various villagers in the eyes as he did. "I will give you all one chance. If you meet any of the definitions of the types of people we seek, reveal yourself now and you will be shown a merciful death. But deny this chance, and it will be slow and painful."

Cora and Leora squeezed their mother's hands, and she pulled them close to her.

Beside them, Geoffrey clung to his mother. "Mama, what should we do?"

"Sssh!" Enheduanna hushed him and put her arms around him.

The coven elders discreetly glanced at one another and then to Enheduanna and Thalia.

Nobody spoke. The villagers, most of whom knew who the witches were, said nothing.

Finally, Carlos Herrero stood.

The tall soldier turned to him. "What say you?"

Carlos made his way out of the pew and into the center aisle. He approached the tall soldier until the soldier's sword touched his chest. "Like the Father said. There are no witches or harborers of witches, pagans, heretics, or any of the sort here, so I suggest you take your men and move along to the next village, where you may be more useful to his royal highness."

The tall soldier sneered, pulled his sword back, and struck Carlos on the forehead with the hilt. Carlos fell to the floor, unconscious. Blood pooled on the wooden planks, seeping through the cracks. Some villagers gasped. A woman shrieked and fainted into the arms of her husband. Father Julian rushed toward Carlos but was stopped by the tip of the tall soldier's sword.

The tall soldier sheathed his sword. "Our scouts have been watching this village for some time. They have observed witchcraft. We know there are witches among you! So speak now, or you will regret your decision to stay silent!"

Thalia thought about the tall soldier's words: *The coven's rules are strict. Nobody uses magic in the open unless it is absolutely necessary. The only way they could have seen magic was if they had been watching the students practice in the forest.*

But then they would not be asking - they would already know.

Cora's mind raced. *Did they see me in the forest last night? No, I would have felt their energy. Did they see us practicing yesterday? No, how could they? Mother Isabella would have known.*

Isabella's heart pounded as she replayed the previous day in her head, hoping it was not her fault the inquisitors had come. *There's no way they saw the children practicing. I'm certain of it. And what about our concealment enchantment? How did they get past it?*

The soldiers waited, but nobody spoke.

Thalia looked at Enheduanna, who was staring at her with her lips parted. Thalia's heart palpitated. *She wouldn't dare,* she thought. Enheduanna remained silent.

Leora found the Lorenzo-Vargas family in the congregation. Anabella held her brother, Ricardo, tightly, and their mother had one of her arms around both of them. Their father held their mother's other hand and kept his head down. In the furthest pew behind them, she saw Francisco and his father wearing their dirty farm clothes. They had their heads down, too.

"Very well," the tall soldier said. "We will stay in your village for one week while we investigate. You will provide quarters for my men. If we find you have withheld information just now, you will be punished without a gram of leniency." He made his way down the aisle toward the exit, pausing one more time before he left to give the villagers a final chance to speak. Still, nobody spoke.

The soldiers along the sides of the church filed out and returned to their horses and equipment on the road. Some villagers rushed into the aisle to help Carlos.

Thalia's eyes flicked from soldier to soldier, sizing them up. Enheduanna noticed.

"No Thalia," she whispered, as if she knew what her sister was thinking. "There are too many of them."

"Ma, I'm scared," Leora stated, succinctly capturing the feeling of everyone in the church.

Thalia comforted her. "It's ok, Leora. We just have to wait it out. They will find nothing and they will leave."

Enheduanna heard and nodded, "Yes, yes, we will wait it out." She stroked Geoffrey's head. As she looked around the room, she caught Mary staring at her from a few pews back. Mary tilted her head in a subtle gesture toward Thalia. Enheduanna understood her intention and pursed her lips, while discreetly shaking her head.

Father Julian stepped back into the front of the church and put his arms out, gesturing for everyone to sit as he spoke, "It's alright everyone. It's fine. We will give them food and shelter for one week, and then they will move on to the next village. In the meantime, we must be sure to carry on as normal, with our very *plain, normal* lives." He looked to Enheduanna and then to Isabella as he spoke, to make sure they got the message. There would be no talk of magic or practicing witchcraft until the soldiers had gone. He continued, "I ask that you fill your hearts to the brim with empathy and kindness this week. Remember Matthew seven, verse twelve: So whatever you wish that others would do to you, do also to them, for this is the Law of the Prophets." He looked into the fearful eyes of his neighbors, "Our village has endured worse, and we will endure this too."

***

The soldiers made their stay difficult for the villagers. Every family was required to provide the soldiers with quarters and food. They ate ravenously, depleting the reserves that families had prepared for the coming winter.

Isabella canceled school, as she feared the inquisitors would deem the uncommon practice of co-educating the peasant class heresy. The soldiers imposed a curfew and patrolled the valley at night. This confined the villagers to their homes at night, but even during the day, they remained in their homes or within the boundaries of their farms, unless it was absolutely necessary to venture out. The exceptions were the children of the village, who would go out during the day to play. The soldiers overlooked the innocent playtime of the children, which made it a forum for the villagers to communicate via their children as proxies.

A conversation between Geoffrey and Leora

revealed the name of the tall soldier who read the scroll in the church: Lieutenant Antonio Garrido Delgado. On the first day of the occupation, he and his sergeants seized control of the Ortiz Estate. Enheduanna and Geoffrey became servants in their own house, moving to the middle bed chambers where their butler Enrique and other servants lived. Enheduanna was humiliated.

Clara provided an update on Carlos Herrero, as her family had taken him in to help him recover. He had regained consciousness, but the blow to his head had rendered him unable to stand. Without children, or anyone else to manage the Herrero farm, the soldiers commandeered it and claimed his horses for the service of the Spanish army.

Soldiers occupied every house in the valley. Two sentries were assigned to the Neumann's roundhouse. To keep her children safe, Thalia enchanted the two soldiers, putting them into a catatonic state. They appeared to stand watch outside the door all hours of the day, but they were completely unresponsive. She would only release their minds when it was time for them to give their daily report. Since they never witnessed anything while they were enchanted, their reports were always clear. Nevertheless, Thalia forbade the girls from practicing witchcraft, even in their house, until the tercio had departed. She also denied Cora's requests to go on any evening walks in the forest. Consequently, Cora and Leora were bored at night. Thalia did her best to keep them occupied by telling stories. The girls would also bring stories of their own back from their limited interactions with the other children.

One evening, after returning home from their playtime discussion with the other children, Cora and Leora were deeply disturbed. Thalia pressed them to find out what they had heard. Leora filled her in. "Ricardo and Anabella didn't come to the main road to play today. Rafael lives next to their farm. He said he saw the soldiers using their cows as targets to practice shooting their crossbows. They killed three of them! Señor Lorenzo-Vargas tried to stop them, but they beat him. Rafael said later he heard shouting, and when he looked outside, he saw a group of soldiers taking Anabella to the barn. She was screaming. Señora Lorenzo-Vargas came outside screaming at them too, but señor Lorenzo-Vargas stopped her, shutting her inside the house. A minute later he went out to the barn with an ax, and then..." she teared up and struggled to continue. "The soldiers k-killed him! Rafael saw them drag his, his body into the field and, and, and leave it for the crows."

Thalia put her hand on her heart. Leora's crying prevented her from saying any more. Cora and Thalia both hugged her.

"Is Ricard...going...to be o-o-ok?" Leora asked, her chest heaving in between her words.

Thalia opened her mouth and looked at the floor. She did not know how to respond.

Cora responded for her. "Yes, Leora, he's going

to be fine. He and Anabella still have their mother."

Leora squeezed Cora and settled somewhat. "But what about Anabella? Why...why did the soldiers hurt her?"

Tears streamed down Thalia's face as she heard her daughter ask. She looked at Cora. Cora's expression told her they both knew what had happened.

Thalia replied, "The soldiers are cruel. They hurt her for their own enjoyment. That is why we must be very careful around them."

Cora added, "We're lucky we don't have animals they can kill, or crops they could destroy. I heard they held a horse race in the field on the Alvarez family's farm, and it destroyed all of their potatoes."

Thalia spoke with gravity, "Girls, if I am not around, and any of the soldiers touch you in any way, I want you to fight hard to escape and run straight home, ok? Use witchcraft if you must, and come straight home to me. Do you understand?"

Cora nodded.

Leora detected the seriousness in her mother's voice, but Thalia's order to use witchcraft surprised her. "But mother, if we use witchcraft, they'll kill us!"

"That is why you need to come home immediately if you must use it. I will handle the fallout. But promise me, whatever they do...if they grab you or try to take you off somewhere, or if they tear at your clothes, you will do whatever it takes to escape them." Thalia looked at Cora, "Cora, watch after your sister and make sure that you do this."

"Yes, mother," Cora replied.

"Leora?" Thalia waited for her affirmation.

"Yes, mother. I promise," Leora replied. She then asked, "But why is that so important? If we use witchcraft, we would put the entire village in danger."

Thalia thought about how to convey her point so that Leora would understand enough. "The soldiers hurt Anabella in a way that she will never fully recover. Her pain will last the rest of her life. I don't want that to happen to either of you."

Leora nodded and said no more.

After one week, Lieutenant Garrido Delgado was not satisfied, and he declared the tercio would remain in Estrelle for a second week. His subordinates passed the message to the soldiers quartered at every house. They also spread word of a new promise: there would be an unspecified reward for providing information that led to the discovery of a witch. To further isolate the villagers from one another, the lieutenant suspended Sunday mass. He hoped they would stew in their seclusion and become less trusting of one another, making it more likely that someone would betray their neighbor.

As the second week passed, Ricardo and Anabella had not showed up at the main road when the children would all meet, and Leora grew increasingly concerned. She asked Thalia if she could visit them. Thalia refused to allow her to go, but consented to investigate herself. She took one guard with her as her spellbound escort. When she returned home, she reported that Ricardo, Anabella, and their mother were safe. She said that Ricardo and Anabella were mourning the loss of their father, and that was why they had not left the house. The inquisitors permitted Father Julian to perform a private funeral with the family, so señor Lorenzo-Vargas could be laid to rest.

Leora imagined Ricardo's pain and cried at the news, but she was glad he was safe.

While the villagers hunkered down, Enheduanna had had time to think, and became more comfortable with her plan to banish her sister. She wrote a letter to her contact in Barcelona, explaining that her sister had been stricken with hysteria, and requesting a prisoner transport to take her to the harbor. She also requested passage for Thalia on a merchant vessel from Barcelona to Rome. In a second letter to a priest in Rome who had been friends with her father, she requested the Catholic church keep Thalia in a holding cell and examine her for demonic possession. She offered payment for the services. Enheduanna dared not send the letters in the presence of the inquisitors, so she held onto them until she would be able.

At the end of the second week, there had still been no signs of witchcraft, and nobody had informed on the coven. Lieutenant Garrido Delgado gave the order that the tercio would stay for yet another week and again suspended Sunday mass.

In the third week, the inquisitors' patience dwindled. They withheld food to pressure the villagers and interrogated some of them. Pillories were erected in the village center; the T-shaped intersection between the two main roads in the valley where the church sat, with the schoolhouse beside it. Two men, both farmers, were stripped, flagellated, and left in the pillories over night for unnamed offenses. The men died from exposure to the cold autumn air. Their bodies were left to be discovered by the children, much to their horror. Father Julian berated the soldiers for their cruelty. By the end of the week, many of the inquisitors openly voiced their desire to move on from the valley, as still nobody had come forward to provide accusations or evidence of witchcraft.

Lieutenant Garrido Delgado announced the tercio would leave the valley on Sunday, following a compulsory gathering of everyone in the village center before mass. Despite the promise of the tercio's departure, and the chance for the villagers to reunite at church, the mood leading up to the final day was one of apprehension. Rumors of a witch trial spread, and Sunday loomed over the valley like a dark cloud.

15

The eve of the last day of the inquisitors' occupation of Estrelle was a dark and quiet night with a new moon. The Neumanns sat in their roundhouse telling stories, as they had done every night for the last three weeks. Their two spellbound sentries stood mindlessly outside the door. The crackle of the fire, Thalia's voice, and the girls' laughter were the only sounds that cut the silence.

Suddenly there was a whisper from the open window around the side of the roundhouse, "Thalia!" Thalia and the girls looked up from their beds. A woman's face filled the window, glowing in the orange light from the fire. Thalia stood and approached the window.

"Dolores, what are you doing here!? It's dangerous for you to be wandering all the way out here at night," Thalia scolded her. As she got closer, she noticed the fear and the tears in Dolores' eyes.

Dolores Lorenzo-Vargas begged, "Thalia, please, I must ask a favor of you. I have no right to, but there is no one else I could turn to. Can you come out here?"

Thalia hesitated, remembering the outcome of the last favor she granted to a villager who came to her door in the night. Ultimately, she replied, "No. But you may come inside. The soldiers by the door are enchanted. They cannot see or hear. They will not notice you."

In another minute, Dolores entered their roundhouse. Clinging to her side, wrapped under a shawl, was her daughter, Anabella.

"Anabella!" Leora exclaimed when she saw her. "Are you alright?"

Anabella looked at Leora but did not respond. She clung to her mother, trembling.

Thalia now understood why they had come. Dolores tried to explain, "The soldiers...they..."

"Yes, I know," Thalia replied.

Dolores continued, "Never in my darkest fears, nor in my wildest imaginations, did I ever think I would come to want such a thing, but my heart has broken for my daughter. I cannot let their violation poison our family. When I heard what you did for Rosa..."

"You heard?" Thalia interrupted. Shock and

terror flashed across her face. Her mind raced for an explanation of how the word could have gotten out, how far it could have spread, and what it might mean for her. *The village is to gather in a compulsory assembly*...Lieutenant Garrido Delgado's orders reverberated in her mind. She swallowed and looked down as she felt the world collapsing around her.

"Yes, and while I cannot condone it, it has given her husband peace. I only seek the same peace for my family." Dolores rubbed her daughter's head with one hand and placed her other hand on her daughter's belly. "Can you fix it?"

Thalia did not hear what Dolores said. She felt like a fish that had been trapped in a net; cold and exposed, unable to breathe.

"Mother?" Cora called out.

Thalia snapped out of her thoughts.

"Can you fix it?" Dolores repeated.

Thalia sighed. "I can."

Dolores sighed in relief. "Oh Thalia, thank you." Her eyes filled with tears and she looked up at the ceiling. "May God forgive us for this treachery."

Thalia turned to her daughters. Remembering how ineffective it was to have them wait outside when the Herreros were there, she opted for a more foolproof method of secrecy. "Girls, I need you to sit in bed and put a blanket over your heads."

Cora began to protest, but Thalia's insistence

silenced her. "Not now, Cora. I need you to listen to me."

Cora groaned and got into the bed with Leora. She pulled a blanket over them both. Thalia cast a spell to turn the blanket into a magical bubble. Inside the blanket, the girls could only hear their own breathing. There was no light or sound from the outside of the blanket, despite that they were in a room with a burning fire. The blanket had become a veil, under which they could not witness what their mother would do.

"I'm scared," Leora declared. "What does she want mother to do? Will Anabella be alright?"

Cora embraced her tightly. "It's ok. Mother will take care of her. She's going to heal what the soldiers did to her."

As they hugged one another, Leora thought about what their mother had said before, about what the soldiers did to Anabella. *How could magic heal her wounds if they would last the rest of her life*? She wondered.

Thalia pulled the blanket off of her daughters, and they were back in the orange glow of the fire. Dolores and Anabella were gone.

"What happened?" Leora asked, "Did you heal her?"

Thalia responded, "She will be ok. It would be kind of you girls to play with her and include her in activities that you do with other students. Never ask her about what the soldiers did - that would be rude of you and painful for her. Just be her friends.

That is what she needs now: the comfort of friendship and time."

The girls nodded.

Thalia sat on the bed next to them. "And there is one more thing I must ask of you tonight. Whatever happens at the assembly tomorrow, you are to be strong for me. Let your bodies be like stone so that, despite what you may see, you do not act impulsively. Do not speak. Do not defy the soldiers and do not use witchcraft for any reason. Understood?"

The girls nodded. Cora studied her mother intently, attempting to decipher what Thalia was trying to hide. Thalia turned away from them, mainly to hide her face from Cora's observant eyes. She stared into the fire, as if watching something in it with her full attention. In her mind, she imagined various futures for her family and entertained the idea of fleeing the valley. *They would hunt me*, she thought. *My girls deserve a better life than that. They would never be safe*. The three of them sat silently for a full minute. Then Thalia spoke, "Girls, you remember what I told you to do if something ever happened to me?"

Leora answered, "Yes, mother. We are to go live with Aunt En and cousin Geoffrey."

"Very good. I wish there was another possibility, but Aunt En is our only family. She would protect you."

"Why are you asking us this, mother?" Cora asked.

Leora perceived an ominous energy coming from her mother. "Mama, are you in danger? Here, take your pendant back!" She lifted the pendant from around her neck.

"No!" Thalia replied quickly to reassure them. She took Leora's hands and put the pendant back around her neck. "Oh no, girls, I'm just thinking of the poor Lorenzo-Vargas family. If anything bad ever happened to us, I would want you to be prepared." She smiled. "But I will never let anything like that happen, and I am not going anywhere." She leaned in and hugged them tightly.

With her chin resting on her mother's shoulder, Cora looked into the fire. She remembered what she had learned from her teacher about her mother's love for Leora. *Even if he is right, I don't care*, she thought. "I love you, mother."

"I love you too, Cora." A tear ran down Thalia's cheek.

16

The morning smelled like damp earth as the overcast skies drizzled light rain over the valley. Dark, low-hanging clouds loomed overhead, threatening heavier rain at any moment. The villagers made their way to the church, stepping over puddles of mud to protect their Sunday attire. Soldiers escorted every family, marching alongside them. Lieutenant Garrido Delgado stood in front of the church, flanked by his sergeants. Father Julian stood near them. He wore green robes in preparation for mass. Their breath was visible in the cold air.

As the villagers arrived, the soldiers arranged them in two lines on each side of the dirt road leading up to the front of the church. The lines faced each other and left enough room in between them for new arrivals to walk several abreast. A soldier lined up behind every villager. When the line lengths reached roughly twenty people, the soldiers began arranging them into new rows on the insides of the others. The result was two rows of villagers on each side of the road, facing one another and backed by lines of soldiers, and a small gap in between them in the center of the road.

By the time the Neumanns arrived, most of the villagers were already lined up. The Neumanns joined their neighbors on one of the inner lines, with Thalia in the middle of the girls. Soon after they arrived, the soldiers indicated to Lieutenant Garrido Delgado that everyone was in attendance. The lieutenant directed Father Julian to stand at the end of the row closest to the church.

"Kneel!" Lieutenant Garrido Delgado commanded. The villagers hesitated.

"Kneel, I said!" the lieutenant barked. Several of his soldiers struck the backs of some of the villagers' knees, causing them to drop down. One soldier pushed Father Julian's shoulders down, forcing him to kneel and dirty his robes.

Once the villagers had knelt, all the soldiers drew their swords, sparking audible distress from the crowd.

Lieutenant Garrido Delgado shouted, "Silence! Everyone remain calm and remain on your knees! Anyone who does anything other than kneel in silence will be punished!"

The villagers calmed down. Some of them whimpered. Others closed their eyes and began to silently pray. Thalia gripped her daughters' hands tightly. "Be strong," she whispered.

Cora scanned the villagers. She saw some of her classmates. Maria was terrified and clutched her mother's arm. Francisco, who had not joined the rest of the children for daily playtime during the occupation, had his eyes closed. His face was dirty, and he appeared to have lost several pounds. His father looked the same way. Cora's eyes met Miguel's, who stared at her absent-mindedly. There was no trace of the mischievous grin that he usually wore when he looked at her. Enheduanna had her arm around Geoffrey's shoulders, and he leaned against her. Both of them had their eyes closed. Dolores, Ricardo, and Anabella were near the front of the line opposite Cora. They cried openly, struggling to remain silent. Clara had her hands folded in front of her and her eyes closed in prayer. Clara's mother, Josephine, knelt between her daughter and her husband. She was trembling. Her husband had his arm around her and was squeezing her shoulder. Cora could see his white knuckles all the way from where she knelt. Conspicuously absent was Carlos Herrero. Cora realized that a few of the oldest villagers were missing, too.

Thalia noticed her daughter looking around. "Stop looking, Cora. Don't make eye contact. Just look down," she whispered.

Lieutenant Garrido Delgado strutted slowly up the center of the road between the villagers with his arms behind his back. As he walked, he randomly selected villagers to scrutinize. He leaned over in front of one man and put his face up to the man's, challenging the man to look at him, but the man kept his eyes on the ground. The lieutenant stood upright again and continued walking. When he got to the end of the lines, he turned around and announced, "I am disappointed with you all." He took another few steps before continuing, "It has come to my attention that there is indeed a witch among you! And as a matter of fact, I know exactly who it is!"

Cora and Leora squeezed their mother's hands tighter. Their palms were sweaty. All three of them remained silent and frozen, staring at the ground.

The lieutenant continued taunting them, "Three weeks ago, I gave you all the opportunity to come forth, and none of you did. You sat there knowingly harboring a witch, knowingly spitting in the faces of our Lord and our king, and said nothing. I warned you of the consequences of this. You knew what would happen if we discovered you had lied. Well...in the example of Jesus Christ, I am merciful, and I will give you all one last chance. One. Last. Chance. Surrender your witch to me, or I will hold you all equally guilty of witchcraft."

Another lie, Thalia thought. *The truth of Rosa's death has not reached them, or they would have come straight to me. There is still hope, as long as nobody panics.*

Cora's heart pounded in her chest. *Does he know? He can't know. We've been careful. I've been careful...haven't I? Did somebody rat on mother?* Her mind raced as she waited with dread at what might happen, but nobody spoke. She heard whimpering from the crowd. She shivered as she felt the rain fall harder, gradually soaking through her clothes and cooling her sweaty body. Suddenly, she heard a girl cry out louder, and the sound of a human voice made her jump. Her heart came into her throat. But when she realized the girl was just crying, she calmed slightly.

The lieutenant slowly stomped between the villagers, forming a rhythmic squishing of his boots in the mud. Every step was like the hand of a clock, counting down to an alarm that signaled doom. As he drew nearer to Cora, it sounded like he was slowing down. The sound of his steps echoed in her mind, and it was all she could focus on. Squish, squish, squish, his boots clomped in the mud. When Cora realized he had passed her family, she relaxed a little, and felt warm urine running down her thighs.

The sloshing of his boots faded as he reached the other end of the lines. Nobody had spoken. He obnoxiously sighed. "Aaagh, I admire your loyalty to one another. I really do. But I am growing tired of this." He stormed forth with speed and stopped in front of señor Serranos, the village surgeon. Rafael was in the row directly behind señor Serranos.

"Bring him to me!" the lieutenant commanded. The soldier standing behind Rafael sheathed his sword and pulled Rafael up from under his arms.

Rafael's mother screamed in protest. His father stood and grabbed the soldier who had taken his son before two other soldiers restrained him. The soldiers took both of them to the end of the lines of villagers and stood them in front of the church.

Lieutenant Garrido Delgado stood off to the side and pointed to them with his sword. "Listen, carefully. I will *kill one of them* unless somebody confesses. Who among you is the witch?" He emphasized his words to evoke fear.

"Nooo!" Rafael's mother wailed from the crowd. She stood up and tried to run to them, but another two soldiers quickly stopped her by seizing her arms to prevent her from moving. "My baby!" She howled, "please no!"

Many of the villagers closed their eyes. Some wept.

"Please! Somebody do something!" Rafael's mother wailed.

"You heard the woman. You can stop this," a sergeant said.

Nobody came forward.

Thalia twiddled her fingers in her daughters' hands and puffed. Both Cora and Leora noticed a difference in their mother's energy compared to everyone else's. Of all the people who had been submitted on the road, Thalia was the only one who felt rage instead of fear.

The lieutenant sneered, stepped forward, and ran his sword through Rafael's father. His mother howled.

"Papa!" Rafael screamed. He struggled against the soldiers who held him. The soldiers holding his father let his body fall to the ground. As he lay with one side of his face in the mud, he looked up at his son. He tried to speak, but could only cough up blood before his eyes went cold and he was dead. As Rafael saw the life leave his father's eyes, he went limp. His body would have collapsed if he were not being held up by the soldiers.

Lieutenant Garrido Delgado stepped back and put his hands in the air. "Is this what you want? You would rather watch your neighbors die than condemn a blasphemer, a consort of Satan?" He paced back and forth. The crowd had gone silent, except for the sobs of Rafael and his mother. "Oh, shut up!" he spat at Rafael's mother, motioning for his men to bring her forward. They dragged her to the front and held her next to the body of her dead husband. "You better stop crying or your son will be next," he rasped in her ear. She closed her mouth, but continued to sputter and whimper.

The lieutenant faced the villagers. "I guess you need more motivation." He sheathed his sword and marched between the lines of villagers. This time, he stopped in front of Enheduanna and Geoffrey. He grabbed Geoffrey's arm, hoisted him up, and hauled him toward the church.

"No! No, please! Take me! Take me instead!" Enheduanna pleaded, walking her knees forward and reaching after them. Her dress caught under her knees and tripped her, forcing her to put her hands on the ground to catch herself. The soldier positioned behind her stepped forward and struck her in the back of her head. She collapsed, face down in the mud.

Mary opened her eyes to find her friend, Enheduanna, in the crowd. She looked at the officers holding Geoffrey in disbelief.

The lieutenant handed Geoffrey over to another soldier and drew his sword again. "Who is the witch?"

Before anyone could answer, he spun around and swung his sword at Rafael's mother, beheading her. As Rafael watched his mother's head and body fall to the ground separately, he screamed so hard that he retched. He gasped to catch his breath in between sobs.

"Are you willing to sacrifice a child for an evil harlot? Who is the witch?" the lieutenant shouted again. He drew his sword back, this time preparing to swing at Geoffrey.

Thalia suddenly dropped her daughters' hands, rose, and shouted, "Enough!"

"No, mama!" Leora pleaded.

Thalia put her hand out to stop her daughters from reacting. "Remember what I told you, girls. Courage."

"Aha! We finally have someone who is willing

to speak!" the lieutenant exclaimed.

"I will tell you who the witch is," Thalia said.

The lieutenant smiled and stepped away from Geoffrey. "You will be rewarded for doing so. Now please, point us to the witch!"

Enheduanna felt her heart rise into her throat, fearing what Thalia might say or do. Before her rational brain could react, and before Thalia could speak, she scrambled to her feet and pointed at her sister. "It's her! She is the witch!"

Cora and Leora were too stunned to react. The lieutenant looked perturbed. "Is this true? Speak, woman, are you the witch?" He directed his question at Thalia and put the tip of his sword to Geoffrey's neck.

Enheduanna began walking toward the front of the lines where her son was being held. "I beseech you for my child's sake, take her! She is the witch, I promise you. She made a deal with the devil for power."

"Is this true?" the lieutenant asked again. He looked around at the villagers. "I will kill every last one of you and burn this village to the ground if I must. Is she the witch?"

"Yes," said Mary, "she whores herself for power."

"Yes, she killed Rosa," said Josephine, who had learned the truth about Rosa from Carlos while he recovered in her house.

Enheduanna smiled as her friends backed her up. She hopefully looked toward Geoffrey, trying to assure him with her eyes that what they had said would save him.

"Yes! She's a witch!" another villager shouted.

"Witch!" said another.

"Yes! Yes! Witch! She's the witch!" The villagers gradually began affirming, one by one. Their confirmations grew louder and more confident as more of them joined in the betrayal.

Constantina joined them, "Yes, she corrupts children in the name of Satan!"

Isabella gave her voice, liberally utilizing what she knew about Thalia's knowledge of botany. "She collects poisonous plants from the forest to use in potions!"

Even Thalia's closest friend, Elise, joined them. "Yes, she's the witch."

Even Dolores, who had begged Thalia to help her daughter only hours before, shouted, "She's a witch! She kills the innocent! She kills babies!"

Even young Anabella, who Thalia had spared from raising the bastard of an anonymous inquisitor, joined in, "Witch! She's the witch!"

The only villagers who did not speak out against Thalia were Rafael, Ricardo, and Father Julian, the latter of whom knelt with his head hung in shame.

Cora regarded her neighbors and classmates with contempt. "How could you!? You fucking cowards!" she shouted, bursting into tears.

Leora wept aloud, deeply hurt by the village's

betrayal.

Thalia said nothing to defend herself. She regarded her neighbors with a complex mix of surprise, anger, pity, and sadness. None of them made eye contact with her. She cursed them, "That's right, denounce me, you pious servants of Christ, and may you bear the cross of your betrayal to the end of your days."

Lieutenant Garrido Delgado directed his men. "I want to be sure she is the one. Seize her."

As soldiers apprehended her, Cora and Leora called out to their mother, but she shot them a look to remind them of their promise to her the night before. Two soldiers took Thalia's arms, while the others stood by. She went with them without a fight. She walked with her head held high between the villagers, who dared not look at her. As the soldiers escorted her toward the front of the lines, the lieutenant added, "And bring her children, too."

Suddenly, the rain stopped falling, as though turned off by a spigot. Everyone gazed around in confusion and went silent. Sound itself seemed to be sapped away, as though drawn into a sponge. Thalia's eyes widened with manic rage. Her emerald irises dissolved into rings of fire that surrounded her black pupils. She wrestled free of the soldiers holding her arms and looked directly at Lieutenant Garrido Delgado, "That...will be your final order, lieutenant. You wanted a witch. You have found one."

The lieutenant's eyes grew wide with fear.

"Kill h..." he began to shout, but the words died before they left his mouth. He dropped his sword and clutched his throat with both hands. His face turned red as his fingers squeezed his own throat with inhuman strength. He collapsed to his knees, while involuntarily choking the life out of himself. He kicked his legs and flailed in the mud, trying to do anything to regain control of his hands. Suddenly, his waist raised off the ground, lifted by an unseen force. His knees bent unnaturally backwards and broke. His torso and hips whipped around in opposite directions, as if his body were a wet rag that was being wrung out, snapping his spine. He fell back to the ground, no longer able to move his lower body, but his hands still gripped his throat like a vise. He choked one last time before his body went limp and he gasped no more.

The soldiers all watched Lieutenant Garrido Delgado in shocked horror, unable to react because none of them had ever witnessed witchcraft. Thalia took advantage of their paralysis and acted quickly. She placed her palms against the sides of the two soldiers who had been restraining her. They stumbled back in pain. The armor of their uniforms melted onto their bodies, burning their flesh until it fell from the bone. She then pointed her fingertips straight out at arm's length in front of her, sending bolts of white lightning into the sergeants in front of the church and the soldiers restraining Geoffrey and Rafael. Their bodies jerked uncontrollably before dropping to the ground, dead and smoking.

Thalia spun around in time to dodge a soldier who thrust his sword at her. She flicked her fingers at him, flinging him high into the air. Three more soldiers charged at her with their lances. She sent an invisible shock wave at them from her palm that threw them back tens of meters. Several soldiers charged at her from her other side, and she levitated herself to escape the reach of their swords. She held her arms out to her side with her palms facing the sky, and fire ignited from them, forming into balls. She lobbed them at the soldiers. The fire balls blasted heat shock waves when they contacted the soldiers, just like the one from Leora's spell at school weeks ago. But unlike Leora's spell, Thalia's fire engulfed the bodies of those it touched, burning them to ash.

The villagers observed the scene before them in shock. The coven elders, Cora, and Leora, were awestruck by Thalia's power.

The soldiers backed away from her, realizing they were outmatched with melee weapons. Their bowmen took up positions all around her and began firing at her with crossbows. Thalia deflected a couple arrows that came at her from the front, but then an arrow pierced through her abdomen from behind, breaking her focus and causing her to fall to the ground. The rain fell with her, crashing into the ground with greater intensity than it had rained before. When Thalia landed, her left ankle broke, and she fell hard, face down into the muddy road. The soldiers closed in around her.

"Mama!" Leora shouted. She and Cora ran to help her, readying spells of their own.

Thalia raised her head out of the mud and shouted, "No!" She thrust out her hand at them to stop. A wave of energy washed over them, freezing them in place. They involuntarily dropped their spells and were rendered motionless.

The soldiers that had encircled Thalia stabbed their swords into her, repeatedly. As her body was ravaged, she used her last bit of strength to telepathically speak to her daughters, "Be strong, my darling girls."

Cora and Leora felt the very moment their mother's life left her. The spell that had them frozen in place ceased, and they dropped to the ground, sobbing.

The rain settled into a drizzle. Enheduanna collected her crying son, telling him it was over and that he was safe.

With the lieutenant and sergeants dead, the chain of command was broken. So the remaining soldiers collectively decided it would be safer to burn the bodies of the deceased villagers rather than bury them. They forced the villagers to bring firewood from their homes to build a pyre, onto which they put the bodies of Thalia and Rafael's parents. After the fire had consumed the bodies, the tercio unceremoniously left the village, departing the valley with their dead comrades, and making their way to their next destination.

Cora and Leora remained sitting in the mud long after the rest of the villagers had gone back to their homes. The pyre burned into the evening, and they simply remained next to it, with no will to go anywhere else. Rafael sat with them.

Father Julian emerged from the church, still wearing his muddy green robes for the mass that was never had. He sat with the children and watched the remnants of the fire reduce to embers in the rain. He said nothing.

PART TWO

4 years later

17

The tallest peak around Estrelle was called La Montana del Trueno, named for the thunderous clouds that often obscured it. La Montana was like a block of swiss cheese, with caves and caverns of ice beneath its glaciers. On a warm spring day, the glacial melt would trickle down to the tree line in the montane, forming small streams that combined to feed the creek that ran through the village.

The glacier-fed creek entered Estrelle from the east, where it passed the village church, in front of which sat two four-year-old tombstones that were conspicuously separate from the graveyard in the back. The creek exited the village in the west, passing by a dilapidated roundhouse at the edge of the village. The abandoned house showed no signs of human care, except for a handmade pile of rocks where the tall grass around it met the forest's edge. A bundle of freshly picked forget-me-nots lay at the base of the rock pile, on a well-trodden patch of dirt. The forest behind the old house was filled with a chorus of birds and the faint laughter of two teenage girls.

"Hrrmph!" Cora strained herself, sweat beading on her forehead, with her hands positioned straight in front of her as if she were holding a heavy ball.

"You look like you're constipated," Leora teased.

Cora laughed and momentarily broke her concentration. "Stop it, you're not helping," she said, as she regained her focus and mentally pushed again.

"Don't try so hard!" Leora instructed. She sat on a rock behind her sister. In front of them, jutting out of the hill, was a massive boulder. While the exposed part was as large as a dairy cow, it appeared like the majority remained buried in the hill.

"Errph! How am I...supposed to...move it without pushing so hard?"

"You have to connect with it."

"I am!" Cora insisted, straining harder.

"No, you're trying to force it to move. You have to listen to it and feel its energy come to you. Remember what it was like before, when we had to close our eyes and quiet our minds in order to connect with nature? Do that! Just because it's so easy for us to connect with it now doesn't mean we can forget how to listen."

"Aagh!" Cora dropped her hands to her knees, leaned over and panted. "It's...it's just too big to move," she said in between breaths.

Leora got up and went to her. She put her hand on Cora's back and leaned over so that her head was next to Cora's. She flipped her long blond hair around and looked at her sister. "Come on, C, let me help you."

Cora let out a deep breath and stood, nodding.

Leora positioned her feet to steady herself and reached out to the boulder with her right hand. "There you are," she said. "Here," she took Cora's hand with her left, "feel what I feel."

When their fingers interlocked, Cora felt the familiar rush of her sister's energy course through her. She felt her sister's very being within her - all of her playfulness, her kindness, the heartaches and sadness that she had endured, all the soul and body scars - they became one with her, and she became one with her sister.

Cora felt the boulder too, just like she had moments ago, but it was different. This time, she detected a shyness, as though the boulder were an old hermit who longed for companionship. There it sat, waiting on this hill for somebody to notice it. Cora realized it was this sensation that she had failed to hear, as Leora put it. The boulder was filled with warm, welcoming energy, and when Leora invited it, it flooded into her and Cora. Its energy opened up completely, prattling on about its existence on the hill that it had waited so long to share with someone, not through words, but a series of experiences and visions of the eons that had passed around it. The boulder had witnessed so much change. The girls saw their entire childhood as a fleeting moment in the existence of the boulder.

It makes me feel insignificant, Cora thought.

No, Leora mentally responded, *it's just a different wavelength. It doesn't diminish the meanings of our lives. Scoop a fish out of the sea and the water in the cup is just a drop in the ocean, but to the fish, the water in the cup means everything.*

Her sister's analogy impressed Cora. It made her realize that even the experiences of the boulder, while expansive in time, were limited to the boulder's immediate surroundings. Its existence was insignificant from the perspective of a continent. Thinking of the boulder in this way made it relatable, and its weight seemed to vanish.

Leora telepathically asked her sister, *In the vastness of space and time, for any two energies to come together at one precise moment and one precise time is extraordinary, don't you think?*

When you put it like that, yes, Cora responded.

Leora and Cora lifted Leora's hand together. As they did, the dirt around the boulder crumbled away, and the boulder slowly slid out further from the side of the hill. Cora smiled. When the boulder had fully emerged from the hill, its size became fully apparent. It was much larger than Cora had imagined. They held it in the air for a few seconds, and then slid it back into the cavity in the hill where it came from.

Cora sensed that the release of the builder and their temporary bond was a melancholy experience for her sister. To Leora, that moment carried the same weight as saying a final goodbye to a friend. *She really holds nothing back. She gives herself completely to her connections*, Cora thought.

With the boulder and their connection to nature released, Leora let go of Cora's hand. "Just like that!" she said.

Cora looked at her with amusement. "Why do I get the feeling you could have done that by yourself?"

Leora smiled. "You could too." She coyly walked around beyond Cora. "But I know one thing you can't do."

Cora took the bait. "What's that?"

"Catch me!" Leora said, snatching the amethyst colored bonnet from Cora's head.

"Hey!" Cora shouted. Leora ran off. "Come on, Leora, we're too old for this game," she said while grinning. Then she took off sprinting after Leora, quickly catching up and snatching her bonnet back.

"Aw, you got me," Leora surrendered.

Cora smirked. "Now it's my turn!" She lunged

at Leora to snatch the ivory hair pin from her chignon.

Leora ducked to the side. "Too slow!" She then tried to steal Cora's bonnet again and failed. They both laughed. Cora took off running through the forest. Leora followed closely behind. They weaved in and out of the trees, leaped over a small stream, and brushed through the undergrowth to come up to a tall rock wall. Cora was cornered with her back to the wall. Leora stopped running and closed in.

Cora smirked and began to move her hand, threatening to cast a spell. Leora giggled and did the same in response. They circled one another, waiting for the other to make the first move. Finally Cora did, sending a small spark at Leora's left foot, shocking her gently. She sent one back in response and Cora narrowly dodged it. Cora generated a gust of wind to blow Leora back, but Leora swirled her hand in a circular motion, causing a ripple of energy through the air and dissipating the energy from Cora's spell, just like her mother used to do. She then raised her hand up, using a growth enchantment to summon thick vines from the earth. They coiled around Cora's legs like snakes, working their way up her squirming torso until she was bound in place by them.

"Alright! You win," Cora conceded, with mild frustration in her voice. "Let me go!"

Leora released the vines, and they receded back into the soil.

Cora put her bonnet back on and beheld the

rock wall. She picked the top ledge of the wall as a target and focused on it, allowing the world to fade as her vision tunneled solely on the ledge. She felt the earth pushing up against her feet where she stood, and the surrounding air became thick like water. Squatting and raising her arms, she jumped while thrusting her arms down to her side, as though she were kicking off of a lake bed to swim to the surface. This caused her to float up to the top of the rock wall, where she stepped onto the ledge and out of Leora's sight.

Leora copied her and followed. When she got to the top, Cora took her hand to help her onto the ledge. They sat on the ledge with their legs dangling over the side and looked out over the forest. From that rocky outcropping, they could see across the entire valley and the village of Estrelle.

"What an incredible view!" Leora remarked. "We need to come here more often." Cora nodded. They sat silently next to each other, swinging their legs.

"You're so lucky," Cora said while observing the valley. "You're just a natural born witch. I'll never be as strong as you and mother."

Leora regarded her. "Don't say that. Of course you will. You just overthink things because that's what you're good at: thinking. I wish I were as smart as you."

Cora silently looked toward the setting sun in the west.

Leora followed her gaze. "We should get back

soon before Aunt En notices how long we were gone."

Cora snorted, "Ha! Aunt En? Notice us? She wouldn't notice if we walked in dragging chains along the floor." Leora laughed. Cora qualified her hyperbole, "Well, she wouldn't notice me at least."

"She notices you." Leora tried to sound confident.

"That's not what I meant. I don't care if she notices me. In fact, better that she doesn't."

"Why do you say that? She cares about you!"

Cora scoffed, "Cares about me? Where ever did you get that impression?"

"Admittedly, she's not the most demonstrative with her affection, but she does care about you in her own way. I think you remind her so much of mother, and it makes her uncomfortable."

"Uncomfortable, huh? I hope so. Maybe she will follow in the footsteps of her kindred spirit, Judas."

"You don't mean that, do you C? I know you still hold her and the rest of the village accountable, but they were scared. We all were."

"Absolutely, I still hold them accountable! So should you! They should pay for what they did!"

"They will answer to God for it," Leora asserted.

"Ha. That's always the answer, isn't it? Come on, Leora, wake up. God is a tool for the powerful to rule over the poor. All we have ever been taught has been to obey our elders and follow God's rules - the rules that the church interprets as they see fit. They label women as witches because they don't understand us, or they see us as threats to their authority, so they kill us and say it is God's will. God is their scapegoat; their moral crutch. They say do as we tell you and God will reward you in the next life. The next life is supposed to be all that matters, and yet they never forget to remind us to give offerings as we leave mass. The church is always the largest, most ornate building in every village, town, and city. If that is God's will, then Aunt En is the holiest in our village, and he would never punish her."

"But Father Julian..." Leora began.

"No, Father Julian is different. I'm talking about the church in general, and Aunt En's version of Christianity. They have much in common, aside from their position on witchcraft."

"But how do you know what the church is like outside of our village?"

"Because...never mind," Cora said. "I just wish there would be retribution. I'm sorry, I didn't mean to vent on you."

"It's ok," Leora replied, "I understand."

The two of them sat in silence for a while. The sky's colors turned from red and orange to violet and indigo, and then the sun's light vanished entirely. Leora stood and offered a hand to help Cora up. "Come on, C, let's go home."

Cora stood and said, "You go ahead. I'll be

there shortly."

"Where do you always go at night?"

"None of your business!" Cora teased.

"Excuse me! I just want to know if you have a secret boyfriend who I don't know about."

Cora laughed. "I just like to go for a walk at night. That's all. It's calming and helps me wind down before sleep."

"Can I come?" Leora asked.

"No. It's something I prefer to do alone."

"Ok. Well, see you at home." Leora stood up and stretched. Then she looked down at the village from their perch. "Hey, get me a stick. I want to fly in like a proper witch!"

Cora laughed, "You're stupid. Go home. I won't be far behind."

Cora waited until she could no longer hear Leora walking through the forest. Then she waited a few minutes longer, before heading off to the grove with the monoliths. When she got close, she deliberately went in a different direction, passing a thicket of red brush where she could hide. She had begun doing this to make sure nobody followed her. When she was sure she was alone, she doubled back.

"Teacher?" she called out as she entered the circle of monoliths. She knew he was there, as she had grown accustomed to his distinct lack of energy presence. Without waiting for his reply, she started the night's lesson in the usual way: talking about her day. She told him about moving a boulder with her sister in preparation for their upcoming magical aptitude test, and about their sparring session where Leora won again. "I can never beat her! It's so frustrating! She has so much power, but all she wants is to be Aunt En's perfect little witch. It's like she forgot that woman betrayed our mother."

"Your sister's weakness is her relationship with authority. She trusts it too much and has an innate desire to please it. This clouds her ability to see it for what it is: the wills of the powerful imposed through social conditioning," Cora's teacher explained.

"She always chooses to believe people are better than they are. It's like she sees all of their strengths but none of their flaws."

"Indeed," her teacher agreed, "and that could be her undoing, if you exploit it."

"How do you mean?" Cora asked.

"You want to beat her in sparring, but you hold yourself back. Stop using cheap tricks and use some real witchcraft. She would never expect her sister to cast a spell against her that could actually harm her."

"But I couldn't! If I actually hurt her...I just could not bear it."

"Then you will never win. If you want something in life, you must commit to it. Take what you want. Hold nothing back."

Cora pondered his advice, considering what it meant for everything she wanted in life. She recalled what she had noticed about Leora's connection with nature earlier, how Leora gave herself completely, lending every ounce of her strength to it. *How is she not exhausted all the time?* She thought, *That's probably why she goes to bed early but still wakes up when I do.*

Her teacher interrupted her thinking, "That is all for tonight, Cora."

"Wait! What if..." Cora began, but realized her teacher had abruptly departed.

Cora had been so lost in thought that she failed to notice Leora had indeed followed her.

Leora arrived within earshot of the grove, just in time to hear Cora ask her hidden conversation partner to wait. *What are those?* Leora thought, upon seeing the monoliths that surrounded her sister. Unable to tell who her sister was talking to, she waited until Cora was gone before creeping into the grove.

She examined the monoliths and took notice of the runes engraved on them. *These must be ancient! I wonder what they mean?* Running her fingers over the symbols, she saw a vision of their creation: a stout, hairy hominid with simian facial features and a hood of animal fur chiseled the stone with another rock. She perceived a sense of fear and uncertainty, and that the individual carving the symbol was hoping it would provide protection from something as a sort of bargain. She then saw the monoliths being erected by several of the hominids. Later, they gathered in the circle to give offerings. The visions dissipated and Leora realized the stones had been there far longer than the village of Estrelle.

She searched the surrounding trees with her eyes. "Hello?"

There was no response. She resolved to follow Cora to the grove again to learn the identity of her sister's secret companion, and see if she would learn any more about the stones.

18

"Wake up! Wake up, mother. Bella and I have to go, and you promised you would ask señora Matisse about a seamstress job." Ricardo gently shook his mother.

"Aagh. Just go on. I can get up on my own," Dolores replied.

"That's what you said yesterday. Please, mother..."

"Get out! I ought to whip you for speaking to your mother that way! Get out! Get out! Get out!" Dolores rolled over and slapped her son's hand away. Her abrupt change in demeanor caused him to stumble back in surprise. Her movement in the bed pushed an empty wine bottle out of the sheets and sent it clunking onto the floor. He fled the room, chased by the rolling bottle, and shut the door behind him.

Anabella touched his shoulder, causing him to jump. "It's no use, Ricky. She's a lost cause." They made their way down the hall to the main room.

"I can't believe that. The Lord is near to the brokenhearted and saves the crushed in spirit. Psalm thirty-four, eighteen."

Anabella rolled her eyes. "You've been spending too much time with Father Julian."

"She's our mother!" Ricardo believed that was sufficient justification for his actions.

"Yes, and you are her son. She is the parent and you are the child, not the other way around." Ricardo did not respond, so after a second, she added, "Even if she acts like it."

Ricardo looked down and said nothing. Anabella frowned. She realized he would not stop trying to recover the mother they had lost, and nothing she could say to him would change that.

"Come on, Ricky, we have to go or we'll be late. If she hasn't gotten out of bed by the time I come back for lunch, I'll make sure she does."

Upon leaving the house, they saw their neighbor, Jose Cervantes, mending the fence around the front of his property. His eyes snapped from his work to Anabella, as though his labor was merely a convenience for him to observe her leaving the house.

"Looking good today, sweets," Jose hollered.

Anabella ignored him.

Jose was perturbed that she did not acknowledge him. "Hey! I said you're looking good. Like a vision of the Virgin Mother Mary herself!" He cackled until he began to wheeze, "Hehehe, virgin, hehehe hah heh cough, cough."

Ricardo shouted, "My sister is grateful for your compliment, but may I remind you of Christ's words about gazing with lustful intent in Matthew five, verse twenty-eight?"

Jose gained control of his coughing to reply, "I wasn't talking to you, you flappy-eared dung nibbler."

Ricardo took his sister's arm in his as they walked away, ignoring Jose when he called after them.

"I wish you would never have laid with him," Ricardo lamented.

"Me too. But we needed the money, and you know after what happened I'll never be able to..."

"Yeah, I know."

They walked in silence until Anabella split off and Ricardo continued toward the school.

"Have a good day at school!" Anabella said.

"Adiós, Bella!"

Leora stood in a circle of girls who were chatting outside the schoolhouse until it was time to go inside. When she saw Ricardo approach, her eyes fixated on him, staring through her friends as if they were invisible.

Clara noticed Leora gawking at someone behind her. She turned around to see what had captured Leora's attention and smirked when she saw Ricardo.

"Hey Ricardo, how's Anabella?" Clara asked.

"Fine. She is learning a lot under señora Bellarose."

"Wonderful. I have been meaning to catch up with her. I have not seen her in so long. I hope she is not too good for us now that she has become a servant."

Ricardo suspected Clara intended her comment to be an insult, but he was not sure. "Of course not. She has always spoken highly of you all. You remain her dearest friends." He approached the entrance to the schoolhouse, discreetly stealing a glance at Leora. His eyes met hers and she smiled at him. He nervously smiled back and his heart leaped.

Leora felt butterflies in her chest, too.

The youngest girl in the group covered her gaping mouth with her hand. "Ricardo smiled at Leora!"

"He likes you," Maya said.

"You think so?" Leora asked.

"Duh!" Clara remarked. "You two have danced around it for years. It's insufferable. Honestly, you need to get it over with and ask him to be your boyfriend already, before someone else does."

Isabella emerged from the schoolhouse and rang the bell to signal the beginning of class, which interrupted their conversation. They filed into the classroom.

Cora sat by herself in the far front corner of the classroom, as she usually did, dressed in black from head to toe. Over the last few years, she had taken to wearing dark-colored dresses. She stared at the other girls when they entered and followed Clara to their seats like a row of minions, which made Clara uncomfortable. Clara smiled awkwardly as she passed Cora's desk.

"It's such a bright and sunny morning, isn't it?" Maya asked Clara. "Days like this always put me in the mood for a black dress." She and Clara snickered.

Isabella entered the room with a young girl who had never attended class before. She had long brown hair and a fair, narrow face. Isabella spoke over the various conversations that the students were having. "Class, I would like to introduce you to Emilia Estevez. Emilia is seven years old. Her family lives on the northern side of the village. They are related to the late Estevez's who lived next to Clara's family. Dear Rafael was Emilia's cousin." She crossed herself as she spoke of Rafael. "With the support of her parents, she has decided to start coming here to gain an education and learn witchcraft. I'd like you all to give her a warm welcome." The class haphazardly greeted her. "Emilia, there is a seat over there beside Maria. Why don't you sit there?" Isabella pointed.

Emilia took her seat, which filled the only empty chair in the classroom. The students watched her with curiosity.

Isabella continued, "It's wonderful to have a full classroom again. Since we have a new student, and because many of you have a magical aptitude test coming up, why don't we begin today's class by reciting the coven's bylaws? Who can tell me the first one?"

Nobody said anything.

"Come now, I know you all know them. What is the first law of our coven?"

Leora spoke up, "Magic is a gift from God, and witches must only practice in accordance with the Bible and in Jesus' name."

"Very good, Leora," Isabella commended. "Who can tell me the second?"

Leora answered again, "Only the coven elders may practice witchcraft outside the valley, and only the elders can grant approval for such use of the craft."

"Correct again, but I know Leora is not the only one who knows the coven bylaws. Somebody else tell me the third."

"When the time is right, witches will become the missionaries of our creed," a young boy answered.

"That is true, Alfonso, but that is the fifth and final bylaw. Does anybody know the third?"

Nobody responded. Leora began to speak, but Isabella silenced her. "Since Leora is the only one here who seems to know the coven bylaws, I will make it your homework assignment tonight to memorize them."

The class groaned.

"You should all be prepared to recite them tomorrow."

***

Elise picked a cluster of small, brown mushrooms with dome shaped heads to put in her basket. Holding one between her thumb and forefinger, she turned to Anabella. "These are the ones we want."

Anabella scanned the ground for more. She had a hard time telling the difference between the mushrooms that Elise had found and the other brown ones that grew around them. "What about these?" she asked, kneeling beside one.

"No, they look similar, but they're different. We are looking for the ones that grow from excrement. See, that is how I found these over here."

Anabella scrunched her nose.

Elise laughed. "It's ok, we will rinse them off."

They continued searching for mushrooms where the pasture met the edge of the forest.

"Oh! Look here!" Elise shouted. Anabella went to see what Elise had found. "Do you see this plant with the flower buds? That's deadly nightshade. In a few months, it will produce berries that are toxic enough to kill. It's best to avoid touching them, unless that is your intention." She winked.

Anabella grinned at the wickedness of Elise's joking suggestion. "How did you learn so much about plants?"

"There are witches throughout the world who possess this knowledge. I have always loved nature. It is a love I inherited from my mother. I learned a lot from her, and a little from my own exploration."

"Do the witches in other parts of the world know magic, too?"

"No, as far as I know, the witches in our valley are the only ones in the world who can actually use magic. All thanks to Faustus Neumann. It's ironic, isn't it, that the church hunts people like us, but none of them actually use magic?"

Anabella nodded.

Elise continued, "My mother was burned for witchcraft. That was why my late husband and I moved to Estrelle. We needed somewhere remote to escape. My husband told me it was for my protection, but truthfully, it was more for the protection of his reputation. God forbid people think he married the daughter of a witch."

"I'm sorry about your mother," Anabella said.

"It was a long time ago."

"You must have married young."

"I did. My mother raised me herself, so she was eager to marry me off to a gentleman of wealth. I was promised to him when I was fourteen."

"Wow!" Anabella's eyebrows raised. "I'm eighteen and I don't feel ready for marriage. I cannot imagine being married at fourteen!"

Elise nodded. "I did not have much of a choice in the matter, though. Sometimes we have to do whatever it takes to survive."

Anabella thought about the men she had slept with over the last few years for money and favors for her family. "Yeah, I get it."

Elise smiled. "I think we have collected all we need. Let's take this back to the house."

They cut through a field of grapevines, carefully stepping over a puddle of mud.

"You know, Anabella, you don't have to stay with me so late in the evening. You should have a life too. And you're young! I'm sure there must be some young man who would enjoy walking with you while the sun sets."

Anabella frowned. "I don't mind. I don't have anything else to do, and I would rather not spend any more time around men than I must."

Elise raised her brow and studied Anabella briefly. "What about men displeases you?"

"Ha. Where should I start?"

Elise grinned and waited for her to continue.

"Well, I'm sure you have heard the rumors about me."

"Oui, I have."

"Then you must know why I do not wish to spend my time around men."

"Understood. But men have their merits. And certainly your time with them has shown you how they can bend to your will."

Anabella scoffed. "I guess. They're all the same. But what does it matter if I can make them work for what they want, when they can just hold me down and take it, anyway?"

Elise stopped walking. "Anabella, I'm very sorry about what happened to you, but you cannot let it define you. You are a woman and a witch. That combination should make you a masterful manipulator." She saw Anabella lower her head and qualified her statement. "I'm not saying you could have done anything to prevent what happened. You couldn't. It was not your fault. I would know better than most." She looked away as she recalled a painful memory. "What I'm saying is that with proper training in witchcraft and seduction, no man should be able to take *anything* from you. Did Isabella teach you nothing?" She pursed her lips. "Ça suffit. From this day forward, you are not just my apprentice botanist. You will be my apprentice witch. I will teach you everything I know, and you will learn how to wrap men around your finger."

"Ok," Anabella accepted. She liked the idea of learning how to take advantage of men, because it felt justified after they had taken advantage of her. But what she would not admit to Elise is that she also felt she had nothing to offer any man who she might be attracted to. She had none of the traditional skills that other women had. Her abortion had left her infertile. She had always wanted a family of her own, with a man she loved, but she feared her dream would never actualize.

Elise added, "And I'm sure you have the rumors about me, too."

"I have."

"Then you must know I get what I want from the men in this village."

Anabella smiled. She had heard Elise referred to as a slut, but she wondered if the label was merely defamation. She did not know of any man in the village who had slept with Elise, yet many catered to her, as if their words and actions would give them the opportunity. She wondered if the same was true of her late husband. *Her husband!* "Elise, are *all* the rumors about you true?"

Elise smirked. "When we get back, we should check on the mash. It has been fermenting for nearly a week and should be ready."

***

The great hall of the Ortiz manor house was second to none. It had a vaulted ceiling and tall pentagonal windows. Muntins in each window divided the panes of glass into diamond shaped grids. The room was painted white, with gold leaf trim on the ornate crown molding. The dining table sat on a Persian rug that laid on the hardwood floor. White cotton cloth that matched the drapes of the great room covered the dining table, and gold leaf porcelain plates and glasses, and golden flatware sat upon it. The room was lit by several golden candelabras on the walls and table.

Enheduanna sat at the head of the table. Geoffrey sat to her left, with Leora next to him, and Cora across from Leora. There were several seats that remained empty. Enrique stood behind Enheduanna, ready to serve. The manor house's lead footman, Javier, entered the room, followed by Julio, who held the dual role of gardener and second footman. They delivered and served several dishes and then exited. Nobody spoke during the process.

Cora and Leora sat up straight, without touching their seat backs, as Enheduanna had taught them. They and Geoffrey waited for Enheduanna to say grace. Once she had, and after she had folded her napkin and placed it on her lap, they all did the same.

"What did you learn in school today?" Enheduanna asked, as she always did.

"Mother Isabella spent a lot of time on geometry with the older students. We learned about the Pythagorean theorem," Geoffrey answered. "I don't completely understand it, or why we need to know it, though."

Enheduanna answered without looking up from her plate, "You learn it because some of you may need to survey land or build maps one day." She looked up at Leora and Cora, "And for the rest of you, it is good to learn a variety of subjects to strengthen the mind. What else did you learn?"

"We reviewed the coven bylaws," Leora answered.

"Ah, very good. It is important that you remember them if you wish to join the coven."

"When will we be able to join the coven? When we graduate?" Leora asked.

Enheduanna swallowed. "Your magical aptitude test begins soon. You will know after that."

Leora's face lit up. She looked at Cora, who was indifferent.

"Cora, I have heard from Geoffrey and Leora. What did you learn today?"

Cora swirled her fork in her mashed potatoes. "I learned Rafael had an aunt and uncle living in this village who could have taken him in after the inquisitors murdered his parents, but for some reason they did not."

Enheduanna stopped raising her fork to her mouth and stared daggers at Cora. Leora looked down at her plate, hoping to avoid another unpleasant family meal.

Geoffrey noticed his aunt's reaction to Cora's comment and tried to diffuse the tension caused by Cora's crassness. "That just speaks to señor and señora Matisse's generosity in taking him in. And it must make you feel fortunate to have an aunt who was willing to take you in."

"Oh yes, cousin, very fortunate indeed," Cora replied with exaggerated enthusiasm.

Leora kicked Cora's shin under the table,

hoping she would not provoke their aunt. Cora, however, could not resist. "It just makes me feel sad for them. I mean, I'm sure they were devastated a couple of years ago when their nephew took his own life. To think that they could have helped him, but didn't..."

Enheduanna interrupted, "That's enough, Cora. I will not hear slander spoken at this table." She turned her attention back to her food.

Cora opened her mouth to speak, but Leora kicked her again, harder. Cora winced, and her eyes met Leora's cautious glare. She smirked and took a sip from her glass.

Cora's antagonism had the intended effect and killed conversation for the rest of the meal.

"May I be excused?" Geoffrey asked as he finished his dinner.

Enheduanna sighed in exasperation. "You may." As he slid his chair out and stood, she slapped her fork down on her plate hard enough to make a loud clank that captured the attention of everybody in the room. "I just wish we could..." she stopped speaking to choose her words, but decided not to finish her thought. "Never mind. I'm glad you all had a productive day at school. Good night." She abruptly stood to leave. Enrique reached out and asked if she was alright, and she batted him away. "I'm fine, I'm fine."

Geoffrey awkwardly left in the opposite direction to go up to his room.

"What?" Cora asked when she noticed Leora

staring at her.

"Must you always be so difficult?"

"Oh, come on, I wasn't being..." Cora felt Leora's judgment boring into her. "You know what? Yes. Yes, I will be difficult, because she doesn't care about us. That's what she was going to say. She just wishes she could have dinner with her son, alone, like she used to before we moved in."

"That's not true," Leora protested. "Did you not see her sadness? For some reason, she has high emotional walls that make it hard for her to communicate with people. But I sense her, I feel her, desperately wanting to reach out to us."

Cora partially shook her head and looked into the corner of the room. She felt a touch of shame and regret.

Leora continued, "When we were on the cliff rock last night, you said you did not care if she notices you, but we both know that was a lie. If you want to have a better relationship with our aunt, you will have to forgive her and get out of your own way. Then you will have to make the effort to reach out."

"Why though? Why should I have to be the one to reach out to her?"

"Because she doesn't know how, and you do. You and I have our mother's empathy. It's not always fair, but sometimes having that gift means we have to set pride aside for the benefit of connection."

Cora was taken aback by her little sister. She

chuckled. "You always say I'm the smart one."

Leora shrugged. She looked at Enrique, who stood vigil through the entire conversation. "I'm sorry to have burdened you with our family business."

"I heard nothing, señorita."

Leora smiled at him. He smiled back.

"I'm going to bed," Leora declared. "Are you coming?"

"In a minute," Cora replied.

Leora left, wondering how long it would be until her sister snuck out to go into the forest. She decided she would wait and try to follow her.

Cora thought about what Leora had said about their aunt. *It's not fair. She has never even acknowledged what she did to our mother. Until she does, I cannot forgive her. I will not. And Leora is wrong. I don't care what she thinks of me.* She stood, sliding her chair back noisily on the hardwood floor, and went to her room to change her clothes.

***

Ricardo waved goodbye to Alfonso and Pablo, who were going to Pablo's house for after school studying.

"Are you sure you don't want to come?" Alfonso asked.

"Yeah, I have chores to do."

"Ok then, see you tomorrow."

"Adiós," Ricardo replied.

Ricardo looked over at his neighbor's house as he walked to his front door. He saw a flash of motion from the window, as a curtain was drawn shut. He sighed in dismay at his neighbor's nosiness.

"Whoa there!" a voice boomed as he opened the door. His neighbor, Jose Cervantes, had his hand on the knob, ready to leave, when Ricardo opened the door. Ricardo jumped.

"Hahaha. A little jumpy there, aren't you, kid?"

"What...what are you doing here?" Ricardo asked.

Dolores came into the main room and answered for him, "Señor Cervantes was here to help us with some repairs."

"Uh huh," Jose confirmed. "Some repairs." He snorted snot up his nose. "Everyone knows that without your father around, this house has fallen into disrepair. It desperately needs a man."

Ricardo looked at his mother, who did not make eye contact with him. He looked back at Jose, who looked at Dolores, and back to Ricardo.

"So, uh, are you gonna let me pass, kid? I need to get home."

Ricardo felt his temperature rise. He glared at Jose and stepped aside to let him leave. "Of course, neighbor. I'm sure your *wife* is waiting for you."

Jose grinned and stepped outside. He paused next to Ricardo at the entrance to look him up and down. "You tell your sister I said hi." His grin grew wider, revealing yellow teeth nested in a bushy black beard.

Ricardo's clenched teeth and balled fists were his efforts to hold back the fury that burned inside him. He took several deep breaths as he watched Jose walk away, repeating Proverbs twenty nine, verse eleven, in his head. *A fool gives full vent to his spirit, but a wise man quietly holds it back.*

"Mother?" Ricardo called out as he shut the door. When she did not answer, he called to her again, letting a touch of anger elevate his voice, "Mother!"

"Do not raise your voice at me!" Dolores hissed as she came out of her room. "Hasn't Father Julian taught you what the Bible says...about respecting your elders?"

Embarrassment muted Ricardo's anger. "I'm sorry, mother, I just..." He saw his mother take a sip from a bottle, and then felt foolish for apologizing. His embarrassment gave way to indignation. "Did you fulfill your promise to speak with señora Matisse today?"

Dolores scoffed. "Ha. It's aaalways about money with you, isn't it? You and your selfish sister. Do you realize..." she stumbled forward, catching herself by putting her hand on the wall, "what I've done for you? Do you?"

Ricardo rushed over to help steady her.

"Don't touch me!" She waved the bottle at him. "I can manage just fine on my own. You'll be happy to know I got us some money today. I even got that spot on the roof fixed."

"Ma, I wish you wouldn't..."

"Wouldn't what? Make us money?"

"No, that's not..."

"How else am I to pay for your education? We don't have *anyone* to farm anymore."

Dolores continued to deliver slurred complaints, but her words faded into the background of Ricardo's mind. His eyes filled with tears. He wanted to run away, to go anywhere but stay in the house - the house where inquisitors bludgeoned his father to death and raped his sister, where his mother lost herself to alcohol, and where the people he loved the most had resorted to selling themselves to keep food on the table and a roof over their heads. He looked up at the ceiling, hoping for something; some kind of respite, explanation, or hope itself to be granted from above. When he received none of what he hoped for, he clenched his eyes, tears streaming down his face. Amid his anguish, the memory of Jose's grin seized him. Jose's words, *this house needs a man,* reverberated in his mind. His mother's disparagement echoed back: *we don't have anyone to farm anymore.* He became aware that his mother was asking him something and finally snapped out of his reverie.

"Are you even listening?" Dolores asked.

He wanted to express his regret for everything that had happened to them, and for not being the son she wanted, but all he could think to say was, "I'm sorry, ma."

"Agh. I'm going to bed," she declared.

Ricardo sat listlessly at their dining table for half an hour in silent reflection. Then he picked up a Bible. He hoped that reading it would calm him, but all he could do was stare at the words, reading the same passage over and over but remembering none of it.

Anabella opened the door to find her brother at the table. She knew something was wrong when he merely glanced at her without welcoming her home. "What's wrong, Ricky?"

"I'm sorry, Bella."

"What do you mean?"

His red eyes teared up again when he made eye contact with her. "I'm sorry I couldn't protect you." His voice softened to a whisper at the end of his apology as he struggled to hold back sobs.

Anabella shook her head.

"When the inquisitors..."

"No. No, Ricky, don't you utter the words. There was nothing you could have done. None of it could have been prevented. It was not your fault."

He cried, and she embraced him, pulling his head into her belly.

"Mother hates me," he cried.

Anabella pieced together what must have transpired to cause her to find him in the state he was in and hugged him tighter. "Oh Ricky, she hates me, too. Our mother has failed us. She may as well have died with father that day." She cried too.

"I pray every day for our family. I don't know what else I can do. I can't farm. I can't work stone, metal, or cloth. I can't cook. All I do is study!"

Anabella's heart sank as she heard her own insecurities reflected in her brother's words. She offered the only advice she could think of: "You do your best. Learn witchcraft, learn from Father Julian, and leave this place. There is nothing in this valley for you but pain."

"I can't leave, not as long as you're still here, and..." Ricardo thought of Leora.

"You don't need to worry about me. I can take care of myself," Anabella avowed for her brother's benefit, while also hoping that hearing herself speak the words would boost her confidence in them. She patted his head and sat down across from him. "What did mother do to make you so upset?"

Ricardo recounted the evening to her, ending with, "I can't stand it. What you and her have had to resort to is a shame. There has to be a better way for us to get by."

Anabella interpreted his statement as moral condemnation. "Well, I'm sorry I'm a shameful embarrassment for you."

Ricardo reached his hand out to touch hers. "No, I didn't mean it like that. I'm not embarrassed by you. I love you. I meant it is a shame to have been put in our situation. I know the Bible says prostitution is wrong, but I don't know what to believe about it. How can God condemn someone if their intentions were good?"

Anabella shrugged. "That is a question for Father Julian."

"But he won't understand. He hasn't lived with it."

They sat together for a minute longer before Anabella got up. "It's late, Ricky. We should get to bed."

He nodded.

"Don't worry about mother. Tomorrow is another day for her to break another promise. Just pray for her like you have been. There's nothing else we can do."

Anabella went to her room and shut the door. Ricardo rested his chin on his hands.

19

Leora woke up to the sound of the church bells signaling the first hour of the day.

"Oh, no!" she exclaimed. She jolted herself up and saw the early morning sunlight creeping in from around the curtains. *I must have fallen asleep while I was waiting for her to leave,* she thought. She had not changed out of her dinner clothes. She quickly dressed herself and splashed scented oil under her arms and between her legs. Then she made her way downstairs, passing the servants praying Lauds in the lower hallway, and to the great hall. Nobody else was awake yet, so she went to the parlor to play a game of chess with herself.

Geoffrey was the next to come down. When he saw Leora playing chess, he sat down across from her.

"Do you need a competitor?" he asked.

"Sure."

They reset the board and began a new game. Leora was playing white, so she moved first. She opened with a pawn to g3; the king's fianchetto. Geoffrey countered with a pawn to g5. Leora moved a bishop to g2. Geoffrey moved a knight to f6. Leora thought for a moment before moving her knight to f3.

Geoffrey smirked. "I have taught you well, cousin."

"Or maybe I have just learned well," Leora said facetiously.

"Either way, the advantage is mine, because you know only what I have shown you."

"Or maybe the advantage is mine, because I know everything you have shown me."

Geoffrey laughed. "Quit distracting me with your logic!"

Leora laughed, too.

Enheduanna appeared in the entryway to the parlor. Leora looked up at her. They smiled at one another.

"Good morning. Gabriella made us some porridge, eggs, and bacon. Finish up your game and join me at the table."

"Did you hear that? Your mother said to finish up our game. We can't do that if you take forever to make a move," Leora teased.

"Agh," Geoffrey complained. He hastily moved a pawn. Leora quickly and absentmindedly moved a pawn in response. Geoffrey did the same. Then Leora illegally moved her queen to the opposite side of the board and knocked over his king.

"Checkmate!" she declared, grinning widely.

"You cheater!" Geoffrey swiped his hand, knocking over several of her pieces. They laughed together.

From the great hall, Enheduanna smiled at the sound of her son and niece playing together. She recalled a memory of her and Thalia playing knucklebones in the street outside their childhood home. "You cheater!" she said to Thalia, before they began throwing the bones at one another and the game ended in a bout of laughter.

"Would you care for a cup of milk, señora?" Enrique asked her.

"Yes, please."

Enrique poured her a glass of milk, just as Cora lumbered into the room, rubbing sleep out of her eyes to help them adjust to the sunlight.

"Good morning, Cora," Enheduanna greeted her.

"Good morning," Cora replied. She sat in her usual seat. For a couple of minutes, she was alone with her aunt. Neither of them spoke. When Geoffrey and Leora joined them, Enheduanna made an announcement.

"I spoke with Isabella yesterday, and she has agreed to open up this weekend's witchcraft practice to the entire village. Anyone who is interested can witness it. The visibility may help capture the interest of some of the other children who are not currently attending our school. It will also be a chance for you to showcase your skills, as you practice for your aptitude test."

"Why would we want more people to learn witchcraft?" Cora asked.

Enheduanna frowned. "Well, as you know, it has always been our goal to share witchcraft with the world. I thought there would be no better place than to start here in our village!"

Leora asked, "Does that mean we will start evangelizing our creed?"

"Soon," Enheduanna replied. "We still need to grow our ranks. The events that happened a few years ago caused division in our village. Some people saw witchcraft as a way to defend ourselves from future incursions, while others denounced it as the cause of our suffering. We reached an accord, but it has been a while and I feel the villagers need to be reminded of the peacefulness and usefulness of our craft."

"Hmm," Cora remarked.

Enheduanna looked at her expectantly.

"Events? *The events of a few years ago* is quite a euphemism," Cora said, before taking a bite from a bread roll.

"Yes, you are right, Cora. Let me rephrase. The tragedy that happened a few years ago."

"Happened...you make it sound like it was out

of your control, as though you contributed nothing to it."

"Well, there was nothing I could have done to stop the inquisitors. What do you want me to say, Cora?" she regretted her choice of words as soon as they left her mouth, realizing that she had opened the door and Cora was about to force it all the way open.

Cora slapped her palm against the tabletop, causing the dishes to wobble and clang. "I want you to admit that you betrayed your own sister; that you are responsible for her death! You sat there and did nothing to help her! You..."

"She was trying to save me!" Geoffrey interjected.

Enheduanna stood up and threw her glass of milk against the wall, shattering it. Geoffrey, Leora, and Enrique flinched. "I have had enough of your condemnation! For years, you have shown me nothing but hostility! I took you in! I have given you food, clothing, a life you never would have had, and all you have shown me in return is hatred. I am your aunt, your elder, and I will not stand to be treated this way any longer!"

Cora stood up from the table and glared at her. Her irises lit up with a florescent fuchsia ring.

"Don't you dare!" Enheduanna warned, pointing at her.

"C, stop!" Leora pleaded.

Cora looked at Leora with surprise. The pink light in her eyes faded. *How could you support her!?* She thought. Her sister's lack of support acutely stung her.

Javier rushed into the room with a broom to clean the broken glass. As he started sweeping, Enheduanna went to Cora and firmly gripped her hair, yanking her head down to pull her into the other room.

"Let go of me!" Cora screamed. She flailed her arms, scratching her aunt's cheek. Enheduanna shoved her into the wall and put her finger in her face.

Leora and Geoffrey sat frozen in their seats as they watched the scene unfold in front of them. Leora cried.

Enheduanna growled, "If you ever threaten me with magic again, I will have you sent to Rome, where you will be imprisoned and tried as a witch. Do you understand?" Cora did not respond, so Enheduanna asked again, "Answer me! Do you understand?"

"Yes," Cora muttered.

Enheduanna stomped up the stairs, leaving them. Leora meekly approached her sister and reached out to her. Cora pulled away, turning toward the wall. Then she ran down the hall and out to the courtyard to cry by herself.

"We should get to school," Geoffrey told Leora.

"Yes," she agreed. She decided to let her sister be, and she left with Geoffrey.

***

* * *

The school bell sounded faint from the inside of Father Julian's office abode. Ricardo imagined his classmates settling in for the day. He stoked the fire to warm the room and went to Father Julian's bed to pull his blanket up further. Father Julian weakly looked at him with gratitude.

"What shall I read today, father?"

"The book of Acts I," Father Julian spoke in a raspy, whispery voice. "Read about the apostles' mission to spread Christ's teachings and baptize all nations."

"Is this what your sermon will be about this Sunday?"

Father Julian nodded.

"Have you written it already? I can read that too, to prepare to read it at mass."

Father Julian nodded again.

Ricardo began to read. The previous night still loomed in his memory. He would have preferred to give confession and ask Father Julian for guidance, but he feared Father Julian was too weak for long discussions. *I will have to find solace in the good book*, he thought.

After more than a half hour, Father Julian interrupted Ricardo's silent reading, "What is it that is troubling you, my son?"

Ricardo looked up in surprise.

"I can tell something is on your mind. You keep looking out," Father Julian motioned toward the school.

Ricardo took a slow breath. "Father, I am useless to my family. I have no skills. I cannot provide what my family needs. I spend my days in school, or studying divinity with you. All I do is learn. I have no purpose."

He shook his head. "Your purpose is to serve God. For that, love is the only skill you need."

"But it's not enough!" Ricardo cried. "Love cannot put food on our table. It cannot save the people I love from hardship and sin."

Father Julian motioned for Ricardo to hand him the Bible. He opened it and flipped through until he found what he was looking for. He handed it back to Ricardo, pointing at a passage.

Ricardo read aloud the fifth chapter of Romans from the beginning. Father Julian held out his hand to stop him when he finished the fifth verse.

"Love is enough," Father Julian said.

"I understand we are tested and that suffering can bring us closer to God, but what if it doesn't? What if suffering pushes someone away from God instead?"

"God's faith in us remains, even during suffering, and even when we turn from Him."

Deep down, Ricardo was not completely convinced, but he wanted to believe Father Julian. He trusted Father Julian's experience and position, so he decided that Father Julian's interpretation of the Scripture must be correct, which comforted him. This renewed his hope that his mother might overcome her alcoholism, and that they would find a way to make money so she and his sister would no longer have to prostitute themselves. *Maybe I can't help physically, but I can help spiritually instead, by supporting them and reminding them of God's love,* he thought. *Father Julian is right. Faith and love will sustain us.*

The end of their time together coincided with the conclusion of school. As he exited Father Julian's office, he saw a group of girls walk in front of the alley between the school and the church. They noticed him approaching.

"Ricardo!" Clara shouted.

"Hi Clara!"

"How was your priesthood practice, or whatever?"

"Fine, Father Julian is so knowledgeable. But it's not priesthood practice. I'm just helping him while he is sick."

"If you say so. He has been sick for a long time. If you keep at it, you may as well become our new village priest!" She giggled. "Can you imagine that?" she asked her friends. "Ricardo wearing those giant robes?" They all laughed.

Ricardo smiled and scratched the back of his head. "Yeah, I would have big robes to fill." He had intended his tweak to the common idiom to be taken as a joke, but nobody laughed, except for Leora, who put her hand over her mouth to hide her amusement from her friends.

Clara looked at Leora and nodded her head at Ricardo. Leora did not react, so Clara did it again more vigorously, but again Leora did not react. "Ricardo," Clara began, "What do you think of Leora?"

Ricardo's face turned red. "What do you mean?"

"I mean, do you like her?"

"Yes," he replied. The girls giggled. Leora blushed. Upon seeing their reaction and fearing he had made a fool of himself, he qualified his answer. "She's a good friend."

"Only a friend?" Maya asked.

He did not respond.

"Leora has a crush on you," Maya stated.

"Hey!" Leora started, "I don't..."

"Yes you do," Clara said. She took a couple steps closer to Leora and spoke to her quietly, "Come on, now is your chance! Tell him how you feel and see if he likes you back."

Everyone stared at Leora, and she froze.

"Let's go everyone. Let's give Leora some space to talk to him on her own," Clara said. She winked at Leora as they left.

Leora remained frozen, unsure of what to say. Her heart pounded, afraid that Ricardo would reject her. They had become friends at an early age and grew into teenagers as friends. Her crush on him started very early in their friendship and had only recently blossomed into romantic interest.

Despite this, she had tried to hide the intensity of her feelings toward him, fearing he would not reciprocate them.

Ricardo's heart pounded too, but Maya's statement invigorated him, and he hoped it was true. His anxiety about his family and his discussion with Father Julian vanished from his mind. After years of secretly pining over the girl who stood in front of him, he finally had a chance to see if she felt the same way about him. He asked, "Would you like to go for a walk?"

"Yes," she answered.

They walked the main road leading out of the village toward the west, passing the Ortiz Estate and crossing the wooden bridge over the creek.

"So how is Father Julian?" Leora asked.

"Not well. It has become hard for him to speak."

"Oh no, I'm sorry to hear. I did not know how bad his condition was."

"Yes, he seems to grow weaker with every passing month."

"Oh dear. Perhaps I can gather some flowers to cheer him up. We could deliver them together on your next study day, if you'd like."

"That's thoughtful. I'm sure he would love that."

Leora smiled, and Ricardo smiled back. "So, what do you study with him?" she asked.

"Mostly preparation for mass every week, and

interpreting the Scripture."

"Interesting. You always do such a wonderful job. Clara may have been joking, but I really could see you becoming our village priest."

Ricardo laughed. "Well, I have always been interested in the Scripture." His face fell. "And I'm not good at much else."

"Of course you are!" Leora insisted.

Leora spoke so exuberantly that she sparked curiosity in Ricardo. "What do you think I'm good at?"

"You comfort people," she said. "The way you read the sermon at mass...it gives people hope. You make God seem closer to us, like an invisible friend who walks beside us."

"Wow, really? That's exactly what I hope people get out of them! I mean, Father Julian writes them, but I help. And to be honest, sometimes I stray from what he has written."

Leora laughed. "Yes, I know."

"How do you know?"

"I know your sense of humor, and I can tell when you say something to capture the congregation's interest, to prevent them from tuning out."

Ricardo smiled, "Well, it usually doesn't work like I hope."

Leora laughed. "No, not at all, Rico. It takes a unique person to appreciate your sense of humor."

"Unique? Gee, thanks, I guess."

"Haha, no, I mean I like your sense of humor."

Ricardo smiled as if he had just won a prize. "Oh!"

"But I might be the only person in the village who does."

They both laughed. Ricardo said, "Well, I know one person who does not like it for certain, and that's Mother Mary. Every time I look at her while I'm up there speaking, her face is stone. I think she has frowned so much that her face is permanently stuck that way."

"I know!" Leora said. "Her marionette lines make it worse, but she looks like she has not had a moment of happiness in her life."

"She's close with your aunt, isn't she? Have you ever seen them joke around?"

"No," she leaned closer to him, "and do you want to know a secret?"

Ricardo instinctively recalled a verse from Proverbs that discouraged the discussion of secrets and gossip, but his desire to be closer to Leora trumped his desire to adhere to the Scripture, and the idea of sharing a secret with her thrilled him. "What is it?" he asked.

"I'm pretty sure that Mother Mary does not know magic."

"What!? How can that be? She's a coven elder!"

"I don't have proof. It's just a feeling. But also, I have seen all the coven elders use magic before, and I don't remember ever seeing her use it."

"But why would the other elders allow someone who doesn't know magic into the coven at all?"

Leora shrugged. "If I had to guess, I would say my aunt must have something to do with it."

"Wow," Ricardo marveled.

They had walked far enough to come to Leora's old house. "Hey, come this way!" Leora said. They took the overgrown path to the roundhouse.

Upon seeing the condition of the house, Ricardo commented, "Wow, it looks…" He hesitated, not wanting to hurt Leora's feelings.

"Run down," Leora finished his thought for him. "Nobody takes care of it anymore. I often wonder if this is what the entire village would look like after a few years, if everyone suddenly left."

"Yeah, probably," he said.

Leora went to the pile of stones around the side of the house where her mother used to hang clothes out to dry. He followed her.

"What is that?" When he saw Leora stand before the pile of stones and noticed the flowers laid at its base, he suddenly realized that it was her mother's grave. "Oh, I see."

"This is where we buried mother. Cora and I often come here to bring her flowers, or just to talk to her."

Ricardo did not know what to say. He saw the pile of stones that had clearly been made by hand, and he knew the villagers would never have buried someone like that. He crossed himself.

"I miss her terribly."

"I'm sure you do," Ricardo said. "I miss my father, too. But...I should be thankful to have a place to pay my respects to him behind the church. It's not right for your mother to be buried way out here."

A tear ran down Leora's cheek. "They blamed her for what happened. And my aunt..."

Ricardo put his hand on her shoulder. "People do foolish things when they're afraid."

Leora nodded. "It makes me so sad the villagers would not bury her next to father. They loved each other so much. This pendant I wear is a symbol of their love. My father gave it to my mother, who gave it to me. It is all I have left of them." She held the pendant out for Ricardo to see.

"It's beautiful," he said.

They stood in silence before the grave for a minute, before Leora broke the silence. "I'm sorry for getting emotional."

"Do not apologize. I'm honored that you were comfortable sharing your feelings with me."

Leora looked into his eyes.

"I like you," Ricardo blurted out. When the words left his mouth, he felt as if they demolished a wall that he had kept around his heart, and his feelings flooded out of him, "Not just as a friend. I don't know if what Maya said about you having a crush on me is true, but I hope it is. I've liked you for a long time, and when I look at you now, I feel... like I'm melting. I think...I think I'm in love with you, Leora."

Leora smiled, "I'm in love with you too, Rico." She briefly touched his hand with her fingertips, causing them to momentarily connect with one another like they would connect with nature to use magic. A flash of a mutual feeling of joyful bliss and intense attraction passed between them, causing them both to gasp.

The feeling filled Leora with excitement, and she wanted more. She looked into Ricardo's eyes, hoping he would kiss her.

Ricardo was overwhelmed by what he felt. He wanted to touch Leora, to kiss her, to feel her body against his, but his desire conflicted with his religious beliefs, tainting his excitement with shame and fear. He took a step back.

Leora's heart fell. "What's wrong?"

"Nothing," he replied.

Leora's own emotions encumbered her ability to read him. She knew something had set him back, but his refusal to share his thoughts with her hurt her.

"We should get home before it gets dark," Ricardo said.

"Yeah," Leora agreed.

They walked back to the village in silence. When they said goodbye at the gates of the Ortiz Estate, Leora quickly rushed into the courtyard so Ricardo would not see her cry. Ricardo went home frustrated and sad.

20

Clara, Maya, and Maria had gathered outside the schoolhouse before class. Leora, Geoffrey, and Cora arrived at the same time as Ricardo and Pablo.

Leora joined her friends as Cora and Geoffrey went into the building.

"Hi Leora," Ricardo said as he approached.

Leora ignored him. He sullenly passed her and plodded into the building. When he disappeared from sight, Leora's friends looked at her with open mouths.

"Oh my goodness," Maya said, "What happened!?"

"You totally shut him down," Maria added.

"What was that about?" Clara asked. "Did you talk to him after school yesterday? What did you say?"

"Yeah, tell us what you both talked about," Maria demanded.

Leora sighed. "We went for a walk and things seemed to be going well. He told me he was in love with me..."

"No way!" Maria interrupted. Clara's eyes widened.

Leora continued, "So I told him I was in love with him too..."

Maya interrupted with a giddy, "Yay! You finally did it!"

"Ssh, let her finish," Clara said.

"Then I touched his hand. I didn't mean to connect with him, but I was so caught up in the moment, I was already synchronized with nature, and he must have been too, because as soon as we touched, we entered that state. We felt everything that each other was feeling. It was...magical! So intense...just so much happiness and excitement."

As Leora spoke, her friends smiled with fascination, glancing at one another with shared excitement. She continued, "It was just for a second, but then he pulled away and I saw this look on his face like he was...uncomfortable. I didn't understand, so I asked what was wrong, and he said, 'nothing'. Then he said we should get home and didn't speak to me the entire way."

Maya gasped.

"Oh no, I'm sorry Leora," Clara said.

"Boys are stupid," Maria declared.

Leora frowned and her friends patted her back to comfort her.

"It doesn't make sense!" Leora exclaimed. "I don't know what I did wrong!"

"You didn't do anything wrong," Clara said. "He's a fool."

Maya agreed, "No, it's not your fault. Maybe he's never been that close to a girl before, other than his sister, and he didn't know what to do."

"Whatever the reason, it's his loss. There are plenty of other boys in this valley. You're better off without him," Clara said.

"Yeah, just find one that doesn't know magic and you can bewitch him!" Maria joked.

They all laughed. "You're right," Leora confessed. "I'm just going to forget about him." Her words were a dagger to her own heart, and she forced a smile to dam the tears that pooled in her eyes.

Isabella began ringing the bell to signal the start of the school day.

"That's right," Clara encouraged, "you still have us, and we'll help you find someone better."

The girls lined up behind Leora, following her into the classroom and patting her back. Each one gave a mean look to Ricardo as they passed.

Ricardo looked away from them, embarrassed.

"What's that about?" Geoffrey asked him.

"I don't know," Ricardo answered.

Cora noticed all of this and felt a tinge of envy. Leora had told her nothing, so she did not know why they would be upset with Ricardo. Her sister's kinship with Clara and Maya also made her uncomfortable. *Everybody loves Leora. Perfect, innocent little Leora*, she thought.

When school ended, Ricardo lingered to speak with Leora, but her friends blocked her off from him by escorting her out of the classroom.

"Leora," he tried.

"She has nothing to say to you," Clara declared.

Ricardo was left in the room with Isabella and Cora. He turned to Cora, "Is Leora ok? I didn't mean to upset her last night."

"I have no idea," Cora replied, "Why don't you ask Clara? Apparently, she and Leora are closer than sisters now." She brushed past him and left.

Ricardo looked awkwardly at Isabella, who was doing her best to ignore the conversation by pretending to be engrossed in something she was reading. He followed Cora out of the building.

When he was about fifty meters from his house, Ricardo saw the door to his neighbor's house open. Anabella emerged, carrying a basket of goods. She did not see him. Jose then appeared in the open doorway. He watched Anabella walk back to their house. Then he saw Ricardo approaching, pointed at him and winked, before closing the door. The day's events had already pushed Ricardo onto a knife's edge, and Jose's actions tipped him enough to send him plunging into a pit of anger. Without thinking, he marched straight to his neighbor's door.

"Jose!" he shouted, abandoning all cordiality and respect for his elder as he pounded on the door. "Jose, get your greasy cow head out here!"

"Ricky?" Anabella had heard him and stepped outside to see what he was doing.

"Jose!" Ricardo shouted as he pounded again.

"Ricky, what are you doing? Stop that and come home!"

"No, Bella. This ends now."

"Ricky, don't."

Ricardo's patience had run out. He took a step back and closed his eyes. As he settled his thoughts, his perception of the world opened up. Time seemed to slow. His body tingled as his sense of touch expanded to feel the surrounding energies. The hair on his arms stood up. When he opened his eyes, they had rolled up into his head, filling the visible parts of his sockets with white sclera. With energy flowing through his body, he thrust his hand out, sending a blast of wind into the door of his neighbor's house, blowing it off its hinges and causing it to fall flat onto the floor inside.

"Ricky!" Anabella shouted. She rushed over, but it was too late.

The door had fallen at Jose's feet. He stood paralyzed in fear, like a plump rabbit whose shelter had been torn away by a fox. Ricardo deftly rushed inside. He channeled the surrounding energy through his body to enhance his physical strength and shoved Jose into the wall.

Ricardo screamed at him, spitting in his face as he spoke, "Listen, you dirty sack of dung. You will never touch my sister or my mother again! Do you understand?"

"Y-y-yes," Jose stuttered, scared by the superhuman strength of the scrawny boy.

Ricardo was not satisfied with Jose's response, as anger had consumed his rational mind. He stepped back, releasing Jose from the wall, only to step forward again and punch Jose in the gut, causing Jose to double over. Ricardo then kicked him, sending Jose careening into a wooden chair, knocking it over.

Señora Cervantes watched the scene unfold from the opposite side of the house, shrieking all the while.

Anabella appeared in the doorway and beheld the scene in front of her. "Stop it!" she shouted.

Ricardo approached Jose, readying another strike.

"Stop it, Ricardo!" Anabella shouted more forcefully, using magic to reinforce her command and freeze Ricardo in place, so that he could not move. "This isn't you, Ricky. You are better than this."

Ricardo's eyes rolled back down, and his body relaxed. He saw Jose cowering in front of him. Shame overtook him. He looked down at his balled fists, slowly unfurling them and staring at his hands as if they were foreign objects. *My God, what have I done*? He thought, stepping back like a drunkard, running into the wall and slumping to the floor.

Anabella approached him and knelt beside him. "Let it go, Ricky. You're better than this."

Ricardo looked at his sister with tears in his eyes. At that moment, Anabella appeared to him as a younger version of herself. He saw his big sister, who would pick him up whenever he fell. "So are you."

She shook her head and began to cry. "No, Ricky. I went to him. I chose to start sleeping with men for favors. They didn't force me to do it. I chose. I'm not who you think I am. I'm not a good person."

"You're my sister."

"Oh Ricky," she took his hands in hers and lowered her face, pressing her cheeks into his palms.

"What's going on here?" Dolores asked from the doorway. "What have you done?"

Anabella stood and faced her. "We had a misunderstanding. That's all."

"A misunderstanding..." Dolores looked at Jose, who had pulled himself up. He leaned against the wall to brace himself as his body trembled. Dolores surveyed the damage to the house and glared at her children. "This man, our neighbor, has shown nothing but kindness to us, and this is how you treat him? Shame on you two!"

"Shut up, mother," Anabella spat.

"You rotten girl..." Dolores began, but was cut off when Anabella put her hand in the air and closed her fingers into a fist, as if she had caught an imaginary ball. Dolores found herself unable to speak, instead uttering unintelligible sounds. She put her hand to her mouth in confusion before realizing what her daughter had done. She scowled at Anabella.

Anabella did not see her mother's reaction to her spell, as she had already turned her back to help her brother stand up. She spoke to him, "All I can promise you is that it won't be him again, ok?" She gestured at Jose.

Ricardo nodded.

Anabella addressed Jose, "Señor Cervantes, whatever arrangements you and I have had in the past are done. You are never to speak to me..." she looked at her disaffected mother, "or our mother, ever again. Stay away from our house, or my brother and I will repeat this *misunderstanding* with a hundredfold increase in severity."

Jose nodded. Anabella turned to his wife. "Señora Cervantes, I offer my deepest apologies." Señora Cervantes whimpered. She and Ricardo took their mother's arms and escorted her home.

21

Geoffrey, Leora, and Cora arrived at school the following day at the same time as Anabella, Ricardo, and Pablo. While Leora went to meet with Clara, Maya, and Maria outside the schoolhouse, Cora approached Anabella.

"Hey Bella," Cora said.

"Hey there," Anabella replied. They kissed each other's cheeks.

"What are you doing here?" Cora asked.

Anabella glanced behind Cora to see if any of the girls were listening. When she determined they were engrossed in conversation and would not notice, she whispered, "Skip today and come with me."

Cora smiled and looked behind her. Isabella

was inside and would not see them leave. Anabella took her hand, and they slipped into the alley between the schoolhouse and the church.

Leora noticed them leave, but said nothing. She was glad her sister had grown closer to Anabella, since Cora had drifted away from Clara and Maya.

Anabella and Cora went to Elise Bellarose's house. Along the way, Anabella told Cora about Elise's promise to teach her how to bewitch men, which delighted Cora. When they arrived, Elise opened the door to greet them.

"Good morning, Anabella. Oh, Cora! Welcome!" They kissed each other's cheeks. "Please come in. I was going to ask Anabella to help me with alchemy today, so you may help too, if you'd like."

Elise Bellarose's house was alive. It breathed cool air that smelled like the forest, with perfumed scents from various flowers. Vines grew up the mossy stone walls like veins. Greenery hung from the wooden rafters, making the ceiling seem like a tree that had grown over the tops of the walls. Plants set in clay pots filled every corner and shelf. A small black cat fled the room as they entered. It was not the house Cora expected for someone who had inherited wealth, but it was befitting of Elise's exuberant personality.

Elise led the girls through her house, out the back door, and into her garden. Her garden was filled with fruit trees, many of which were flowering. "Help yourselves to anything," she offered. "The apricots have already started to ripen."

Cora stopped to admire a patch of irises that grew in a rainbow of colors. Each one was more beautiful than the last. Cora knelt down and fixated on a violet one, losing herself in its furled petals and fuzzy, yellow anthers. She heard Elise and Anabella speaking, but their voices faded as her surroundings blurred. She heard a high-pitched ringing coming from the flower. As she focused on it, it grew louder. More tones began to accompany it from the other flowers. They sounded like pure tones at first, but gradually gained resonance and depth until they became angelic voices, singing chords that alternated as they gently swayed in the breeze. Cora felt her body sway with them. Their sweet scent filled the air. She closed her eyes to allow her other senses to take over, until her thoughts silenced, and she was filled with ethereal peace.

Anabella called out to Cora.

"Give her a moment," Elise said. "They love an audience, and they put on quite a show."

Cora slowly opened her eyes and smiled. The flowers had calmed her and refreshed her spirit.

"Don't you just love nature?" Elise asked.

"That was wonderful!" Cora remarked. "I can see why you live with all of this around you."

"In France, we say nature is une symphonie permanente."

"It's true," Cora said, inferring what Elise meant by the sounds of the words, despite not knowing French.

They proceeded to a small stone building that Elise used as her kitchen. Inside, there were several large barrels along the back wall. Along the front wall, to the right of the door, was a copper alembic still.

"What is all of this for?" Cora asked.

"It is alchemy," Elise replied.

"This is how we make whiskey and oils," Anabella clarified.

Cora's eyebrows raised. She marveled at the equipment.

"We put the mash in here and heat it up," Elise said, using her hands to demonstrate on the alembic. "When it reaches the right temperature, the vapor goes through this pipe, where it cools back down and condenses into this jar. Then we put this back into here and do it again."

"That's so cool," Cora commented.

"Shall we begin?" Elise asked.

Cora nodded, "Yes!"

Anabella smiled at Cora's enthusiasm. "See? I told you this would be better than school."

They gathered materials to make a fire and set up the still. When everything was in place, Elise announced, "Now it is only a matter of time."

They sat in silence for a moment. Then Anabella said, "Actually, Cora, I did not invite you here today only to practice alchemy with us. I need to ask you a favor."

"What is it?"

"Ricardo has been struggling to cope with the fact that my mother and I sleep with men for money. I know it must be hard for any boy to see his sister and mother become prostitutes, but it's especially hard for him because of his faith. Last night he attacked our neighbor, señor Cervantes."

Cora's eyebrows raised. Elise looked at Anabella with concern.

Anabella continued, "If I had not arrived in time to stop him, he may have gone too far. I know Ricky, and that would have unraveled him. God forbid he follow in Raphael's footsteps." She crossed herself. "But after we got home and talked for a while, he said that he and Leora professed their love for one another."

Cora's jaw dropped.

"Apparently they had a moment together, but the intensity of what he felt frightened him, so he withdrew from her. As you can imagine, she did not take that well and has been cold to him ever since. And he, of course, had no idea what he had done, or why she would act that way."

Anabella paused before continuing, "Now we both know those two have been like bread and butter for years. Everyone in the valley knows. It's about time they finally recognized it themselves. But I think the misunderstanding between them was the tipping point that triggered Ricky to take out his feelings on our neighbor."

"So, what are you getting at? What do you want *me* to do?"

"I want you to speak to Leora and let her know Ricky did not intend to hurt her. And let's help them reconcile. Get them somewhere together and let them work it out. It would be one good thing in my brother's life, and he needs one right now. I'm sure Leora could use one, too."

"Hahaha. Good things are not scarce in my sister's life. Have you seen her with her friends? They're practically their own coven. And our aunt adores her. She sees my sister as her perfect instrument for whatever plan she has been cooking up all these years." Cora cautiously looked at Elise, uncertain of what was safe to say in her presence, lest she report it back to Enheduanna.

Anabella listened with anticipation, hoping Cora would not decline her request.

Cora, however, was caught up in her complaints about her sister and continued, "And my sister is too stupid to realize that they're all using her."

Anabella saw a chance to push her idea. "But not Ricky! He genuinely cares about her."

"Well, *I* genuinely care about her, and it makes no difference to her. It seems she has a penchant for driving those who love her away, while being suckered by those who only pretend to care."

Elise butted in, "If I may weigh in..."

Cora nodded.

"Love is a rare, precious thing. If you love her, you should help her, even if she refuses. She may not recognize it now, but she will be grateful in time, and so will you."

"Why should I be obligated to help her simply because I love her?"

Elise shook her head. "No, it has nothing to do with obligation. It is for your own benefit. You will regret it if you don't."

Cora considered Elise's advice.

"So will you do it?" Anabella asked.

"Fine. Yes."

"Hooray!" Anabella rejoiced. "I have wanted to see them happy together for so long."

Cora smirked. "I have too," she admitted.

"Wonderful!" Elise commented. "I'm proud of you both."

Cora went back to what Anabella had told her about Ricardo. "So Bella, if your brother hurt someone with magic, that breaks one of the coven's bylaws." She turned to Elise. "What does that mean? What will happen to him?"

Elise frowned and averted her eyes from them, which concerned Anabella.

Anabella pleaded, "Elise, you can't let the elders punish him for it. He has endured so much, and señor Cervantes had it coming. If Ricky had not beat the arrogance out of him, another man would have done it, sooner or later."

"I will do what I can. All I can say is that the last time something like this happened was when Leora injured Francisco. Enheduanna called for harsh punishment, not for her, but for your mother." She looked at Cora.

You will do what you can. Ha. A lot of good that did for my mother, Cora thought.

There was a distant knocking. Elise got up. "Somebody is knocking on my door. I will return shortly."

After she left, Anabella said to Cora, "Ricky is hard on himself. He already told me he feels horrible about what he did. He was going to confess to Father Julian today and determine his penance. I really hope the elders show him mercy."

Cora did not speak. She simply nodded. Internally, Anabella's hypocrisy enraged her. She thought, *how dare she ask for mercy for her brother, but condemn mother to death?* Cora recalled the memory of the day the inquisitors lined everyone up in the muddy street in front of the church. Anabella joined the rest of the village in their betrayal. Cora remembered all their faces and clearly visualized them shouting, "Witch!"

Several minutes of uncomfortable silence passed, broken only by the slow drip of alcohol into the collection jar.

Elise returned and announced, "That was Enheduanna. Señor Cervantes went to her this morning and filed a complaint. Enheduanna canceled this weekend's public witchcraft demonstration. She fears it would be too inflammatory after what happened. She wants the coven elders to convene this evening to discuss how to handle the village's response."

"What did she say about my brother? Will he be punished?" Anabella asked.

"No. She understands why he did it. She is going to speak with Father Julian, but she does not think it is necessary to punish your family."

Anabella sighed in relief. "Thank God."

Cora looked at Elise in disbelief. *That bitch violently shook my sister after she defended herself against Francisco, but shows mercy for someone she is not related to for an unprovoked attack*, she thought. While Anabella and Elise continued speaking, Cora zoned out. After a few minutes, she stood up and made up an excuse to leave.

"I worry about her," Elise said after Cora left. "I have heard she became more withdrawn after her mother passed."

"She's fine. She might keep to herself, but she knows she has me to confide in. She's like the sister I never had."

Elise smiled. "Tres bien. Do you also confide in her?"

"Yes, but not all the time. I don't tell her about some of the men I've slept with. She's still a virgin, and it seems to make her uncomfortable to talk about it. I would venture to say she may even be disinterested in sex."

"I cannot imagine what that would be like! I

cannot go a single day without the rush of an orgasm."

Anabella looked at her mentor in shock. "Seriously?"

"Oh yes! You don't think I have sex with men only to get something out of them, do you?"

"Well...I guess I did," Anabella replied. They both laughed. "I just don't know any man in the village who has said they slept with you."

Elise laughed. "That's because the ones that have don't remember it. I give them a drink, we have some fun, and they go on their way. Sometimes they go with a desire to do something for me, and they have no idea where the impulse came from."

Anabella laughed again. "I see. So is that the type of bewitchment you promised to teach me?"

"Of course. I will show you many things," Elise smiled devilishly, while subtly running her fingers along the inside of her thigh.

***

Cora upheld her promise to Anabella and told Leora why Ricardo had gone silent during their walk. Leora was elated to hear why he had done it and relieved that it was not because she had repulsed him. She even found his inability to communicate the intensity of his feelings for her endearing, which made Cora roll her eyes. Cora did not have to convince her to meet with Ricardo. Leora decided to do it on her own.

Instead of going home after church, Leora went to the Lorenzo-Vargas' house. There was a large rock sticking out of the ground in front, and she sat on it to wait for Ricardo.

Anabella and Dolores arrived first. Dolores asked Leora what she was doing there. Anabella answered on Leora's behalf and led her mother inside. "He'll be here soon," she promised Leora, smiling widely.

A short time later, Ricardo came around the bend in the road that led from the village center to his house. As soon as Leora saw him, she jumped up. He stopped walking when he saw her. She approached him, quickening her pace until she was running. She ran to him and threw her arms around him. He hugged her in return, cautiously at first, but tightened his arms when he felt the strength of her embrace.

"I wish you had told me how nervous you were on our walk. I thought...oh I just didn't know what to think. I was confused and sad that you ignored me on the way back."

Ricardo responded, "I'm sorry. I was not nervous at first, but when we connected when we touched, it was so intense. I was embarrassed, like how Adam must have felt after he ate the fruit."

"You don't seem to be embarrassed now."

Ricardo blushed as he realized she must have been able to feel his erection through their clothes. He tried to pull away, but to his surprise, she squeezed him tighter.

"No, I like it," she whispered.

Hearing her whisper in his ear and feeling her body pressed against his sent a wave of euphoria through him. Like before, he heard his inner voice warning him of the sin of lust, but this time, he ignored it.

They separated. "How about we retry that walk?" Leora suggested.

He agreed, "Yeah, let's do that." He offered her his hand, and she gleefully took it. They walked down the road toward the east end of the valley, passing the Matisse's house and the farm across from it that used to belong to the Herreros.

"Are you ready for the aptitude test this week?" Ricardo asked.

"Yes! I can't wait!"

"You can't wait for a test?" Ricardo chuckled.

Leora grinned. "No, I can't. But that's because I know something you don't."

"What?"

"You'll have to wait and see. Aunt En would not want me to tell anyone else."

"Fine. You can have your unfair advantage. I'll just have to work harder to score higher than you." He smirked.

"Haha. No! It's not like that. It's about the reward for passing. I don't know what we will have to do for the test, but I do know what happens if we pass."

"Hmm, I see." Ricardo veered off the road

toward a grassy pasture that went up a hill to meet the forest. He pulled Leora's arm. "Let's go up there." He helped her over the wooden fence around the pasture.

"Hey watch out!" Leora exclaimed as she noticed Ricardo stepping toward a cow pie.

"Oh my, that was close! Thanks!"

They continued up the steep hill. The afternoon sun warmed the grass. A couple of yellow butterflies passed over them, playfully swirling around one another.

In between breaths, Leora said, "Clara says I should ask you to be my boyfriend."

"Oh?"

"So...what do you think?"

"About what?"

"About being my boyfriend, dummy!"

Ricardo laughed. "Haven't I been your boy friend since we were little?"

"No...well yes, but that's not what she means. She means you should court me."

"Like with the intention of marriage?"

Leora giggled, "Yes!"

Ricardo smiled. "Would your aunt agree with that?" They had nearly reached the tree line, and the hill had leveled. They turned around to walk along the hilltop, where they could see the entire village.

"I'm certain of it! You will inherit your family's farm, so I could come live with you." She gestured with her free hand toward Ricardo's family farm.

Ricardo's smile faded. He had never considered his inheritance when he imagined his future. He hated that farm. He had not thought about where he would live after finishing school, but he did not want it to be in the house he grew up in. Part of him wanted to follow his interest in the divinity, and another part wanted to be with Leora. He began to realize that these goals might not be compatible.

"What's wrong?" Leora asked after seeing the look on his face.

"It's just a little much."

"What do you mean?"

"Marriage. Moving in together. We're still so young."

"We're fourteen. Almost fifteen. There are plenty of people who get married at our age, with their families' blessings. And I'm not saying we have to do it right away. We should finish school first."

"But that's only two more years. I don't even know if..."

Leora stopped walking to turn toward him. "Don't know what? What do you want us to do?"

Ricardo let go of her hand and threw his arms out. "I don't know!" He circled around in the other direction.

Leora followed him. "Give me your hands. It would be easier to understand if we connect."

"No."

Leora grabbed one of his hands, anyway.

"No! Stop it!" Ricardo pulled away.

Leora was stunned.

"You can't just read my mind!"

"Then tell me what you're thinking!"

Ricardo looked at her. Her blond hair glowed like gold in the sunlight. He felt his frustration sink into the ocean of her big blue eyes. Those eyes looked at him expectantly, longingly. "I want you," he said softly. "But I can't live here. Not in my family's house. Maybe not in Estrelle."

Leora smiled and stepped closer to him. "Oh Rico, we don't have to live here. We can go wherever we want!"

"And I don't know what I will do for a living. I've thought about becoming a priest," he admitted, "but that would prevent us from..." He could not finish the sentence.

Leora's heart sank, and she looked away. *He would make an excellent priest*, she thought.

"Hey, nothing is decided," he took her hand and put it on his heart. "The only thing I know for certain is that I love you."

Leora smiled. "Love is enough. We can figure the rest out."

Ricardo smiled back at her. Her words brought tears to his eyes.

He's overwhelmed, Leora thought. *I get it. I will help him*. "Let's not talk about the future. For now, let's just enjoy our walk."

"That sounds great." Ricardo put his arm around her. She rested her head on his shoulder, and they gazed over the valley.

22

Thursday marked the first day of the magical aptitude test. Shortly before the midday Sext bell, Isabella waited in front of the schoolhouse with Clara, Maya, Maria, Emilia, Alfonso, and Esteban Hijo.

At age six, Esteban Hijo, the son of Esteban Padre, was the youngest student in the class. Despite his and Emilia's youth, Enheduanna had insisted on granting them the opportunity to take the test.

Enheduanna, Geoffrey, Cora, and Leora came walking up the road from the Ortiz Estate to meet them. Ricardo and Pablo rounded the bend in the road and came around in front of the church.

"Will Anabella be joining us?" Isabella asked

Ricardo.

"No, she's not feeling well," Ricardo replied.

"She was ill when we practiced for the test last weekend. I hope she's alright," Isabella said.

Ricardo covered for his sister. "It's nothing serious. She has just been dealing with melancholia." He had decided on this excuse, rather than tell Isabella that Anabella saw no point in taking the test, or in wasting time preparing for it.

Isabella pouted. "Poor thing. I will let Father Julian and señor Delgado know so they can stop by to check on her." She turned and addressed all the students, "Alright, as you are all aware, today you will have a magical aptitude test. The goal of the test is to assess your current abilities and identify which areas you could improve. But what you might not know is what happens if you pass the test. Sister Enheduanna, would you like to make the announcement?"

"Certainly," Enheduanna said, "Students who pass the test will be deemed skilled enough to join the coven!"

Several students gasped. Leora beamed with excitement. She looked at Cora, who smiled at her to acknowledge her excitement, but Cora felt none of her own, and her smile vanished as soon as Leora turned her head.

Isabella described the test. "All six coven elders will observe the test. We will wait here for the rest of them to join us before we go to the forest, and in the meantime, we can review the tasks. There are four total tasks. The first one will test your ability to connect with nature. You will be blindfolded and taken to a place in the forest where you will need to describe the world around you in detail. The second task will test your ability to influence objects through telekinesis. You will need to move a large boulder. The third task examines your mastery of the elements: earth, fire, water, and thunder. You will need to cast elemental spells to navigate an obstacle course. The final, and most important task, tests your loyalty to the coven. I cannot provide details on this task ahead of time. Anyone who cannot complete a task will not move on to the next one. Today, you will attempt the first task. Tomorrow, those remaining will attempt tasks two and three. We will conclude Saturday with task four. After Sunday mass, there will be a celebratory feast at the Ortiz Estate."

The students brimmed with excitement.

"Ah, perfect timing. Here come the other elders now," Isabella said. The students turned to greet the other five elders. Mary led the way. She looked sternly at the children, eager to judge them. She was not fond of children, especially Thalia's girls, but they did not care much for her either. The other elders followed, with Elise bringing up the rear. Elise wore a corset that accentuated her figure, and her dress was cut low enough to reveal the tops of her breasts. The boys in the group gawked at her as they all approached.

"Is this everyone?" Enheduanna asked.

"Yes," Isabella replied, "Anabella is feeling under the weather. The only children who are not here today are the ones who do not practice witchcraft."

Enheduanna frowned. "Pity." She had had high hopes for Anabella. *We need numbers for my plan to succeed*, she thought.

Isabella corralled everyone. "Well, now that everyone is here, let's go to the forest!"

Isabella stopped the group after they had walked deep enough into the forest that they could no longer see church's steeple. She reiterated the instructions for the first task: "For the first task, you will each be blindfolded and paired with an elder who will take you somewhere in the forest. You will need to describe your surroundings using your senses and connection with nature to guide you. Let your senses be your mind's eye, projected into the world through magic." Turning to the coven elders, she addressed them, "Sisters, please take a blindfold and pair up with the students." She took a handful of rags from her satchel and held them out.

One by one, the elders took a blindfold, picked a group of students, and blindfolded them. Constantina chose Clara and Maya. Josephine chose Esteban Hijo and Alfonso. Mary chose Maria and Geoffrey. Enheduanna took a blindfold from Isabella and hesitated to evaluate her options.

Cora averted her eyes, hoping her aunt would not choose her. She noticed the other students were doing the same. *Nobody wants to be paired with the coven leader*, she thought, *or maybe it's that nobody wants to be stuck with Aunt En*. The thought made her smile.

"Leora," Enheduanna said while approaching her. Leora smiled politely as Enheduanna put the blindfold on her. She vigorously yanked it and tied it so tightly that Cora could hear the abrasion of the fabric from a meter away. Leora flinched.

Isabella waited for Enheduanna to take a second student before handing a blindfold to Elise, but Enheduanna did not. "Ok...Elise?"

Elise took a two blindfolds. Pablo looked at her with anticipation, eager to be blindfolded and led into the woods with the beautiful witch. She walked over to Ricardo and asked, "How about it, pumpkin? Can I evaluate you today?" Ricardo agreed enthusiastically.

Cora smirked and glanced at Leora, knowing how irritated she must be that the beautiful Elise chose Ricardo.

"And you too, darling," Elise looked at Pablo, who had glued his eyes to her. His smile extended from ear to ear.

"So that leaves you two with me," Isabella said to Cora and Emilia. She blindfolded each of them, and the group divided into the forest.

Enheduanna held Leora's hand tightly as she led the girl up a slope, out of the tree line, and into an opening in the rocks at the base of one of the mountains that surrounded the valley. The opening led to a small cave, just large enough for the two of them to stand inside. Leora noticed the change in the sound of her environment as she stepped into the cave. Her breathing echoed back to her. She noticed the cooler air and the drier, harder feeling of the ground beneath her feet that the rain had not wet in a long time.

"I can tell we're in a cave without using witchcraft." Leora confessed.

Enheduanna laughed, "Well, I should hope so. The sound alone should have given it away. Your test is not about this cave, though. It's about what's in it." She knelt down and waved her hand over a bundle of tinder that had been prepared in the cave ahead of time, setting it alight. She used the flame to light the end of a stick and held it up. The light from her makeshift torch revealed paintings on the walls of the cave. The paintings, thousands of years old, were crude depictions of animals, people, and events. "Alright, Leora. I have high hopes for you. Tell me, what do you see?"

Leora had already begun to look around the cave in awe, with her mouth slightly agape. "Wow," she commented. It did not matter that she was blindfolded, Leora could see beyond the rock paintings in the physical world. She sensed the intent of their ancient artists, feeling the messages they wanted to convey. She could feel them so vividly it was as if the spirits of the artists had joined her in the cave, whispering the stories of their lives into her ears and pointing to the paintings as testament to what they said. Leora walked over to the rock wall and touched a black ash painting of a bull with her fingertips. Enheduanna held the torch up to see what she was touching.

"Oruk," Leora spoke in a foreign manner, changing the sounds of the vowels from her native language to have more of a deeper, hollow resonance in her mouth, and the k consonant to have more of an airy, softer sound. She ran her fingers along the back of the animal as if petting its back. She then looked to the right, where there was a human figure drawn in red ochre. The figure faced the bull with its arms out. She put her fingertips on the figure's chest. "Amakti," she said in the same manner of speech. She brought her left hand up and touched the bull again. With one hand on each figure, her body connected with them. She then said, "Amakti ra anan und oruk."

Enheduanna's face gradually went from curiosity to surprise as Leora spoke. Leora began touching other paintings, describing them in an ancient, forgotten language, and explaining how they related to one another. Enheduanna's eyes went wide. Leora moved from one to the next, faster and faster. Finally, she turned and grabbed Enheduanna's hand that was not holding the torch, finding it as easily as if she had not been blindfolded. She put her aunt's hand up to a painting of a deer, leaving her hand on top of her aunt's. "See what I see."

"Aagh!" Enheduanna cried out in shock. She dropped the torch and stumbled back into the opposite cave wall. "Impossible!"

Leora extended her hand, "It's ok Aunt En."

Enheduanna picked the torch back up, but did not take Leora's hand. "Amazing," she remarked. "Thirty-four years I have communed with nature, and never have I experienced a connection like that."

"Did I pass?" Leora asked.

Enheduanna laughed, "Yes dear, of course you passed! Well done! Here, let me help you outside and remove that for you." She guided Leora to the exit, helping her duck her head under the rock. When they emerged, she removed the blindfold to reveal Leora's bright smile. Enheduanna could not help but smile back. "I'm so proud of you!" She hugged her niece.

Her aunt's embrace suddenly reminded Leora of her mother. It was the most genuine hug she could remember ever receiving from Enheduanna, and it was exactly the same way Thalia used to hug her. Her memories, and her emotional response to them, were powerful enough to be felt by anyone sensitive enough, and Enheduanna noticed. Enheduanna's eyes suddenly grew wide, as Leora's memories took her right back to that day. The lieutenant's sword pointed at Geoffrey's neck. "Witch! She's the witch!" the entire village shouted in a fever of desperation. Thalia used her last ounce of life to protect her daughters as the inquisitors ran their swords through her body again and again.

Enheduanna let go and backed away from Leora, looking at her as if Leora had just stabbed her in the heart. As much as she wanted to, she could not break her eye contact with Leora. She had just felt what Leora had felt, and it had opened a door that would never close - a door that Enheduanna had known about for years, but did not have the courage to acknowledge.

"I..." Enheduanna attempted to explain herself to her niece, grasping for a reason she had betrayed her own sister. "I couldn't let him..." The recognition of what she had done was too much for her to bear, and she began to cry. Despite every ounce of her intuition nudging her, and despite the mountain of repressed guilt whose weight she had suddenly remembered, she could not tell Leora that she was sorry. She could not ask for forgiveness. She could do nothing, and it made her feel just as helpless as she had been that fateful day.

Leora felt every one of her aunt's emotions and heard all her thoughts. Enheduanna was as transparent as glass to her. For years, she and Cora had sought some sort of closure for that day. Leora wanted reconciliation. Cora wanted retribution. But standing there in the forest, looking into the small, sad eyes of her aunt, Leora realized that neither of them would get what they wanted from her.

"I know," Leora said. "Geoffrey is your son.

You couldn't let him die." The excuse Leora provided for her aunt was no consolation for her. She had waited so long for this moment. She had wanted to say so much, but after gaining a deeper understanding of her aunt, she realized none of her words would make a difference. She would get no reconciliation, because Enheduanna simply did not have the capacity for it. The excuse Leora provided was also a release of her hopes. The pain would endure, and that was the closest Leora could offer to forgiveness.

Enheduanna nodded.

Leora finally broke their eye contact and looked down, making Enheduanna feel liberated from accountability, and she took a few deep breaths.

After her aunt had had some time to collect herself, Leora asked, "Should we find the rest of the group to move on to the second task?"

"Yes. Yes, let's do that," Enheduanna replied.

***

Cora laid on her back in the grassy area in the middle of the monoliths, looking up at the stars. Her hands were behind her head.

"Nobody looked at her. Nobody wanted to deal with her," she smirked. "She picked Leora, of course. That left me and Emilia with Mother Isabella. She took us to a giant rock with trees growing out of the cracks in its surface. Emilia tried her best, but she's just too young. She has not yet learned to see the ether. She knew we were on a rock, but that was all she kept saying. I don't think she used magic at all." Cora closed her eyes, remembering her experience. "It was not so hard for me. I saw everything. Even with the blindfold, I could tell what everything was around me. I passed easily." She opened her eyes again. "And that reminds me: we have been talking for years, and I still have never seen you."

"I told you I would reveal myself to you when you were ready," her teacher said.

"Am I not ready?"

"Not yet. But you could be, soon."

Cora sighed. "Of course, that's what you always say when I ask about it." She rolled over and stood up. "Hey, you know what else was funny today? Elise picked Ricardo, and he loved it. I looked at Leora, and she was clearly jealous. Only a few days ago, they went for a walk and Leora boasted that they talked about marriage, but today he was ogling Elise. Maybe poor Leora won't get everything she wants." She paused to think before continuing. "What makes it even better is that Elise sat right next to me when Anabella told me how important it was; how much it would benefit Ricardo to make up with Leora. She knows, hell, the entire village knows, how those two have always seemed like they were meant to be together. Even so, she wore a low cut dress and deliberately chose to take Ricardo and Pablo off into the woods with her. It showed her true character. She wanted to see if she could capture the interest of a boy who was in love with someone else."

"Does that trouble you?"

"No. Yes. Maybe both. I like that she doesn't give a damn - that she takes what she wants, but she was my mother's closest friend. I watched her betray her supposed best friend, and do nothing while the inquisitors killed mother in front of us all. And today I watched her deliberately do something that she knew would hurt my sister's feelings."

"She deserves to suffer. She should know betrayal before she dies," Cora's teacher asserted.

"Yes," Cora agreed, "that would be fair."

"And her protégé, Anabella, what of her?"

Cora sneered. "She's even worse. She's *my* best friend. My mother spared her from raising the bastard child of an inquisitor, but she joined the rest of them, nevertheless. She betrayed both my mother and me, and she had the audacity to act like her request for me to encourage Leora to make up with Ricardo was for Leora's benefit. It was for *her* benefit! She wants her brother to be distracted so he won't cause trouble for her, like beating the shit out of one of her customers."

"She deserves the same fate as Elise, no?"

"Yes," Cora agreed again.

Her teacher issued a command that sounded like a question, "And it must be you who delivers that fate."

"Yes."

"But are you committed enough to deal it? After all, she is, as you said, your best friend."

Cora thought for a moment. "You once told me the best way to beat an enemy is to make them your friend."

"Yes. But the danger in doing so is forgetting they are your enemy."

"I have not forgotten," Cora insisted.

"Prove it. Kill Anabella."

It made Cora feel strong to say that people like Elise and Anabella needed to be killed for what they did to her mother, and she had even taken pleasure in imagining herself doing it. However, her teacher had challenged her to act. His challenge brought her revenge fantasies closer to reality and forced her to consider the consequences. *Could I actually do it? Would my conscience allow me to be a murderer, even if the murder is justified?* She could not respond with conviction, so she blubbered, "Wha...you want...now?"

"This is not something I want. It is what you want. I am only asking you to do what I always have: to choose your path. Prove your loyalty to yourself. Do as thou wilt."

Cora put her forehead against the nearest monolith. *I do want it*, she thought, *but...*

Her teacher continued, "If you do it, you will have your revenge, and you will be a person of conviction. If you do not, you will never have revenge, and you will forever doubt yourself in everything that you do. Revenge is what you have wanted more than all else for the last four years, is it not?"

"It is," Cora confessed.

"Then if you do not take it, how will you trust yourself again? Prove to me, and to yourself, that you are a person who commits to action. Kill Anabella."

"When?"

"Now. You choose the time and place, but the longer you delay, the less likely you will follow through."

Cora mulled it over and bit her lip to calm her anxiety.

"If you do it, you will finally be ready to complete our contract. Your time as my student will come to an end, and I will reveal myself to you."

Cora looked up in surprise. She scanned the forest, as if she would see her teacher and see whether he was serious. She asked for clarification. "Come to an end? What do you mean? What will happen then?"

There was no reply. Her teacher had left her with that promise.

23

On the second day of the aptitude test, the students and coven elders assembled at the pond in the forest, where Isabella preferred hosting many of the students' practice sessions. Rumors had already circulated about who passed and failed the first task, but the students watched one another closely for clues. They did not have to wait long to find out, because Isabella read the names of the students who would proceed to the second task. She had them line up.

"When I read your name, please step forward," she said. "Clara, Cora, Geoffrey, Leora, Maria, Maya, Ricardo."

I shouldn't be surprised, Cora thought as she looked at the other students who passed. *It's the most experienced of us.*

Isabella asked the students who did not pass to stand aside. Esteban Hijo wiped his eyes and kept his head down, trying to hide his tears. Ricardo had been standing beside him and noticed he was crying.

"How are you doing, Esteban?" Ricardo asked.

"Fine," Esteban replied, kicking a stone into the pond.

Isabella patted Esteban's head, "It's alright little one. You have years to improve your skills."

"Yeah, it's ok, big guy. I was the same way at your age. It took me a long time to be able to connect with nature, and sometimes I still struggle with it," Ricardo encouraged him.

Geoffrey overheard the conversation and snorted. "Only sometimes? Your spell casting is as limp as a noodle." He took delight in his insult and looked around to see if anyone else thought it was clever. Nobody did. Ricardo ignored him.

Isabella provided the instructions for the next task. "Alright students, well done on your first task. Seven of you will proceed to the second task, which will require you to lift the boulder from the edge of the tree line over there, move it over the pond, and place it on the other side there. You will try one at a time, starting with..." she looked down the line, "Geoffrey."

Geoffrey moved up to the edge of the pond as the other students fell back to watch. He appeared to be nervous about going first.

Leora encouraged him. "You can do it, Geoffrey!" She whispered to Cora, "Remember, don't force it. It's just like how we practiced together." Cora gave her a thumbs up.

Geoffrey closed his eyes to calm his mind and prayed under his breath.

Enheduanna watched him from the other side of the pond, whispering words of encouragement to herself, as if it would somehow help her son.

Geoffrey opened his eyes and reached out toward the boulder with his palm facing up. He remained in this position as he tried to connect with the boulder. When he did, he lifted his hand, and the boulder floated off the ground with it. He carefully turned, moving the boulder through the air over the pond. When he got it halfway across, he squinted and bit his lips.

"Don't force it, relax!" Leora shouted. "Come on guys, encourage him!"

Some of the other students started shouting words of encouragement, and it seemed to help Geoffrey. He got the boulder to the other side and dropped it down. It hit the ground with a loud thud, shaking the ground and nearby trees and sending ripples across the pond.

"Careful, Geoffrey! You passed, but set it down gently next time. That goes for all of you, too," Isabella instructed. "Ok. Leora, you're up next."

Leora moved the boulder across with ease and set it down gently. Clara, Maria, and Ricardo all got it across, too. Maya followed them, showing visible strain from the very beginning. She lifted the boulder, but dropped it into the pond less than halfway across. Last up was Cora.

"Remember, C!" Leora said.

"Yes, I got it, Leora!" Cora said, exasperated.

Cora calmed her mind and lifted the boulder. She drifted it across the pond and set it down perfectly. Leora gave her a high five.

Isabella wasted no time and explained the rules for task three. "That concludes our second task. Six students will proceed to the third task: the obstacle course. This course will require you to use the elements of earth, fire, water, and thunder. First, you will need to push the water in the pond aside to reveal the mud at the bottom. While holding back the water, move the earth until you reveal one of several wooden boxes buried in the mud. Some boxes have keys in them. Search until you find one, and retrieve it. Once you have the key, cast a thunderbolt to break apart the boulder that you have all just moved over the pond. Inside the boulder is a safe that requires the key to open, but the key will not fit. Cast a fire spell to mold the key to fit the lock. Inside the box is a blue ribbon that indicates you have successfully completed the task. The elders will reconstitute the boulder after every student, and put the safe back inside. Is that understood?"

The students acknowledged and agreed. Maria was up first this time. She walked to the edge of the pond and brought her hands together in front of her as if she were about to pray. She pushed her arms out in front of her as though her hands were driving a wedge into the air. When she pulled her hands apart, the water in the pond parted down the middle. Maria gradually pushed the water aside, making it run higher up the banks on either side of the middle channel. The pond floor in the middle channel was just as Isabella had described: a greenish brown mud pit interspersed with moss-covered rocks. Maria slowly let her hands down, but the water remained contained by the invisible force field she had put into place. She then cupped her hand and scooped at the air, which caused the earth to scoop and pile up, as if it were being dredged by an invisible shovel. She did this twice, digging into the earth only half a meter. On her second scoop, she uncovered a flat stone that partially covered a cube-shaped object. Maria carefully stepped down the bank, into the muddy pond floor, and went to the stone. Underneath the stone was a wooden box. She tried to move the stone, but it was deceptively heavy for its size. She squatted down and used two hands to pull on it. As she strained herself, the water walls around her began to falter, splashing onto the mud.

"Come on, Maria! You can do it!" her classmates shouted. Maria stabilized the water by holding out her hands as if to tell the water to stop. Once it was under control, she focused on the box again. She grabbed hold of the rock and heaved. The moment she did, the rock slid off the top of the box and came unstuck from the mud, but the effort was too much for Maria to maintain all at once. The water of the pond rushed to her and obscured her in a giant splash as the walls came together. When it settled, Maria reappeared, wading to the side of the pond and spitting out water. At its maximum extent, the water went up to Maria's neck in the middle, but it lowered to her waist and then to her ankles as she walked out.

"I'm sorry, dear, but you have failed the second task," Isabella said.

"That was a lot harder than it sounded like it was going to be," Maria confessed, wiping water out of her eyes. She walked, crestfallen, to join the other students who had failed previous tasks.

Clara was up next. She parted the water and moved the mud where Maria had before. She uncovered the box, which was only partially buried now, and stepped through the muck to retrieve it. Maria had done the hard part by removing the stone that had covered it and dislodging it from the muck, so Clara only had to open the box. But when she did, she found it was empty.

"Hey! It's empty! Where's the key?" she asked Isabella.

Isabella shrugged. "It looks like that box does not have one. You will have to keep searching."

Clara turned back to the pond and scanned the dirt. There was no sign of anything buried. She let the water ease back together and opened a channel parallel to the first one she had made, but more to the right. Then she scooped a chunk of mud out of the end of the channel. Nothing. She scooped the mud near the middle. Still nothing. Clara was beginning to sweat. She struggled to hold back the water as frustration set in, hindering her ability to focus on her connection with nature.

"Where is that stupid thing?" she said to herself. She let the water merge, this time not having the patience to ease it back together. The two sides collided in a large splash, and the water sloshed around the banks. Clara took a few steps to her left, strafing around the pond, and opened a channel at a different angle than the first two. She once again began digging, only to find nothing.

"Come on!" she complained with exasperation.

Maria shouted to her friend, "Don't give up Clara, you can do it! Just keep trying!"

Josephine anxiously watched her daughter with her hands tightly clasped in front of her. *Don't give up*, she thought. *Show them what you can do.*

Clara walked further to her left and opened a new channel. She again came up empty-handed after a few digs.

"Jeez, where are all the boxes? There must be at least seven out there for all of us, and more if some are decoys. How has she not found any of them yet?" Geoffrey rhetorically asked Ricardo. Ricardo shrugged.

Before Clara moved to a new spot, she bent

over, panting as if she had been running. She was tiring from the physical demand of spell casting and letting frustration overcome her, making it harder to use witchcraft. Her classmates shouted words of encouragement, and she once again tried a new channel. She dug into the mud nearest to her, almost into the bank itself, and this time a box appeared. It was just like the one Maria had found.

"Thank God!" Clara exclaimed. Her classmates cheered. She went to it and heaved the stone that sat atop the box to the side. The water walls wavered, but she held them back, grunting as she did. She opened the box to find a key. "Ah!" she cried in satisfaction. Then she rushed out of the pond and let the water come together again. Before continuing, she doubled over and took several deep breaths. Then she walked back around the pond to the boulder.

The elders stepped back to give the boulder clearance for when it would be blasted apart.

Clara raised a hand to the sky and forcefully brought it down to the level of the boulder. Nothing happened. "Agh!" she cried in frustration. She tried again, more forcefully, but again nothing happened.

"Dammit, come on!" Clara shouted. She tried again, grunting with effort, only to fail yet again. Her last attempt caused her to fall to her hands and knees in exhaustion.

Isabella stepped up to her and put her hand on her shoulder.

"No! I can do this! I know I can!" Clara said

while panting.

Isabella glanced at Enheduanna.

"Let her try once more," Josephine said. Enheduanna nodded.

Isabella took a step back. Clara strained herself and reached to the sky as if trying to grab a bolt of lightning with her hand. When she brought it down, she roared with effort, moving with enough strain as though she were tugging the lightning out of the sky, but nothing happened. She collapsed.

"I'm sorry Clara," Isabella said. "It's time to stop."

Clara began to cry out of frustration. Her classmates gathered around her and helped her up. Josephine wanted to help too, but held herself back. She was pleased to see her daughter's friends supporting her.

"It's ok, Clara. Who would have known it would take so long to find another key box?" Maria said, trying to comfort her.

"Yeah, you did well. It was just bad luck," Ricardo added.

They helped her to the side of the pond and Isabella called on Geoffrey to go next.

Geoffrey created a channel in the water about one third of the diameter of the pond and dug into it near the opposite bank to the one he stood on, unearthing a box.

"Are you kidding me!? On the first try? And way over there?" Clara exclaimed.

"Yeah, talk about luck," Cora said, glancing at Enheduanna, who smiled at her son. *It's almost like he knew where to dig*, she thought.

Geoffrey retrieved the key and walked over to the boulder. He mimicked Clara's hand motion and a bolt of lightning came from the sky, passing through the boulder, causing it to fracture down the middle. He used telekinesis to pry the fractured halves apart to reveal a safe. Walking over to it, he tried to fit the key into the keyhole as it was. As Isabella had promised, the key did not fit the hole. He withdrew it and held his hand over it. A red glow emanated from his palm and soon the key began to glow a dull red.

"Ow!" Geoffrey shouted, dropping the key.

The students laughed. He had heated it up while holding it with his other hand.

"Put it on a rock and heat it," Enheduanna recommended.

"Mother Enheduanna!" Isabella exclaimed, "Please do not interfere!"

"That's not fair, he should be disqualified for getting help from his mother!" Clara said.

"I apologize. It won't happen again. Sisters," Enheduanna addressed the elders, "do not let my mistake ruin my son's chances."

Mary nodded. The other elders followed suit.

Isabella nodded and said, "Geoffrey, please continue."

Geoffrey put the key on a rock by the side of the pond and tried again. The key heated from orange to yellow and began to melt. Geoffrey stopped heating it and began looking at the key.

"How am I supposed to lift it?" he asked. Nobody responded. He tried using telekinesis, but he had heated the key too hot, and when he raised it from the rock, it bent in the middle, its sides drooping and cooling. "No!" he shouted. He set it down, heated it back up, and lifted it again, only to have it elongate even more. He tried again and by the third time, it no longer resembled a key but a long, amorphous blob of metal.

Isabella looked at Enheduanna, who buried her face in her palm.

"I'm sorry, Geoffrey, but it is clear that there will be no way for you to use the key to unlock the safe."

"Dammit!" Geoffrey shouted in anger, kicking the hunk of metal. He stomped over to join the other students.

"Let me try next," Leora requested.

Isabella consented.

Leora went to the edge of the pond, knelt beside it, and put her fingertips into the water. "Ok," she whispered.

As the students observed, they were awestruck. Even the elders watched with surprise. Before them, Leora raised all the water out of the pond. It floated above the pond like a cloud. She held it there and put her other hand on the ground. The surrounding earth began shaking like an earthquake whose epicenter was in the middle of the pond. The mud vibrated so viciously that its thick consistency broke apart, becoming more like sand. It fell away to unearth all the solid objects that were buried in the pond floor, including stones and all the wooden boxes.

"What the...how are you doing that?" Geoffrey asked.

Cora shushed him. "She's concentrating."

Leora did not appear to be concentrating, though. Her face was serene. She was at peace with nature and completely tuned in to the energies around her. She calmly retrieved the key from one box and let the pond water rain back down to fill it again. Then she turned to the boulder, and with a wave of her arm, summoned a powerful bolt of lightning. The boulder blasted to smithereens, and the safe inside flew out and stuck into the ground from the force of the blast. The elders shielded their faces from the small fragments of the decimated rock that blew past them.

Leora raised the safe and the key into the air. The key began to glow red hot. When it liquefied, she slid it into the keyhole and let it cool inside to mold into the required shape. She extracted the blue ribbon and held it high for all to see. Everyone cheered. She looked at Ricardo, who, much to her satisfaction, was happy for her.

Josephine and Elise reconstituted the boulder.

"I will go next," Cora declared, not wanting to be upstaged by her little sister. She cut a channel through the pond water where she remembered one of the boxes was exposed by Leora. Then she made quick work of the boulder and key, molding it the same way Leora did. She took out the ribbon and held it up. The students cheered again.

"Wow! Well, I guess that just leaves me," Ricardo said.

Ricardo copied Cora's approach to the pond, cutting a channel where he remembered an unopened box had been submerged. It was empty. He tried again, and the second box had a key. His lightning bolt was not as powerful as Leora's or Cora's, but it got the job done, splitting the rock apart. Then he levitated the key while simultaneously trying to heat it. He tried for an entire minute, but nothing happened. The key did not heat up.

"Come on!" he said as beads of sweat collected on his forehead. Suddenly, the key began to glow. Ricardo looked at it with surprise. "Haha!"

The students encouraged him. Cora glanced at Leora, whose silence surprised her. Leora had her hands behind her back and seemed to be fixated on the key. Leora noticed her sister staring at her, but did not react. Cora smirked.

When it was hot enough, Ricardo put it into the safe, copying the same technique he had seen Leora and Cora use. His classmates cheered as he obtained his ribbon.

Enheduanna addressed the class, "Impressive. All of you."

Isabella supplemented Enheduanna's praise,

"Agreed. I'm proud of all of you for what you have accomplished today." She spoke to Ricardo, Leora, and Cora, "You three have been exceptional. For you, there is one final task."

The elders joined the students and congratulated the three who passed, as they all hiked back to the village.

***

Cora went to her room after dinner and waited until she heard the church bell ring to signal Compline, before turning over an hourglass. When the sand had finished dropping into the bottom, she snuck out to meet her teacher.

From her room across the hall, Leora heard the wood creak when her sister crept by. She still had not followed Cora back to the circle of monoliths after she had discovered them. She considered following, but was too tired. *After the test concludes*, she thought, *I'll find out who she has been speaking with.*

"Teacher," Cora called out upon reaching the monoliths. She was eager to tell him about the second day of the test.

"Have you decided on a time and place?" he asked.

Cora had hoped to delay speaking about the subject, preferring instead to discuss the day's events, so his question disenchanted her.

"Yes," she lied.

"Well? Tell me. How will you do it?"

She made up a plan on the spot. "Aunt En told us at dinner tonight that there will be an induction ceremony for anyone who passes the test. It will be next Friday night. Everybody will be preoccupied with the ceremony, so nobody will notice if I slip away in the middle of it. I'll go to the Lorenzo-Vargas house. Ricardo will be at the ceremony, so it will only be Anabella and her mother at home. Her mother will probably be drunk, so it will be easy for me to slip in and out without being seen." She impressed herself with the speed with which she concocted such a scheme.

"Very good," her teacher replied, "and what will you do to her?"

The more Cora envisioned her plan, the more she felt herself committing to it. She wanted to do it, but was unsure whether she actually could take her friend's life. Talking through the steps made her see the deed as a simple sequence of actions; something she could easily handle, and her anxiety abated. "I'll make sure she knows it is me. I'll freeze her in place, and cut open her throat. She will feel the betrayal of her best friend and know that it was I who took her life."

"Bravo. It will be a fitting conclusion for her."

"Yes," Cora agreed. Her teacher's support bolstered her confidence further.

"There is nothing more satisfying that looking your enemy in the eye as you enact your vengeance. You will feel invigorated when the deed is done. It is important that you leave quickly to avoid being caught. Come straight here to me, and I will fulfill my end of our deal."

"You will reveal yourself to me?"

There was no reply. Cora huffed. "Alright then," she said in disappointment. "Goodnight to you, too."

As she walked back to the Ortiz Estate, Cora wondered what her teacher might look like. She imagined him being handsome and mature, with features that were as striking as his intelligence. She fantasized about being with him. She imagined him telling her his secrets: how he could conceal his energy, how he could see into her mind, and why he had chosen her to be his student. Her thoughts excited her, and she looked forward to what she hoped would be a new phase of her life.

24

The students and coven elders met at the school early in the morning of the last day of the aptitude test. It was rare in the mountains, especially in the spring, to have a cloudless sky. The morning sun already baked the land on what would be an unseasonably hot, late spring day.

Isabella followed the valley's creek to lead everyone up the mountain they called La Montana del Trueno. They hiked until midday, when they reached a relatively flat part of the mountain's slope. The flat area jutted out from the mountain to form a shelf, with a cliff edge that dropped hundreds of meters. At the back of the shelf, where it met the mountain, there was a cave. Isabella stopped at the mouth of the cave and turned to face the cliff. She raised her hands with her palms up to gesture at the area. "This is it," she declared.

The students explored the area. Pablo and Geoffrey wandered a few meters into the cave.

"Not too far, boys," Isabella warned when she saw them. They did not need her warning, however, as they stopped before going too deep. There was an unsettling darkness in the cave. It was an absence of energy that seemed to eat any sunlight that dared to enter. A foul smell of rot and damp accompanied the darkness, completely separating the environment of the cave from the world outside. Even at a few meters, the sound of the wind from the outside disappeared, giving way to plunks of water dripping from the stalactites above.

"Creepy," Pablo stated.

Geoffrey shushed him and pointed up. He whispered, "Bats. Do you see them? There must be thousands."

Pablo squinted to peer through the darkness. As he looked closer, the ceiling seemed to move. It squirmed. It palpitated. Pablo gasped and took a step back, tripping and falling onto his bottom.

Geoffrey stifled his laughter. "Careful, man," he said as he held out his hand. "Watch your step." He helped Pablo up.

Pablo stared into the darkness of the cave and began to feel uncomfortable, as though the darkness were staring back. The feeling was so dreadful that when he and Geoffrey exited the cave, he backed up, refusing to turn his back to the darkness.

"Careful!" Geoffrey exclaimed again, catching Pablo's arm to prevent him from tripping over a stalagmite. Geoffrey had to guide Pablo back until the sunlight met their feet, before Pablo finally felt safe to turn around.

"Are you ready?" Isabella asked as the boys exited the cave. Everyone else had already assembled. The elders had grouped on one side of the flattened rocky area, and the students on the other. Isabella stood in the middle.

"Yes, sorry Mother Isabella," Geoffrey said. They rushed over to join the other students.

Isabella provided the instructions for the last task. "Welcome to the ultimate task of the aptitude test. Only the three students who have passed all the other tasks will attempt to complete this one. Anyone who passes today's task will be inducted into the coven."

Leora shook with excitement and nudged Cora.

Isabella turned to Cora, Leora, and Ricardo, who had lined up in front of the other students. "The goal of this task is to defeat Sister Enheduanna, our coven leader, in a duel with witchcraft."

Leora's smile faded. Cora's jaw dropped. Several of the students gasped.

"What!?" Ricardo asked.

"No way!" Geoffrey remarked.

Clara asked, "Defeat the coven leader? But how? She's the most powerful of all the elders!"

Isabella smiled, "It's not quite as it seems. Sister Enheduanna will challenge you, but she will not use her full power. The point of this task is to see if you are strong enough to be a member of the coven, because if you succeed, you will become one!"

Leora had longed to join the coven and become an elder like her mother. This would be her chance. However, the realization of what she would have to do to achieve her goal dampened her spirit.

Cora bit her lip. The shock she initially felt had given way to excitement. *Could I beat her? There is the cliff....* A dark fantasy enthralled her, as she imagined avenging her mother. She looked forward to dueling her aunt, but she wanted nothing to do with the coven. A thought then crossed her mind that she verbalized, "Wait, isn't this task supposed to test our loyalty to the coven? How does a duel accomplish that?"

"To be loyal to the coven is to obey the commands of the elders, whatever they might be," Enheduanna answered. "You all may be reluctant to face me, but Sister Isabella has ordered you to, so the question is: will you do it?"

Isabella initiated the ultimate test. "We will begin promptly so that we may make it back to the village before sundown. Now then, clear away from the edge of the cliff rock so there is room for the duel. Sister Enheduanna, please stand over there," she pointed to her left. Enheduanna took up a position along the cliff rock. "Ricardo, you will go first this time. Good luck!"

Enheduanna stood with her arms crossed, waiting for her challenger to take a position across from her. The edge of the cliff served as a daunting backdrop for the duel. Any spell could push the duelists over the edge, and they could get badly hurt, if not killed. This caused Ricardo to approach the cliff with apprehension. His anxiety was noticeable in his shaky, cautious movement. He walked up to the cliff and peered over the edge. His palms became sweaty as vertigo overtook him. He clenched his eyes shut to force the feeling away. When he opened them, he slowly backed up and turned to face Enheduanna. He dropped one of his feet back into a stance that seemed like he was bracing himself for a physical fight. Enheduanna, meanwhile, stood in a relaxed posture: her feet were together and she never uncrossed her arms.

Isabella explained the rules of the duel. "Students, you are to cast spells against Sister Enheduanna. If one of them lands, you will be victorious. Sister Enheduanna will defend against your spells and cast some in return. If one of her spells lands, you will lose. There are no turns, but the student will cast the first spell to initiate the duel. Is that understood?"

"Yes," Ricardo said. Isabella looked back at Cora and Leora, who both nodded.

Leora was fraught with concern. She worried

about both Ricardo and her aunt. She did not want any harm to come to anyone. "Be careful!" she shouted.

Geoffrey also watched with concern, fearing for his mother's safety. "Mother!" he shouted.

She shot him a calm smile. "It will be alright, Geoffrey."

Ricardo smiled nervously at Leora. *Ok Ricardo*, he thought to himself, in the third person, *she's watching you, so don't embarrass yourself in front of her*. He shook his arms to relieve some tension.

"You can do it, Rico!" Leora shouted.

"Go Ricardo!" Maria shouted from further back. Pablo whistled.

Cora fixed her eyes on Enheduanna, watching her body closely to learn how she might react in the duel.

"Begin!" Isabella shouted.

Ricardo immediately spun his right hand in a circular motion, causing a wave of transparent energy to warp around it. Then he pushed his palm forward, sending a concussive blast at Enheduanna. She acted with surprising speed, unfolding her arms and dropping into a square stance. Her left arm chopped through the air vertically, and it sliced through Ricardo's blast, allowing it to pass around her while she stood safely in the middle. She then stomped her left foot on the ground, causing a fracture in the cliff rock that traveled from her foot toward Ricardo. Ricardo held out his hands to stop it, and the crack in the ground stopped progressing roughly two meters away from him. While he focused on blocking the spell, Enheduanna had flicked her wrist, sending a rush of wind at him. He could not react in time to block the second spell, and it lifted him off his feet and threw him backwards, off the side of the cliff.

Leora screamed and reached out toward Ricardo, but Josephine had already responded, telekinetically catching Ricardo in the air and floating him safely back onto the rock. When his feet touched the ground, he dropped to his hands and knees, trembling.

"The duel has ended. Come join your classmates over here, Ricardo," Isabella said.

Ricardo slowly and shakily rose to his feet and walked back to the group, slightly hunched, as though he were afraid he would suddenly be launched over the side of the cliff again.

Leora went out to meet him and took his hand to lead him back. "It's ok," she said, "This test is dangerously irresponsible. None of us should have accepted it." She turned to Isabella. "And I will not! If the requirement to become a coven member is to risk harming one of us, then count me out. I will never be a member of the coven."

Cora looked at her sister in shock. She wondered, *That is all she has wanted her whole life. Would she really give it up?*

Enheduanna raised her eyebrows. The other elders looked at Leora with curiosity.

"I see," Isabella responded. "Are you certain of this?"

Leora's eyes teared up. She looked at Enheduanna and the elders behind her, and then turned to Cora, and finally Ricardo, whose arm she still clung to. "I am," she replied as she stared into Ricardo's eyes.

"Then there is no need for you to duel," Isabella said. "I'm sorry, Leora, but your forfeit means you have failed the task."

Leora nodded. She turned to her sister. "Cora, don't do it. It's not worth it. What if Josephine could not have caught Ricardo? What if he or Enheduanna had slipped, or if they destroyed the cliff rock? It's too dangerous!"

Cora empathized with Leora. The danger of the final task surprised her, and she shared her sister's belief that it was reckless. But her desire to take a shot at her aunt was too great. "I'm sorry, Leora. I know it's dangerous, but I want to try."

Leora begged, "Please C, I know how tempting it is to have the chance to become a coven member, but this isn't right."

Cora put her hand on her sister's shoulder. "I'm sorry," she repeated. "It will be alright though, you'll see." She stepped forward to the edge of the cliff where Ricardo had stood.

"No!" Leora protested, wiping the tears from her eyes.

Ricardo put his arm around her to comfort her. "Your sister is strong, she will be ok. And the coven elders won't let anyone get hurt," he said. Leora put her hand on top of his. As he felt her hand on his, Ricardo looked at Leora's blond hair. He observed how it softly framed her forehead, how it tucked behind her small, pink ear and sat on her shoulders. He looked at her teary blue eyes and their long lashes, her curved eyebrows, and her button nose. It was the same face he had seen every day since he was little, but it looked different now in a way he could not describe. He felt a warmth inside of him; an intense desire to kiss her soft cheek. But instead of acting on this desire, he became embarrassed by how it had surfaced at a time like this, when Leora was worried about her sister and aunt. His face flushed. He turned back to the duel, feeling ashamed, and removed his arm from around Leora.

Leora discreetly glanced at him. She felt the same warmth inside of her, and she longed for him to kiss her. But when he retracted his arm, the same confusion surfaced in her as the day they professed their love for one another. She wondered if she had embarrassed him or made him uncomfortable. *Why does he keep holding back?*

"Begin!" Isabella shouted.

Cora put her hands out to her side, and balls of fire formed in her palms. She side-stepped around her aunt, staring her down and positioning her with her back to the cliff.

Enheduanna watched her niece cautiously and curiously. *What is she doing?* She thought. She did not have to wait long for the answer.

Cora lobbed a fireball at her with all of her might, causing her body to spin. She spun around and lobbed another, with another instantly forming in her palm behind it.

Enheduanna moved quickly, dodging the first fireball and blocking the second with a puff of wind that dissipated it. She had no time to counter, as Cora continued tossing more and more at her with vicious speed. Enheduanna blocked and dodged as fast as she could. Suddenly, she felt herself get hit by a powerful concussive blast. She had failed to notice that Cora had been advancing toward her as she tossed the fireballs, and by the time Cora sent the blast of energy at her, she was only a meter away. Enheduanna's eyes widened with surprise. She thrust her arms backward to propel herself forward to avoid being tossed off the side of the cliff. The blast was so strong that her feet skidded backwards, only stopping at the edge of the cliff. As soon as she stopped sliding back, she had to jump in the air to avoid a razor wind that Cora had sent toward her legs.

Isabella began shouting from behind Cora for her to stop, as she had landed a spell on her aunt.

Cora did not ignore her, rather, she did not even register Isabella's presence on the mountain. Rage consumed her mind, but rather than breaking her connection with nature, it seemed to nourish it, focusing her concentration.

Enheduanna landed after dodging the razor

wind to find that she was merely an arm's length away from Cora. She gasped as their eyes met, and she saw fiery fuchsia-colored rings encircling Cora's black pupils.

Cora bared clenched teeth and shouted a feral, "Aaagh!" as she swiped at her aunt's face as hard as she could. When her hand connected with her aunt's face, the memory of Enheduanna slapping Leora on the day Leora hurt Francisco streamed through her mind. Enheduanna's head twisted violently to the side, her cheek torn by Cora's fingernails.

"Cora!" Isabella shouted and rushed toward them.

Cora quickly put her palm on her aunt's chest, causing them to psychically connect.

Enheduanna looked at her niece, completely stunned. She saw hatred in Cora's burning eyes and felt it emanate from her niece's palm. She was filled with all the pain, anger, sadness, and confusion that Cora had felt about her and the village's betrayal of Thalia. She felt and understood Cora's need for revenge, causing her to finally grasp the gravity of the position she was in.

Cora felt her aunt's regret. All of Enheduanna's failures and insecurities made her seem smaller, weaker, and more pathetic to Cora. The deeper understanding she gained about her aunt through their connection only served to further her desire to hurt her. Cora's palm heated in preparation for a fire blast, scorching

Enheduanna's tunic.

Enheduanna felt what was coming, but before she could defend herself, she was enveloped by a vision. She saw Cora. Her eyes were closed and her face bore the pale countenance of death. The vision receded into another. It was Cora again, but this time her face was covered in blood spatter and tears. She was screaming a haunting, guttural howl. Enheduanna perceived from the vision that her niece was greatly suffering. Her vision faded to black.

Enheduanna opened her eyes, sat up, and gasped, "Cora!"

"It's alright, Sister Enheduanna, the duel is over. Everyone is ok," Isabella said. She was kneeling at Enheduanna's left side.

"Where is she?" Enheduanna asked.

Mary, who was kneeling at Enheduanna's right side, replied, "She is with the other students. We had to stop the duel. She is a little shaken up, but otherwise alright. How are you feeling?"

Enheduanna looked around. The elders had encircled her to check that she was alright. The students had similarly encircled Cora. "What happened?"

Mary looked up at Josephine, who was standing behind Enheduanna, and then responded, "The girl got carried away. We had to stop her from hurting you. It seems you have grown a little slower in your old age."

The memory of the duel suddenly returned to

Enheduanna, and she touched the deep cuts on her cheek.

"She got you pretty good," Elise said. "It was quite a sight."

Enheduanna's face turned red, and she stood.

"Careful," Isabella cautioned as she and Mary stood with Enheduanna.

Enheduanna scowled. She pushed past the other elders and marched toward the children. "Cora!" she shouted. The children stopped talking and looked at her in fear of the punishment she might dole out. They stepped aside to let her pass. She walked up to Cora so that they were face to face. She stared at her niece, and Cora stared back defiantly.

Elise and Isabella rushed in. "Why don't we all take a step back and calm down," Isabella suggested. She and Elise took Enheduanna's arms and guided her back a few steps. Isabella then stepped in between her and the students. "The final task of the aptitude test has concluded, and it is my pleasure to announce that we have one student who passed all the tasks, and will become a coven member!" The students smiled and looked at Cora. Isabella continued, "And that student is…"

"Leora," Enheduanna interjected.

Isabella turned around, unsure of what Enheduanna had intended. "Leora?" she questioned.

"Yes, Leora," Enheduanna repeated, "She is the only one who passed the ultimate task."

Everyone was silent for a few moments, until Leora asked, "But the task was to defeat you in a duel. I refused to even try. Cora succeeded, so shouldn't she be the..."

"The ultimate task was a test of loyalty to the coven," Enheduanna interrupted forcefully, "and loyalty to the coven means never attacking another coven member or elder with magic. We told you the task was a duel to see which of you were truly loyal. But we were secretly testing to see which of you would turn on a comrade for personal gain. Leora was the only one who remained true."

There were a few more moments of awkward silence before Isabella agreed. "Very good. Our victor is Leora!"

Leora looked around with her mouth agape until she found Cora's nod of approval. Then she smiled and laughed, "I can't believe it! I passed!" The other students cheered. "I'm going to become a coven member!" Leora said.

Cora hugged her sister and congratulated her. She noticed Enheduanna in the crowd of elders, staring at her with fury. *Well played*, she thought.

When the students and the coven elders returned to the village, Enheduanna announced that Leora's induction ceremony would occur the following Friday night with the full moon. The group dispersed.

Geoffrey, Leora, and Cora went home with Enheduanna. The sun had nearly set by the time they reached the iron gate in front of the house. Cora made an excuse about how she left a book in the forest and needed to retrieve it, in case it would rain during the night.

Enheduanna refused to let her go however, "No Cora, after dinner you will go straight to bed. If today taught me anything, it is that your deviance poses a threat to everything we have built in this valley. You need a firm hand and a watchful eye to guide you back to righteousness. So tonight you will go to bed early, and tomorrow we will have a serious discussion about your future."

The four of them went inside to find that Enrique and Julio had dinner waiting for them.

At dinner, Geoffrey and Leora talked excitedly about Leora's induction into the coven. Geoffrey could not hide the fact that he was envious, but he was also curious about what being a coven member would mean. Enheduanna reveled in their curiosity, but held her tongue. "You'll find out soon enough," she said.

Cora remained mostly silent while they ate, occasionally catching stern glances from her aunt. Geoffrey and Leora were too caught up in their excitement to notice the tension between Cora and Enheduanna.

After dinner, Enheduanna escorted Cora to her room on the second floor. She locked the door to the hallway to ensure that Cora could not escape. *Only the Lord knows what darkness has beset that girl*, she thought. She retreated to the master bedroom to think about how she could instill the fear of God into her niece.

A single candle illuminated Cora's room. She laid flat on her bed, staring at the ceiling and waiting. When the moon appeared in her window, and she no longer heard any sounds in the house, she got up and blew out the candle. She cracked her door and looked into the hallway to make sure it was clear. Then she floated out of her room, levitating herself centimeters off the floor to avoid causing any creaks in the floorboards. Her door quietly shut behind her, and she floated to the door at the end of the hall. When she placed her hand on the knob, the lock clicked, and she opened the hallway door. She locked it behind her and floated to the master bedroom, placing her ear on the door. The only sound on the other side was her aunt's soft snoring. Cora smiled. She opened the door and floated to the side of her aunt's bed. "Sleep well, Aunt En," she said while hovering her palm over her aunt's face. Her aunt snorted and her body jerked briefly before relaxing again. Cora dropped to the floor and boldly walked from the room, closing the door behind her without concern for the sound it made. Her aunt would hear nothing until she returned to lift the sleeping spell she had just cast.

The temperature had plummeted from the heat of the day, and it was now a chilly night. A fog had settled into the valley, and the ground was damp with dew. Cora wore a fur-lined cloak with a hood to conceal her identity. She crept through the village, opting to walk through her neighbor's cow pasture instead of taking the road. The cows watched her as she strolled through. "Don't mind me," she said smiling, "I'll be out of your way in a heartbeat." On the other side of the pasture, she hid behind a tree next to the road, peeking around to make sure nobody was watching. Then she dashed across the road and into a vineyard on the other side, making her way to the tree line. She was careful, but failed to notice a smaller hooded figure following her at a distance.

When she got to the monoliths, she dropped her hood and called out to her teacher, "Teacher? Are you there?"

"I am," her teacher replied from the shadows.

Cora immediately began to recount the duel. "I beat my aunt in a duel today! It wasn't even close. She is supposed to be the most powerful witch there is, but I demolished her!" Cora gloated. In terms of importance to her, her duel with her aunt dwarfed the other events of the last week.

"Hmm," her teacher mused.

His reaction disappointed Cora. "Don't you have anything to say about that? I defeated the coven leader!"

"No. You beat an old woman who was unprepared for her niece's ferocity. Then you were subdued by the other elders. I would hardly call that a victory."

Cora protested, "What do you mean!? She

couldn't even respond to my attacks. Isabella said she would hold back, but I pushed her to the edge, and she could not respond!"

Her teacher explained, "Your aunt was caught off guard. You did indeed beat her, but if she had planned for a stronger challenge from the start, it would have ended differently. Next time, she will not underestimate you. You played your hand too soon, Cora."

Cora was crestfallen. She realized the truth in her teacher's words. He continued, "She will watch you more closely now."

"Then I cannot continue to live with her," Cora said. "I'm old enough, and strong enough, to take care of myself."

"That remains to be seen," her teacher stated.

"What do you mean? What else do I need to learn? What else do I have to do?"

"Do you remember the agreement we made when you became my student?"

Cora summarized, "You teach me how to become powerful, and I will be your student."

"No. You will be my *companion*," he corrected. "And you are so close now. All you need to do is show me, and yourself, how powerful you have become, not as a witch, but as a force of will. Seize your vengeance! Kill the friend who betrayed your mother! Fulfill your contract with me!"

Cora sighed, dejected. She paced around the stones, thinking. Then she asked, "Well, this is no companionship. It's just me talking to a voice in the forest."

He did not respond.

Cora sighed, "Aagh! Fine! So that's my lesson for tonight? That I beat Aunt En too soon, and I need to take my revenge? That's stupid. It's not just Anabella, it's Aunt En too! Hell, it's the entire village! They all need to pay!" Her eyes lit up and her body emanated a florescent fuchsia aura when she spoke. Her teacher waited for her to calm down and did not respond. She continued, "When I first met you, I thought you would teach me powerful magic. But all these years, all you have told me is that true power comes from believing in myself."

"That is what I said, but you have not learned it yet," her teacher declared. "Think about it. Do as you promised yourself and come back to me when you understand."

"Forget you!" Cora shouted in frustration. She stomped off into the forest.

Leora got up from behind the tree she had been crouched behind and ran to the monoliths to find the person Cora had spoken with. She did not hear the conversation, but she knew that whatever was said made Cora angry. "Who's there?" she said as she slowed to a stop at the edge of the monolith circle. There was no reply.

She scanned her surroundings and froze her gaze on a spot in the darkness of the trees, behind the opposite side of the circle. Her heart jumped as she recognized a forgotten presence. It was the void; the same void she had witnessed years ago watching her and Cora in the grass beside their roundhouse. "What are you?" she asked.

"Leora, my sweet Leora," Cora's teacher responded in a caring tone that he had never used with Cora. "I have longed to meet you, but Cora has kept my existence a secret from you. I'm so glad you are here. Step into the moonlight so I can better see your face, my daughter."

Leora gasped, placing her hand on her heart. The word daughter lingered in her head. "Father?" she asked, stepping into the circle of monoliths.

"Oh daughter, I'm so happy to see you," he crooned. "You have grown so much since I last saw you."

"I can't remember you. What happened to you, father?" Leora squinted, attempting to espy him through the darkness.

"You were so young when I last saw you. I lost a wager, and this was the price I had to pay," he answered. "I am no longer of this world, and that is why you cannot see me."

"How long have you been here? Are you the reason Cora sneaks out at night? Does she come to talk to you? Why can't I see your energy? How is it possible that I can talk to you?" Leora barraged him with questions, causing him to laugh.

"Such curiosity. You are so much like I was. Yes, Cora has been coming here to speak with me for years," he replied.

Years. The word caused Leora's heart to drop.

How could C have known about the spirit of our father for years and never tell me?

Anticipating her next question, he continued, "Do not blame her for keeping me a secret. I asked her to. I knew you would find me yourself when you were ready, and here you are. You are becoming a young woman." His voice suddenly came from Leora's left side, sounding as close as if he were whispering in her ear, "But you are still so naïve. You have much to learn."

Leora jumped and spun to her left, but saw nothing. She approached the edge of the circle, staring hard into the trees. A cloud passed in front of the moon, blocking its light. A sudden, ominous wind blew through the trees, causing Leora's hair to waft backwards. The hairs on the back of her neck stood up. Leora never knew her father, but the feeling she got was not what she expected her father to feel like. She felt like a deer sensing the hidden presence of a wolf. Her hand unconsciously touched her mother's star pendant. A soft white light emanated from within it. The feeling of the pendant between her fingers calmed her. The wind settled, and the moon emerged from behind the cloud.

He analyzed Leora. "Your faith is strong. You try to live your life to please God, Father Julian, your aunt, and...you try to be someone your mother would be proud of. Isn't that right? That pendant you wear - it reminds you of her pure heart?"

"Yes," Leora replied, surprised how he could

read her.

"Have you forgotten what your mother did to señora Herrero? She killed her," his voice echoed through the trees, making it hard to pinpoint its source. "Just like she killed those soldiers. Remember how she tortured the lieutenant before he died?"

"Yes, but…"

"Do you remember how she helped Anabella? What was it she did exactly?" he asked.

"I…I don't…"

"Ask her," he commanded. "ask Anabella about the innocent life your mother took that night."

"Mother told us never to bring it up. She said it would be painful for Anabella to talk about. And what do you mean? She didn't kill anyone that night. Why are you saying such horrible things, father?" Leora asked in confusion.

"Leora, where is that curiosity you had merely minutes ago? You have just learned your father haunts these woods, and your sister has been keeping it a secret for years. I have revealed to you that your mother's heart was not as pure as she tried to make it seem, and you do not want to learn why, because it could hurt your friend's feelings? Your mother strayed far from righteousness. Certainly you must want to know why. You must want to know that as much as what your beloved Ricardo wants from you, or what your aunt has planned for you. Everybody you know has been keeping you in the dark."

"What do you mean? What Ricardo wants from me?" Leora asked, repeating his phrasing.

"You are becoming a young woman, and he is becoming a young man. It is only natural for a man to desire a woman. Ask Anabella. Ask her what she gives to men, and you will discover the only thing Ricardo wants from you. Ask her what your mother did to her, and you will learn your mother's true nature." His voice faded into the darkness, becoming more distant as he spoke.

"Father, wait!" Leora called out, but he was gone. Leora was left alone in the forest, confused. *Why would father make me feel so uneasy? Why would he say such things about mother?* She did not feel right about any part of her interaction with her father's supposed spirit. On her walk home, she decided to delicately interrogate Anabella.

25

By Wednesday, Leora still had not seen Anabella, so she went to the Lorenzo-Vargas' house after school. She told Geoffrey and Cora that she was going home with Ricardo to check on Anabella's health. Cora teased her, suggesting that she was only making an excuse to spend time with Ricardo.

As Leora and Ricardo arrived at Ricardo's house, a man walked out of the front door. Leora recognized him as señor Lopez, one of the older farm hands who was fond of wine. He ignored the two of them, walking away with his eyes glued to the ground in front of him. To Leora's surprise, Ricardo seemed not to think anything of it.

"What was señor Lopez doing at your house? Is he helping your mother with something?" Leora asked.

Ricardo shook his head. "No, he was probably here to see my sister," he said in dismay.

Leora was confused. "What do you mean?"

He looked at her with surprise. "You have not heard the rumors about Bella?"

"No."

Ricardo lowered his head in embarrassment as he spoke, "Ever since those soldiers raped her, she has been messed up. Mother said the baby was terminated, but the operation would prevent my sister from becoming pregnant ever again. So sometimes, to make us extra money, she lets some men from the village...look it doesn't matter." His voice rose in frustration. He stopped walking and looked Leora in the eyes to make sure his point was clear before they went inside. "She's not like...like Mother Elise. She's just trying to help us get by. Just don't bring it up with her, ok?"

Leora did not know how to respond. She had finally put the pieces together and the significance of what had happened to their family, and what her mother did for them, hit her hard.

"Are you ok? You look spooked," Ricardo said.

Leora broke her eye contact with Ricardo and looked at his house. She stared through the house, as if it were transparent and she was looking far beyond it. The new information overwhelmed her. Ricardo's words, *the baby was terminated,* reminded her of what she had heard in the dark forest the other night. *Ask her about the innocent life Thalia took.* She thought back to the night Dolores brought Anabella to their roundhouse. Dolores had asked Thalia to fix it. Leora had always thought she meant for Thalia to heal Anabella. Even when Cora explained to her what the soldiers did, and she learned the meaning of rape, she assumed it just hurt Anabella. Now, however, she realized Anabella had become pregnant. *Mother killed the baby,* she thought. *Señora Lorenzo-Vargas must not have wanted the spawn of such a cruel man to be reared by her daughter.* Leora understood why Anabella had been traumatized by the experience. *But to lose the ability to have children? What an awful sacrifice,* she thought.

A second realization then dawned on her. *Father told me Ricardo only wants the same thing from me that Anabella gives to the village men. He must have meant sex. But that's not all he wants! Ricardo loves me! Doesn't he?* She looked at him.

"What's wrong?" he asked again.

"I...I don't feel well. I need to go," Leora responded. She turned and ran home.

"Wait! I'm sorry! I just...Leora!" Ricardo called after her, but she ignored him and kept running.

Cora heard her sister run up the stairs, down the hallway, and into her room. Leora slammed the door shut and locked it. Cora went into the hallway and knocked on her sister's door.

"Leora, are you ok?"

"I'm fine! Go away!"

Cora paused at the door, unsure of what to do.

"Just leave me alone!" Leora shouted.

Cora frowned and went back to her room.

Leora laid on her bed and cried. She remembered what her mother had told her and Cora after she had killed señora Herrero; that it was wrong, but she chose to do it anyway. *That's what she did for Anabella too*, she thought. *She killed the baby to spare her pain. She did it out of mercy.* Leora pulled her pillow over her face and sobbed. Everything she had learned from the Bible told her murder was wrong. She now had to come to terms with the fact that her mother sinned with good intentions. *How can God let terrible things happen and punish people who just want to help?* She questioned her entire worldview.

Leora remained locked in her room for hours. When Enrique knocked on her door to let her know that dinner was ready, she told him she was not hungry. Later, when Enheduanna knocked on her door to check on her, she said she was not feeling well and needed to sleep. *What are you planning for me?* She wondered, thinking back to what she heard at the monoliths. *Does Rico really love me, or does he just want to have sex with me?* Her world shrank down to the bedroom she had locked herself in, trapping her in loneliness and doubt.

Finally, Cora knocked on her door one last time before retiring to bed, "Leora, can I come in?"

"No," Leora refused.

"I'm worried about you. I just want to make sure you're alright," Cora said.

I will never again be alright, Leora thought. She waited for Cora to leave, but Cora's stubborn patience outlasted her own. She walked up to the door and spoke to Cora through it, "C, do you think father would still love mother after what she did? After she killed señora Herrero, the soldiers, and Anabella's unborn baby?"

Cora hesitated to answer, wondering what had happened when Leora went home with Ricardo. But the answer to Leora's question was obvious to Cora, "Yes, of course he would! Do you feel any differently toward mother?"

"No," Leora squeaked, "I don't care what she did. She did it out of love, whether it was for us, the village, señor and señora Herrero, or for Anabella and her mother. I'll always love mama."

Cora smiled, "Then there's your answer. Father loved mother more than anything. That pendant she gave you represents that."

Leora touched the pendant and closed her eyes tightly to blink away tears.

Cora continued, "Mother did those things because she was strong, not with magic, but in her heart. She did what nobody else in the village could. She believed in God, but she followed her own path. That's all any of us can really do."

"Yeah," Leora agreed. She paused. "Do you think...never mind."

"Ask me, it's alright." Cora put her hand on the

door.

"Do you think Ricardo really loves me? Or does he just want to have sex with me?"

Cora's eyebrows raised in disbelief at the absurdity of her sister's question. She wondered what had distressed Leora so much. "Of course he loves you! I mean, he probably wants to have sex with you too, but that boy has loved you since he first saw you. If there is such a thing as fate, then you two are fated to be together. Why are you asking these questions?"

"I don't know," Leora whimpered.

The two of them stood facing one another on opposite sides of the closed door in silence for several seconds before Leora said, "Goodnight, C. I love you."

"I love you too, L." Cora said, smiling, emphasizing the L.

Leora smiled at her sister's mimicry of her nickname. She did not see it, but for a moment, her mother's pendant twinkled with a nearly imperceptible flash of light.

Cora waited at the door for a moment longer before going back to her room.

Leora slunk down to the floor with her back against the door, still twiddling the pendant between her fingers. She sat in contemplation of the day's revelations. *Mother was a good person,* she thought. *Her heart was pure. And so is Ricardo's. Even if he wants to have sex with me, he wants it because he loves me. And I want it too.*

"He's not our father," she said to herself. "He's a liar." She resolutely stood up and went to her chest of clothes to retrieve something warmer.

The night was unusually cold for late spring. Snow flurries drifted in the air of the upper foothills as Leora trudged through the forest toward the circle of monoliths. When she arrived, she called out, "Hello?"

"Welcome back, daughter! Did you ask Anabella about her baby?" the voice asked.

Leora ignored his question. "Don't call me daughter. You are not my father. You are a liar."

"What are you talking about, sweet Leora? I am most certainly your father."

"No, you are not. My father would never speak of my mother the way you did the other night. And he would have recognized this pendant as the symbol of their love, not as a symbol of my mother's heart. Who, or what, are you really? Show yourself," she challenged him.

He tried once more to convince her, "I'm sorry if what you discovered upset you. I was just trying to open your eyes to the truth. And that pendant, it has been so long, and in this otherworldly state, my memory is not what once was. Please, daughter, I only want the best for you."

Leora shouted, "Shut up! You do not care about me or my mother! You lied to me about who you are, and about Ricardo. We love each other. He would never do to me what those soldiers did to

Anabella! You are not my father, you are a monster!"

A harsh wind blew through the trees, carrying with it a hissing sound that transformed into the voice, "Silence, girl! Your insolence astounds me! I see now that you cannot be reasoned with. You have closed yourself off to the truth to live in fantasy. You are right - no daughter of mine would abide such delusion. At least I have your sister."

Leora's expression darkened with fury. She dropped the fur from around her shoulders, revealing a long white dress embroidered with silver. Moonlight lit her mother's pendant, reflecting and illuminating a small area in front of her.

"You will never have my sister!" she shouted. Leora reached her fingers toward the sky and raised her head up, absorbing the energy around her and letting the moonlight nourish her.

An inhuman growl came from the darkness of the surrounding trees. The wind blew again at Leora, blowing her hair back behind her, as the presence that she detected as the void approached her with great speed. When it breached the circle of monoliths, close enough to touch her, she opened her eyes and lowered her head forward to face it. A pure white light beamed from her eyes and pierced the darkness like the sun.

"Aaaagh!" the voice howled.

Light continued radiating from Leora, spreading from her eyes to her pendant, and then to the rest of her body. The void in front of her dissolved bit by bit, like a log in a fire reducing into black, cracked, smoldering cinders, until it had degraded to the form of a crusty human figure. The figure cowered and tried to use its arms to shield itself from Leora's light. Its hairless, wrinkled body resembled a hairless rat with pointed ears. It growled and hissed at her like a frightened animal. For a brief moment, it lowered one of its arms enough for her to see a pair of dark, menacing eyes staring at her. The black pupils were five-pointed stars engulfed in irises of rust-colored flames.

The quick flash of eye contact with the creature sent a spike of fear through her, but Leora let it pass and adamantly gritted her teeth to finish her spell.

She shouted, "Whatever you are, liar, you will endanger us no more! I banish you! Be gone from this valley and go back to the shadowy hell from which you came!"

As she cast her spell of banishment, the monoliths around the circle began vibrating. A low frequency hum filled the air. The monoliths shook more violently as the hum increased in volume. The runic symbols began cracking apart and bits of rock fell from them. Leora brought her arms down, causing the monoliths to shatter all at once into countless pieces. The figure in front of her screamed as a wave of light projected out through the forest, carrying with it a great wind. The wave traversed down through the valley. No corner was left untouched. It only faded when it reached the mountains around the valley.

The grove darkened again, no longer illuminated by Leora's light. The figure had vanished. Leora stumbled backward, breathing deeply. The exertion from her spell had exhausted her. As she collected herself, she noticed a silent calm had settled into the forest. The air felt lighter and warmer. *He's gone*, she thought. *Good riddance.*

26

Leora awoke the next day feeling weak, as though she were ill with the flu. Her spirit, however, was full of renewed vigor. Her mood rubbed off on Geoffrey, Cora, and even Enheduanna. Cora was pleased to see her sister happier, and she assumed it was because of their talk the previous night. Their cheerfulness was not confined to their household; the entire village was bustling with life. On Leora's, Cora's, and Geoffrey's short walk to school, they greeted five villagers, which was highly unusual.

Anabella escorted Ricardo to school. Leora saw them arrive. She looked at Anabella with newfound respect, detecting a sadness in Anabella's eyes that she had not noticed before. It was the type of sadness that takes root and grows slowly over time, like a vine that gradually strangles the life out of a tree, but Anabella persevered.

Before class started, Leora spoke with Ricardo, apologizing for fleeing their conversation the previous day. She attributed her retreat to a sudden illness. He believed her.

The school day passed quickly for Leora. In the evening, the coven had planned a dress rehearsal for her induction ceremony.

As Enheduanna and Geoffrey were getting dressed in their rooms, Cora helped Leora get into her ceremonial dress. The dress was crafted from a royal blue fabric that shimmered with every movement. It was accented by a navy blue piece in the front center, and intricate white stitching that ran down its length and arms, tracing patterns along the seams and forming perfect symmetry on each side. The back sported a hood that Leora was to wear until it was time to reveal herself, as they had planned to practice at rehearsal. In its entirety, the dress gave Leora a feeling of elegance befitting of high-born blood.

"There!" Cora said, stepping back to take in Leora's visage. Leora's blond locks and deep blue eyes were a perfect match for the dress, and the sparkling star pendant rested neatly in the navy middle section.

"How do I look?" Leora asked.

"Stunning," Cora replied, "Ricardo's jaw will

hit the floor when he sees you in this."

They both laughed. Cora held up a small mirror for Leora to see.

Leora's appearance impressed herself. She spun from side to side to see the shimmering blue twirl around her. "Wow," she said, "I love it!"

"I bet it looks better on you than it did on Elise," Cora said. Elise had worn the dress when she was inducted into the coven years earlier. Since the aptitude test, Josephine and Mary had worked hard to fit the dress for Leora's body.

Leora looked at Cora with her eyebrows raised. "Oh, it most certainly does," she said with over-the-top haughtiness. They both laughed again. She felt the material between her fingers and looked down at herself. "C, I think this is the nicest dress I have ever worn."

Her comment rang true with Cora. Thalia did her best to provide for them, but the clothes she would barter for were always old hand-me-downs. She would patch them herself. Occasionally, she would have time to sew an outfit with higher quality material, but it retained a handmade look that the other girls in their class would mock. Even Thalia's green church dress, as nice as it was, could not compare with half of the clothes in Enheduanna's wardrobe. This ceremonial dress was the most elegant garment either of them had ever worn.

"It's truly magnificent, and you look so beautiful, Leora. Mother would be proud." Leora's eyes filled with tears. Cora hugged her.

"Now it's my turn," Cora said. "But that thing will not look as nice as your dress." She pointed to the dull brown hooded frock laying on the bed. Brown was the standard color for aspiring coven members. "It is the color of poop," she added.

Leora's laughter at her sister's comment burst through her tears and brought her back to the present.

When Cora was ready, the girls met Geoffrey in the hallway, who wore a brown tunic with a thin leather belt around his waist, and brown pants tucked into his boots. On their way out of the house, they picked up Enheduanna, who wore the white dress of the coven leader and her oak tree pin.

When they got to the forest grove where the ceremony would take place, the coven elders and the other students were scattered around, engaged in conversations while they waited. The lower ranked coven members were also present.

"Ah! Here comes the young woman of the hour!" Isabella announced. Everybody stopped talking and turned to look. Cora had been right: Ricardo's eyes widened when he saw Leora gracefully striding through the middle of the crowd, and they remained fixed on her as she passed. Leora pretended not to notice him, but his reaction was the sole focus of her peripheral vision. She blushed and tried to stifle her joy as she walked past him.

Cora's attention was on the group of Clara, Maya, and Maria, who wore the same brown colored dress as her. Clara looked at Leora with envy. Maria whispered "Wow." Now it was Cora's turn to hide her smile.

Elise approached Leora and took her hands. "You are resplendent in that dress. So graceful and refined. Sisters Mary and Josephine did a fine job. I dare say it looks better on you than it ever did on me."

Mary approached Leora from her other side. She inspected the seams of Leora's dress, nodding.

"We're so glad you will soon be one of us! I will be honored to call you sister," Josephine said, as she approached Leora too, positioning herself between Leora and Cora.

Constantina and Isabella drew closer, too. With all the elders gathering around Leora to dote on her, Cora shuffled off to the side and joined Clara, Maya, and Maria.

"How does it feel to have your sister join the coven, even though you were the one who defeated Mother Enheduanna?" Clara asked Cora.

A scowl flashed across Cora's face, but she quickly adopted a smile. "I'm so happy for her. Leora has wanted this for so long, and she deserves it."

"Me too," Maria said. "Soon she'll be able to go to all the secret coven meetings with the elders, and they'll teach her all sorts of special spells. I'm jealous! Wait, does this mean we'll have to call her

Mother Leora?"

Clara laughed, "No silly, she will be an ordinary coven member, not an elder. So we'll call her Sister Leora."

"Did all of them have to take the aptitude test?" Maria asked, scrutinizing the coven members who were not elders.

Clara replied, "No, they did not. I don't know why we had to. And Elise, who was the last to join, is an elder instead of a regular member, so I have no idea. Do you know, Cora?"

Cora shook her head. She did not know, but suspected it had to do with her aunt's grand plan. *She wants an army*, she thought, *so she would probably want her most loyal followers high in the hierarchy*. Cora watched the elders encircle her sister, and an unexpected feeling of loss came over her. *The closer she gets to them, the further she is from me*, she thought.

Enheduanna approached the large round stone altar that stood in the middle of the grove. "Alright, let's gather around everyone. I want the students lined up around the entrance to the grove and the elders up here with me. We will run through this twice so everyone knows what they are supposed to do. Elise, you stay with Leora and walk her through it. Isabella, you help the other students."

"Yes, mother," Isabella responded. Everyone got into place. The students formed a single line from the entrance of the grove up to the altar, pretending to hold candles. The coven elders stood in a half-circle around the altar, with Enheduanna in the middle on the opposite side from the entrance, so that the altar was between her and the entrance. Elise and Leora stood side by side at the entrance, pretending to hold bouquets of flowers. Everyone put their hoods up.

Perfect, Cora thought, *this is the part when I will sneak away tomorrow night.*

With the students in place, Isabella joined the other elders around the altar. She began to sing "ah", holding a single note. The others joined her, except for Elise and Leora. Instead, they walked silently up to the altar. Enheduanna waited with her back to them on the opposite side of the altar. When they reached it, the elders closed the circle tighter around it. The students rotated their line to face the altar, then bent into a half circle and walked forward. Altogether, they formed a complete circle around the altar, with the elders on one side and the students on the other.

Enheduanna turned to face them, singing in Latin. She walked up to the altar and held a cup in the air, placing it on the stone. Leora put her imaginary flower bouquet into the cup. Everyone stopped singing.

Enheduanna spoke, "We are gathered here tonight under the light of a full moon, and by the grace of our Lord, we will accept our sister Leora into our coven. Leora, can you confirm your belief in God?"

"Yes, I believe," Leora answered.

Enheduanna continued, "Do you swear to obey God and exercise witchcraft, which is one of His many gifts to us, in accordance with His will?"

"Yes, I swear," Leora answered.

"And do you swear undying loyalty to your coven, your sisters, and the coven leader?" Enheduanna asked.

"Yes," Leora answered.

Elise took Leora's hand and held it out above the cup. Enheduanna knelt to pick up a knife. She pretended to slice open her palm and Leora's. Putting their cut hands together and saying, "Now we are sisters. One blood, one coven." She passed the knife to Isabella. One by one, all the elders passed it around, pretending to slice open their palms, taking Leora's hand and speaking the same words. When it came back to Enheduanna, she put it on the stone next to the cup, and rotated Leora's hand so her imaginary blood would trickle into the cup. She held the cup up to the sky and chanted something in Latin. The elders repeated it. Then she tipped the cup, pouring its imaginary contents onto the altar.

Mary came up to the altar, holding a dove. "And this is when you sacrifice the dove. Grasp it firmly and be swift. There is no need for it to suffer," she instructed.

Leora took the dove in her hands and clenched it. She felt its small body squirm in her palms and watched as it studied her with one of its eyes.

Leora's eyebrows wrinkled, and she frowned. "Remind me why I have to do this again?"

Mary replied, "It is a symbol of the surrender of your old life. It's a demonstration of your willingness to obey the coven, as it is the first command that the coven leader will issue to you."

Leora felt the energy of the dove. As she heard its coos, she closed her eyes and felt its being flow through her, seeing its life play out in her mind's eye, and feeling the anxiety it now had in her hands. She wanted so badly to let it go; to raise her hands in the air and help it fly freely into the sky.

Elise raised her eyes from the dove to meet Enheduanna's. Enheduanna noted the concern in Elise's gaze and warned, "You must do this if you want to be one of us. It is the only way. That is what you have always wanted, isn't it?"

"Yes," Leora replied meekly.

"Don't think of it as killing the bird. Think of it as sending it home - back to God's everlasting glory. Do it in the name of God," Enheduanna said.

Cora watched her sister from behind, sensing her sadness. She looked at the coven elders with hatred. *Everything he said about you hags was right*, she thought, remembering what her teacher had told her about the coven over the years. *They're hypocrites. God is nothing but a tool for them.* She felt sorry for Leora. *Is this what you really want, Leora?* She wondered.

Leora picked up the knife and pretended to

cut the dove's neck.

As they walked home after the rehearsal, Cora noticed a somberness in her sister that was not there before. She held Leora's hand. "You did good, sis." Leora smiled at her, but said nothing.

Enheduanna watched the two of them walking ahead of her, hand in hand, and squinted. She remembered what her sister, Thalia, had told her when they formed the coven: she took Enheduanna's hand in hers and said, "Nothing will ever break us apart, En. We are one blood, one coven." *One blood, one coven*, Enheduanna thought, the words echoing in her mind.

***

The previous day's hopeful sunrise now seemed like a distant memory to Leora. The new day brought overcast skies that hovered, seemingly motionless, over the valley like a large gray blanket. She thought about the ceremony throughout the day at school, frequently drifting into deep thought.

After school, Leora and Cora got dressed in preparation for Leora's induction ceremony. While they waited for Enheduanna and Geoffrey, they sat on the fountain's retaining wall in the courtyard of the Ortiz Estate. Leora stared blankly at the water.

"You've been doing that all day. What's wrong?" Cora asked.

"Doing what?"

"Staring off into space. Are you still upset

from this weekend, or are you anxious about the induction ceremony tonight?"

Leora shrugged. "Both, I guess."

"Why were you so upset Sunday evening?"

"It's not important now," Leora tried to dismiss the subject, but Cora would not allow it.

"It certainly seemed like it was important. Come on, what happened to upset you?"

Leora sighed. She explained how she learned about what happened to Anabella and what it meant for their mother's involvement. "And that's why I was feeling sad on Sunday evening."

Cora nodded. "I'm sorry you found out that way. I could have told you, but it's not a subject that would ever have a convenient time to discuss."

"I know, it's ok," Leora said. She drew her finger in a circle in the water, forming a tiny whirlpool. "But there is one thing I wish you had told me," she said while watching the whirlpool.

"What's that?" Cora asked.

Leora made eye contact with her and continued, "That you were talking with something in the forest that you thought was our father."

Cora's heart jumped. "What are you talking about?"

"You've been sneaking out at night for years to go to that circle of stones in the forest. I've seen you."

Cora's face went white as she realized Leora had caught her. "I...did you follow me there?"

"Yes."

Cora was perturbed, "Why?" Leora did not answer for a couple seconds, and Cora added, "Couldn't you let me have one thing for myself?"

"You mean like having secret conversations with what you thought was our father's ghost?" Leora asked.

Cora squinted in confusion. "What do you mean? He's not our father. I don't know who or even what he is, but he's definitely not our father."

"So you figured that out too?" Leora asked.

Cora shook her head, "No! He never said he was! He said he wanted a companion, so in return for keeping him company, he teaches me things. Have you been eavesdropping on us? Why did you think he was our father?"

Leora realized that the thing in the forest must have only tried to convince her that he was their father, and not Cora. *Why would he do that?* She wondered. She answered her sister's question. "No, I followed you one night and spoke to him after you left. He's a liar, Cora. You can't believe anything he says. But it doesn't matter anymore. He's gone now."

Cora reeled back as if Leora's words were daggers. "What do you mean, he's gone?"

"I banished him from this valley."

Cora's eyes went wide. "What!? Why would you...no, you can't!"

"It's true. I cast a spell to banish him from this valley forever."

Cora stood up and backed away from her. "No! No, no, no, no. You can't! I need him! What is wrong with you!? He was the only person I could talk to about things. You have Clara, Maya, Ricardo, Aunt En, Isabella, even Geoffrey. Hell, everyone in the village loves sweet, obedient Leora. But me? The deviant goth sinner? I don't have *anyone!*" she roared her last sentence in anger and despair.

"You have me," Leora said softly, with tears forming in her eyes.

"No, I don't, Leora!" Cora said with her voice cracking. Tears ran down her face. "After tonight, you'll be one of them. The people who killed mother...you'll be *their* sister."

Leora timidly approached her sister and put her hand on Cora's shoulder. "C, that's not true. I'll only ever be your sister. The ceremony is just a custom."

"He has taught me so much, helped me so many times. If he were not there for me, I don't think I could have made it so long living with En."

"Cora, whatever he was teaching you could be dangerous. He lied to me and deliberately tried to turn me against you, Ricardo, and mother. He was the reason I went to see Anabella yesterday. I think he's evil."

Cora looked at Leora angrily. "Well, he was there for me when nobody else was. You wouldn't know."

Her sister's statement hurt Leora. "Haven't I always been here for you?"

Cora shook her head. "No, Leora. You're just little miss perfect, always doing whatever Aunt En says, or what Mother Isabella says, and now you're going to be their sister."

"Stop saying that! Sister is just the word the coven uses to..."

"Just a word, huh? Is that all we are too?"

Leora did not know how to respond, and Cora continued, "You find something that scares you - that has no logical explanation, and you call it evil and try to destroy it. You're no better than En and her zealots! He understood me! He encouraged me to think for myself! And now..." her voice cracked, "I hate you!" she shouted.

Cora's words stung Leora, making her body feel numb. She did not react.

Cora's anger had darkened the cloudy sky. Thunder rumbled through the valley. Her eyes filled with a circle of fuchsia light, and her body began to faintly glow the same color.

"Let's go, girls," Enheduanna called out, as she and Geoffrey exited the house into the courtyard. She closed the door and turned around, bumping into Geoffrey, who stood frozen. Enheduanna took in the scene before her. When she noticed Cora's eyes, she assumed Cora was preparing to attack her sister. She screamed at her niece, "Cora! Stop this at once, you demon child!"

Cora glared at her aunt.

Enheduanna acted to prevent a repeat of their duel. She cast a spell to sweep Cora's feet out from under her, causing her to fall onto her side. Cora's head hid the patio stone and bounced off of it. She winced in pain and grabbed her throbbing head.

Leora screamed when she saw her sister's body hit the ground, and blood pool on the stone beneath her head. Enrique and the other servants rushed outside to see what was happening.

Enheduanna stepped in front of Leora. "Stay behind me, Leora," she commanded. She cast a spell to cause vines to grow out of the ground and wrap around Cora's body, constricting her and preventing her from moving.

"Stop it! Stop it!" Leora screamed from behind. She was too weak from the exertion of the spell she had cast the night before to stop them. Enheduanna motioned for Enrique to assist. He and another servant restrained Leora.

"Take her inside," Enheduanna ordered. They hauled her away as she kicked and screamed, pleading with her aunt to leave her sister alone.

Even with blurry vision, Cora could see her aunt stepping toward her, readying another spell. She channeled all of her might into the earth, causing sharp rocks to jut out of the ground around her aunt. This forced Enheduanna to stop her advance so she could avoid the rocks, which provided enough time for Cora to burn the vines off her body.

While Enheduanna blasted the surrounding rocks apart, Cora tried to stand. She hauled herself up, but doubled over, putting her hands on her knees to steady herself.

When Enheduanna had cleared a path through the rocks to her niece, she sent a concussive blast of energy at Cora, but Cora sliced through it and thrust her hand out to telekinetically push her aunt back. Enheduanna stumbled backwards and tripped over an uplifted patio stone, falling onto her bottom.

Cora looked at her sister, who was struggling to avoid being pulled indoors. She did not speak, but Leora intuitively discerned her intention.

"No, C, please don't! Don't go! I'm sorry!" Leora sobbed.

Cora's eyes teared up, and she screamed in anguish before turning and running away. She ran through the iron gates, doing her best to ignore Leora's cries. She ran until her sister's voice faded away, continuing down the road and up the path into the foothills, stopping at the circle of broken monoliths, and frantically searching the trees for her teacher.

"Teacher?" Cora called out. There was no reply. There was residual sunlight in the sky, so she sat on the ground to pontificate while waiting for sundown. She thought about her plan, about Leora, and about running away. *Can I really leave her here?*

"She has the coven now, so she'll be fine. She doesn't need me anymore. There is nothing left for me in Estrelle." Cora did not fully believe those words, but she wanted to, so she spoke them to herself, hoping that speaking them would help convince her of their truth.

When the sky was completely dark, Cora called for her teacher again, several times, but there was no reply. She cried.

"She really did it. I can't believe it."

She stood and remembered her most recent conversation with her teacher, and her promise of revenge. Rage consumed her, and entrenched in her the desire to cause pain. She marched back to the village and toward her next objective.

***

Leora stood at the entrance to the grove where her induction into the coven would take place. Her classmates were lined up in front of her on both sides, holding candles to light the path to the altar. The elders around the altar also held candles. Everybody's hoods obscured the top halves of their faces so that the candlelight only illuminated their mouths. She watched their mouths move as they sang the Latin chant they had prepared. Leora felt like she was a spectator in her own body, watching herself go through the motions of the ceremony. Her surroundings were muted. She felt trapped in her mind, tying to make sense of everything.

Elise escorted her up to the altar. Leora passed the small gap in the line of students where Cora would have been. Her sister's absence from that spot made it feel like a chasm, begging Leora to stop as she passed it. She wanted to turn and run off to find her sister, but her body kept following the sequence she had rehearsed for the ritual. She heard herself responding in the affirmative to Enheduanna's questions, just like she had practiced.

This is the moment I have waited for all my life, she thought. *I should revel in this moment. I should...* She could not convince herself how she should feel, which forced her to admit to herself that the moment felt unfulfilled without her sister there to support her.

Enheduanna took Leora's hand. "Now we are sisters. One blood, one coven," she said. The other elders did the same.

Leora had not felt the knife cut into her palm. She now held it in her hand, and Mary was handing her the dove.

"Prove your loyalty to the coven," Enheduanna commanded.

***

Cora stood in the doorway to Anabella's bedroom. Her subterfuge had been flawless. Nobody knew she was there.

Anabella laid on her back, sleeping peacefully.

Cora approached Anabella's bedside and looked down at her friend; her target. Her heart pounded. She was now inches away from tasting revenge. Her fingers grasped the knife she had concealed in her garment. She withdrew it and held it to Anabella's throat, trying hard to steady her hand. *Seize your vengeance! Kill the friend who betrayed your mother!* She heard her teacher's voice in her mind as if he were in the same room.

She has to know it was me, Cora thought. *I have to wake her before I cut.* She looked at Anabella's eyelids as if she were looking into her friend's open eyes. Memories flashed through Cora's mind.

"See! I told you! I knew it would look good on you," Anabella had said to her that night they tried on clothes at the Matisse's house.

"Nice one, Cora! You earned it!" Anabella congratulated Cora for winning Capture the Flag at the pond.

"See? I told you this would be better than school," Anabella said the day she skipped school and learned how to make whiskey.

"Witch! She's the witch!" Anabella cried.

Cora's eyes welled with tears. "I hate that you made me do this," she rasped through gritted teeth.

"You will have to forgive her and get out of your own way," Leora's words suddenly crept into Cora's mind.

Cora shook her head. "I can't," she whispered, as if she were replying to Leora.

Anabella's eyes slowly opened. She blinked hard. "Cora?"

Cora froze, tears streaming down her face.

Anabella was still groggy. "Cora? What are

you doing here?" She then felt the sharp blade against her throat and realized she was in danger. She gasped and scooted back on her bed, as far as she could, until her head was against the wall. "Cora, what are you doing? Why are you…"

Seizing the opportunity, Cora pounced on Anabella, pinning her to the bed with her knees on Anabella's chest. She held the knife at Anabella's throat again and put her other hand on the top of Anabella's head.

"You betrayed my mother," Cora spat. "You…" Her emotions broke through her like the breaking of a dam, causing her to sob. She gained control of her breath to say, "She helped you! She helped you and you killed her. Why Bella? Why did she have to die?"

Anabella helplessly watched her assassin, frozen in silent terror.

"I hate you!" Cora sniveled. "I care about you, and I hate that I care about you!"

Despite her surprise at finding her friend with a knife to her throat in the middle of the night, Anabella recognized the pain in Cora. She was familiar with it. She put her hand on Cora's hand that held the knife. "It's ok, Cora. It's ok. I understand." She began to cry too, not out of fear, but in sadness on behalf of her friend, and the tragic circumstances that led them to that moment.

A small amount of blood oozed from Anabella's throat as the knife pressed into it. Cora saw the acceptance in her friend's eyes. *She would let me do it*, Cora thought.

"For years, all I have thought about was revenge. I came here tonight to kill you for betraying our mother four years ago, and for forsaking me, your friend. I wanted you to suffer…" Cora's voice broke. "And you have."

Anabella nodded. "We all have."

Cora nodded. "We all have." She pulled the knife away and threw it to the floor. "We all have," she sobbed. "I'm sorry, Bella."

"Me too," Anabella replied. She sat up and hugged Cora. They cried together for a few moments.

"I have to leave here. I'm leaving Estrelle."

"Good."

"Will you watch after my sister?"

"Of course."

"Make sure Aunt En doesn't dig her claws into her and ruin her."

"Maybe I'll join you someday," Anabella mused, "if you'd welcome me."

Cora smiled and kissed her friend's cheek. She left the house and ventured back into the foothills, following the creek to the east end of the valley. When the forest thickened, she found a tree with a wide trunk, leaned back against it, and went to sleep.

***

Leora set the knife on the altar, and the

lifeless dove beside it. Enheduanna removed her hood, and then Leora's. She turned Leora around to face the students. They all removed their hoods, too.

"I present to you the newest member of our coven: Sister Leora!"

The students hollered and cheered. Leora observed them listlessly. Enheduanna noticed Leora's unenthusiastic demeanor.

"It will be alright, Leora. We will take care of you, and you will help lead our coven to greatness. You don't need to worry about that wayward sister of yours. Wherever she went, it's for the best that she is gone."

***

Cora awoke just as the morning sun peeked over the tops of the nearby mountains. She immediately hiked to the mountain pass where all the traders would enter the valley from the east. Then she turned around to look at her lifelong home one last time. The rising sun lit the picturesque green valley in a golden hue. From this vantage point, Cora noticed how small the village really was. She closed one eye and held up her thumb at arm's length, covering the village with it. *That's my entire life, covered by a single thumb*, she thought. A tear ran down her cheek.

"Goodbye sister," she said, before turning away from the valley and walking toward an unknown future.